I.D. RUSSELL

Beyond the Dark Forest

For old friends who forget themselves

THEN

"This is our newest model," the salesman said, pointing to a fine-looking Zenith television with polished wood finish. "Twenty-three inches. Clear colour picture. Remote control. You won't find a better price on this anywhere in River City."

Jim let the man point out all the features, rubbing his chin to show that he was seriously considering the deal. Next to him, his seven-year-old son's eyes grew in interest.

"Here, let me show you how it works." He clicked the set on. Immediately, a crystal-clear shot of a news broadcast came into focus.

"—park authorities say the creature was shot by a local hunter who wished to remain anonymous. The carcass is being shipped to the University of Manitoba's veterinary studies department for examination, after which we're told the remains will be sent to Hawkins Taxidermy where it can be—"

"Notice the colours," the salesman said. "You can practically feel that blouse of hers, can't you?"

His son, Billy, rushed forward and touched the screen, but Jim was engrossed in the reporting, doing his best to maintain an image of being nonplussed.

"—how common is it for a bear to not only attack humans, but also, if the reports are to be believed, eat them?"

"Well, April, black bears, while still dangerous, are not typically known to kill. They'll get into the trash, knock over fences, steal food left out, but generally aren't harmful to humans. A mother with her cubs, maybe, but this particular bear wasn't a black bear."

"What kind of bear was it?"

"Grizzly. Monster, too. Nearly nine hundred and fifty kilograms. Although some of that weight might be due to the amount of people it ate and—"

"Now," the salesman said, reaching for the remote, "I can show you—"

"Wait a minute," Jim said, holding his hand out.

"That's nearly a tonne," the reporter continued. "Is it unusual for a grizzly to reach such a size?"

"In the Whiteshell, yes. Out west in Alberta? Also yes. Down south? Still yes. Let's just say it was one hell of a big bear."

"Thankfully dead now."

"Too late for all the people it killed, though."

"Is there any theory as to why the bear suddenly began attacking humans?"

"As of now, April, no. Sometimes animals just attack. Maybe it didn't like the smell of someone's perfume or a song playing on their radio or it was just hungry and decided to take a bite."

"Just a bite?"

"One bite that gave it the taste for human flesh, which it then indulged. A lot."

"Would you like to hear about the extended warranty or

payment plan?" the salesman said, mistaking Jim's interest in the news with interest in the set itself.

"I'm not entirely sold just yet," he said. "Give this a second."

"Dad, it's great," Billy said. "Why don't we—"

"Shhh, Billy. I want to test the sound."

"—think I can speak for all of our channel six viewers, Gerry, when I say that I, for one, am glad the thing is dead," the reporter said.

"We all are, April. Well, maybe not the bear or his family."

"Are you suggesting there's a chance for one of the bear's relatives to look for revenge for the death of its, uh, relative?"

"Grizzlies are loners, April. I doubt this bear's family has any idea of what's happened. And unless they're viewers of your channel, I can't see that changing any time soon."

"Luckily bears can't operate the buttons on a television set, right, Gerry?"

"Not as of yet, April. Their paws are just too damn big."

"You can't say that word on television, Gerry."

"What, paw? That's fucking stupid."

"Gerry!"

"So can I get the paperwork started on this model for you?" the salesman asked.

"What do you think, kids?" Jim asked the rest of his family.

"That show was boring," Billy said. "Can we change the channel?"

"Let's see something else on the screen." Jim took the remote from the salesman. "For reference." He changed the channel.

"—Gene, Gene, the dancing machine." Music, applause, garish colours; a total contrast to the drab news report.

"Here we go," Jim said.

"Yay," Billy said happily, bobbing his head to the tune.

"Now tell me that doesn't look great," the salesman said proudly.

Jim nodded. "Okay, ya sold us. We'll take it."

NOW

"Come on, girls, get ready. This isn't sit-down-and-do-nothing time, it's get-your-ass-packed-and-ready-to-go-motherfucking-camping time. Half hour tops. I want to be on the road *before* lunch."

Donna's shouts jerked Mandy out of her deep slumber, but they weren't enough to make her want to move or even give any indication that she was awake at all. Maybe if she didn't react, Donna would leave her alone and let her get fifteen more minutes of sleep. She'd been having such a nice dream.

"Bitch, don't even pretend. I know you hear me."

A pillow bounced off Mandy's head and landed next to the nightstand. She couldn't stop herself from grunting. The game was over. She had no other choice but to roll over and admit defeat.

"Okay, okay, I'm up. Jeez, would you lay off?"

"No, I will not. We are going fucking camping today. You lazy bitches are not going to spoil the plan. I don't care when you went to sleep last night or what you were drinking before you finally did. We're going."

Mandy opened her eyes to see that Donna was already dressed. She wore jeans and a leather jacket over a tight red shirt. She had a "don't try me" look on her face as she stared at Mandy still laying in bed in her ratty old pyjamas.

"Who made you the boss?" Mandy said petulantly as she rubbed her eyes to try to force herself awake.

"Let's see. Maybe the fact that I'm the one who organized this trip by meeting a cute guy at the gym? Or because I'm the one who got him to bring three of his friends—single friends, mind you—to meet three of mine for a nice weekend at the lake? Or how about because this is a vacation, dammit, and we are not going to dick around and waste it."

Donna clearly wasn't going to leave until Mandy got out of bed, she could see that in her eyes.

"You are not going to daydream on me, girl, get the fuck up." Donna threw another pillow and hit Mandy square in the face. It hurt more than it should have.

"I'm up, I'm up, I'm up."

"Good. Breakfast in ten, on the road in thirty. Do what you have to do."

Donna stormed off and Mandy could hear her yelling to wake up the rest of the house.

She rolled out of bed, putting her feet down slowly onto the carpeted floor. The long shirt she wore had bunched up high. Her legs were bare and there was a chill in the room. She walked over and opened the Venetians, the sudden burst of sunlight nearly blinding her.

"Fuck." She turned away from the light she'd been happily avoiding until now.

Her room was a mess, but then Mandy was never the neat one in the family. That always fell to her older sister, Ashley: the one who led the way, the one her parents always compared her to, the one who could do no wrong. Mandy lived forever in her big sister's shadow, subsisting on her hand-me-downs and leftover makeup. But it wasn't all bad. When Ashley had bought a house and needed roommates to help with the mortgage, she'd asked her sister and her friends to move in. That had turned this place into party central and had the added bonus of getting Mandy away from her overbearing parents earlier than she'd expected.

But then was her sister being any different than they were?

Do this, do that, clean this, clean that. There were so many rules; it was like living with Mom and Dad all over again, only without the crushing feelings of being a perpetual disappointment. She scratched her back under the shirt and dug through a pile of underwear on the dresser. She was pretty sure they were clean, but then did it really matter when they were just going out to the woods?

Shit!

She suddenly realized that if Donna was waking them all up at the same time, then it would be a mad dash to the shower, so she grabbed her underwear and ran out into the hall. She spun on her heels, dashed inside the bathroom, and just managed to slam and lock the door before Ashley could get there.

"Hey," Ashley squealed in protest.

"Not my fault you slept in," Mandy taunted her from the other side of the thick white-painted door.

First!

There was makeup everywhere on the countertop of the bathroom vanity. The white plastic bins that Ashley had made them all use with their names stencilled on never managed to stay full for long. Besides, they all pretty much just used whatever they needed, ownership be damned. A lone towel hung on the rack. The labels above each spot, to show whose towel below ostensibly belonged to who, was just another recommendation that went unheeded.

"Nobody needs to know that this is supposed to be Beth's."

Mandy cranked the shower on, glad that she was going to get to use it before the hot water was all used up. The warmth woke her up completely and the satisfaction of getting the last clean towel made her morning. When she was done, she shot Ashley a smug look as she passed her waiting outside the door for her turn.

"Took you long enough, M," Ashley said.

"All yours," Mandy said coyly.

Ashley, her hair matted from a rough night, frowned, trying to figure out what game was being played on her. Giving up, she went inside.

As Mandy returned to her room, she could hear her yelling back, "Where are all the towels?"

She quickly dressed and tossed some clothes into her backpack, then brushed her blonde hair and went downstairs to get something to eat. Donna and the slender, dark-haired Beth were already at the table. The sun was shining brightly in the white kitchen.

"Hey, sleepyhead," Beth said, chewing on a mouthful of toast.

"How'd you get up so early?"

"Alarm a la Donna," Beth replied.

"So you didn't shower?"

"I can wait. I was starved."

"You're gonna miss all the hot water."

"Food trumps—"

"You used all the hot water," Ashley said, coming into the room with a towel wrapped around her.

"Sorry, Mom."

Ashley glowered at that comment but didn't say anything. Even she had to realize how much she was starting to resemble their mom right now. The dark hair, the downturned mouth, the wide hips and bust, the overly serious air that permeated her. Put her in bellbottoms and take her picture with an old Polaroid and she'd fool anyone.

"Shit," Beth said, running out of the room.

Mandy swung into a chair and grabbed a granola bar from a box on the table. As she pulled it out, Ashley swatted her hand. "Those are for the trip."

"I'm hungry now."

Before Ashley could take it away Mandy had it open and stuffed in her mouth.

"Oh, great, now we'll have to stop at the store and get some more."

"So good," Mandy said as crumbs fell from her mouth, covering the counter.

"Hey," Ashley shrieked, "I just wiped that down."

"Where are all the towels?" Beth shouted from behind them.

Ashley turned just in time to see the stark naked and dripping wet Beth run into the kitchen and grab the towel from off Ashley's body. She yanked it away and ran back down the hall, leaving the other girl naked.

"Hey," Ashley said and covered herself.

"Well, that's a whole lot more than I expected to see this morning," Mandy said.

"If you people just did your laundry, this wouldn't have to happen." Ashley grabbed a tea towel and tried to cover herself.

"Your schedule is too hard to follow." Donna pointed to a chore schedule written on a dry erase board hanging from the refrigerator. "How am I supposed to only do my clothes at 2am every Tuesday?"

"That's the optimal time to ensure that we have full hot water every morning for showers," Ashley said. "You find a way to make our hot water tank heat better, I'm all ears."

Mandy tossed her granola bar wrapper in the garbage can and took a drink of orange juice. "Okay, I'm ready, when do we hit the road?"

"When I'm not soaking wet, for one."

"And when you put that phone away," Donna said as Mandy swiped through faces on a dating app.

"We haven't left yet," she said.

"We all agreed to a no-phone weekend," Donna said dismissively.

"I still don't think that's a good idea," Ashley said as she tried to hold two tea towels over her body. "We're going to the woods. We might need one for emergencies."

"There's no signal out in the bush," Donna said. "And besides, we're going to be with four big strong men. We'll have them for emergencies."

"Why the fuck did I ever agree to this in the first place?" Ashley asked.

"Even thirty-year-olds can date," Beth said.

"I'd have preferred if we met these guys somewhere in the city first. What if they're—"

"They're not," Donna said. "Percy told me all about them. Now, let's take a look at their profiles and decide who calls dibs on who."

* * * *

"What's burning?" a voice shouted from the top of the stairs.

"Toast," Aiden called back.

"So I'm not having a seizure," the voice called back matter-of-factly.

"You still could be," Aiden replied. "The fact I'm making toast might just be a coincidence."

Jack came down the stairs and into the kitchen, his short dark hair a mess. He wore fraying smiley face boxers and a torn Nike shirt. He blinked a few times and grabbed the wall, pretending to stumble, then grinned. "Nope. I'm fine. No frothing or nothing."

"It could be an embolism," Aiden said. "Those just come on out of nowhere, I hear."

"Fuck you," Jack said. "Just put another load in the toaster for me."

Jack took out a protein shake from the refrigerator, cracked the top, and pounded it back in one gulp, dripping on his shirt. He wiped his mouth with the back of his hand.

"Are you back on carbs now or not? I can never keep track."

"Then live in the real world," Jack said.

"And disappoint his legions of online followers?" another voice called out.

Percy came into the room, swinging his bulging arms with a confident strut. The owner of the house they all lived in, he was a hugely overinflated man who obviously spent a lot of time in the gym. Between his financial planning job and his workouts, he was barely ever home. He wore a tank-top and sweatpants, and took another protein shake from the fridge to drink.

Aiden shrugged. "What can I say? People seem to want to pay me to live online. I can't help it if I'm just that interesting."

"It's bullshit." Percy belched.

11

A part of him secretly agreed. Aiden lived digitally. He'd created and cultivated an online presence as a minor-league influencer in River City. Restaurant reviews, clubbing, movies, book talk, fancy clothes and recycled life advice; nothing he did was making him rich, but goals were important and every new video he posted was an opportunity to catch fire.

"You're just jealous because you have to go to an office every day."

"Hardly. As long as you can afford the rent, I don't give a shit what you do for money," Percy said.

"I'm jealous," Jack said. "So jealous of all those awkward nerd chicks who crush on you that you never bang. They must be just creaming for it, but you don't even hit them up."

The most popular video Aiden had made had been about a manga series he'd been reading. A high school romance with zombies and mech battles. To him it had just been content, but there were enough fans of the series out there that one had discovered him and decided he was 'cute.' From there he'd enjoyed some peak engagement and dozens of new followers. Keeping them was the struggle.

"Dude," Aiden interjected. "There are boundaries you have to maintain in this game. I don't know if these girls are underage, crazy, actually men or whatever. I say or do the wrong thing, and it goes all over the fucking internet. Then there's protests, dog-piling, petitions. The next thing I know people call me a rapist or a sex predator and my channel is perma-banned. Then bam, out of work and what the fuck do I do?"

"Get a real job," Percy said. "Like the rest of us."

"I don't want a real job."

12

"What good is internet fame if you don't get laid off it?" Jack asked.

"The admiration of my peers, the confidence of my own success, the entrepreneurial ethic," Aiden started, but Jack interrupted him with: "I'd rather have groupies."

"There's no groupies for quote unquote influencing," Percy said, scoffing.

"Not true," Aiden said defensively.

They had this fight all the time. The other guys all had 'real jobs.' Percy and Jack in finance and John in transportation. They didn't get how he could survive by playing the role he played, and he used elements of their lives in his fictional one. The balancing act, for now, was holding. He knew, however, that the day might come when he had to give up his dreams and do something more traditional.

"If you won't fuck your nerd girl fans," Percy said, "they're not exactly groupies, are they?"

"Trust me, it's just way too complicated these days," Aiden said.

"Only because you're a pussy," Percy said. "You're overthinking this. Just let them make the first move and you're off the hook no matter what happens."

"Nerd girls don't make the first move," Jack added.

Percy and Jack had a running competition to see who could get the most women. So far, it was a one-heat race, with Percy so far ahead that he was lapping the guy. But Jack wanted to be Percy in the worst way and lived his life like an echo of the man.

"As if you'd know," Percy said. "Even minor celebrities have super fans going hard for 'em."

"Not Aiden," Jack said, laughing. "His just write fan fiction about him."

Aiden regretted ever having shared that nugget with Jack. "It was only a few pages long, okay? You don't have to keep bringing that up."

"No, I do," Jack said. "It was fucking hilarious. What did that one girl write? That you and some other YouTube guy fucked?"

Percy snorted. "What the shit? Why haven't I heard about this?"

"God, I never should have shown you," Aiden said.

"And she didn't even include herself in the story. That's the kicker. Her fantasy was seeing him fuck another dude."

"Look, can we just forget about that? It's bad enough that it even exists, let alone that I let someone else see it."

"I want to read it," Percy said. "That sounds fucking funny. Aiden getting pegged."

"It was weird, trust me. Just weird."

Most of his interactions with the small coterie of fans who'd liked his manga talk could be classified as similarly abnormal.

"Come on, man, show it to him," Jack said.

"No. Besides, don't we have to get on the road soon? Assuming we are still camping? I told all my followers I was going offline for two days, so I'd like to actually do that now."

"Of course we are," Percy said. "Just get John up and we can be there in no time."

"After we get the beer," Jack added.

* * * *

"Are we packed yet?" Greg called out from the bathroom.

"You could be helping," Sally angrily shouted back from

14

the bedroom as she lay more clothes into the green canvas suitcase. It was neatly filled with clothes of all sizes and for all ages; kids and adults, shirts, shorts, pants, underwear, swimsuits, and all the toiletries an army could possibly need while out on maneuvers. No one could ever accuse her of being unprepared.

Greg entered the bedroom wearing only a towel around his waist. His nearly hairless lanky form was still glistening and moist. Once again, he was avoiding doing any of the actual work involved with travelling. He closed the distance and hugged his wife, soaking her instantly.

"Hey, you're not dry."

"You wanted my help."

"I didn't mean like this."

He kissed her playfully on the neck.

"Quit it, the kids are running around someplace."

"So?"

"So, you're pretty much naked."

Greg dropped the towel to the ground and hugged his wife again, pressing his wet body tightly to her.

"Now I'm totally naked."

"Mommy, Daddy!" Children's screaming filled the air. Greg frantically grabbed the towel and wrapped it around his body just as two kids ran into the room and hopped up on the bed, jumping and causing all of the carefully packed clothes in the suitcase to come flying out in a mess.

"Max, Sophia, get off the bed," Sally shouted at the two kids who'd promptly ruined her meticulous organization.

The boy and his younger sister climbed down, but the damage had been done. The carefully packed suitcase was a disaster. Sally sighed and began pulling everything out to begin repacking.

"Max hit me," Sophia said.

"Did not," the boy replied.

"Did, too."

"Did not."

"Did, too."

"Enough." Greg pulled a shirt over his head. "I don't care who hit who. I just want you guys out of here so we can pack for the trip."

"When are we going?" Max asked.

"When will we get there?" Sophia whined.

"Why do we have to go camping anyway?" Max added.

"Because you two are obsessed with TV and video games. You need to get outside and enjoy nature. Your father and I used to go camping all the time before we had you. It's about time you guys experienced the real world instead of some screen."

"Can we take the DS?" Max asked.

"No, of course we can't," Greg answered. "The whole point of getting outside is to get outside."

"You can play the DS outside. It's portable."

"I mean *out*side. Real outside. Not to just play video games outdoors."

"What about the DVD player? I want to watch—" Sophia began but Greg cut her off with an upraised finger. "No DS, no DVD player, no phones."

"But Greg," Sally said. "We should take the phone. What if we need it for an emergency?"

"No. This is going to be a weekend away from it all and that's final. It's not fair if we don't let the kids bring their screens and then bring ours. So we're both cut off. Besides, there's probably no signal out there anyway."

"I don't know. I'd prefer to have my phone."

Greg shook his head. "We made do without them growing up, we can make do now. It'll be an adventure."

He never put his foot down about anything, but this was not one of the smarter times to finally do it.

"The best adventures are the ones where you've adequately prepared for every contingency."

"Contingency con-shmin-gency. Live a little, honey."

"Yeah, Mommy, live a little."

"You're still not getting that DS," Greg said.

"Awwww, you said to live a little."

Sally said nothing, just went back to refolding and carefully placing their things into the suitcase. She hated having to be the bad guy all the time. She resented Greg's lackadaisical attitude to life that came from being a struggling artist while she had to carry the burden of actually providing for the family and working for a living.

"You're annoying your mother, kids," he said, picking up on her mood for once. "How about this? First one to get your jacket gets a prize."

"I'm going to win," Sophia said and darted out of the room.

"No, I am," Max shouted and followed.

"There," Greg said. "Problem solved. Now you can—"

"I'm taking the phone," Sally said.

"And you think they're addicted to screens?"

THEN

Manfred Schenn stared lazily out the window of the rumbling Greyhound bus. The passing wheat fields blurred into a mass of emptiness as the rumbling forty-seater blazed through the prairies. His stomach growled; the sun was starting its descent, and he hadn't eaten anything all day.

You should have grabbed a candy bar at that last highway stop.

He had some jerky and enough trail mix to last a few days in his pack, but he'd stored that under the bus. To distract from his hunger pangs, he looked around the interior cabin at the others joining him on this trip east. He wondered where they were all going. A pair of men in suits probably heading to Toronto on business, what looked like a tour group of seniors, chatting to the driver.

"—first rode this in forty-two—"

"—should've seen the road then. They'd just paved the lanes and—"

"—but that was after the war—"

A family of Mennonites, backpackers, others minding their own business. Nobody really stood out and neither would he. The man beside him hadn't spoken a word all trip; he seemed lost in some internal monologue, lips moving soundlessly.

"Where ya headed?" Manfred asked the man, deciding that it had been far too awkward sitting next to him in silence for so long.

"Excuse me?" the man asked. He was large, over six feet tall, with dark, sunken eyes and hair pulled back from his face with copious pomade. He had the thick forearms and calloused hands of a labourer or construction worker.

"Just asking where you were headed," Manfred repeated. "All the way to the Maritimes? Stopping in Toronto? Ottawa? Quebec? Thunder Bay?"

"You ask a lot of questions," the man said.

"Heh, sorry, I guess I should have started with one." Manfred chuckled.

"Which one?"

"How about we start with what's your name? Mine's Manfred. From River City. I'm in publishing, mostly industrial safety manuals, but—"

"Hello, Manfred," the man said calmly.

"Hello, Mr....?"

He remained silent and seemed not to be forthcoming with his name, so Manfred switched subjects. "Alright then, how about telling me where you're headed to?"

"Do you really want to know?" The man looked at Manfred with the coldest eyes he'd ever seen. They weren't completely grey, but they had to be close.

"It makes the trip go by faster if you have someone to talk to."

"I thought I did," the man said.

"We've been sitting side by side for four hours so far and you haven't said a word or done a thing. Not even read a book."

19

"I was listening."

"To whom?"

"Just the voices."

"Sure, I get it. Piecing together the stranger's lives, right? What did you pick up?"

"It's hard to make sense of the great jumble. But it'll become clearer the further from the city we go."

"You sound like a man heading to the great outdoors. I can dig that. I'm going camping. Rock Peak Lake. It's beautiful out there. I figured to get away from the grind for a couple of days, sit at the beach, let nature rejuvenate me, that sort of thing."

"Ah yes, I understand. The call of nature, trees and bears and such."

"That's right," Manfred said. "Although I'd hoped to avoid bears on this trip. They don't make the best tent partners."

From the look on the man's face, Manfred had to assume that he didn't understand the joke. In fact, the way the man looked at him, Manfred wasn't so sure he understood English at all. It was as if the words were going in one ear and out the other.

"You know, cos a bear in your tent would make it pretty crowded." He elbowed the man gently in the ribs, to punctuate the joke, but the man just stared at the gesture like it was insane. Blank eyes looked back. It was like talking to a brick wall.

"You still haven't said where you were going. East, I presume. If you've never been, go to Ottawa. See where all the decisions are made, then hop on over to Montreal and check out the girls. They'll do things the ones in River City can't even—"

"I have already been told where to go."

"Alright then. That's good to—"

Manfred trailed off. The strange man was asleep. It was as if a switch had simply been turned off in his head and he was out.

Strange guy, he thought to himself and turned back to the window and the passing prairie.

* * * *

Alice checked and rechecked her bag. She had everything she could possibly need for a weekend alone in the woods; clothes, first aid kit, food, water, map, extra battery, flashlight, bear spray, bug spray, knife, signal flare. She couldn't think of a single thing she'd missed.

"Am I over-prepared? Better safe than sorry."

She slung the pack over her shoulder and tested the weight. It felt heavy, but nothing she couldn't handle. She walked over to the full-length mirror and admired herself. She certainly looked like a regular camper; cargo pants, bandana, solid hiking boots, sunglasses, flannel shirt. You'd never know this was to be her first time out in the woods alone or that she was looking at this trip as an opportunity to get away, slow down and try to bring some sanity into her chaotic life.

Look at you. You can do this.

The dirty-blonde hair, tanned skin, and pert smile didn't show it, but the faint beginnings of crow's feet did. Maybe it was the divorce, the stress from her job, or just that nagging voice at the back of her head that criticized herself for all the bad decisions that had led her to this point. They were all aging her before her time.

Adam, the house, my mom, work, they can all fuck right off for a weekend.

She had to get away, just had to. She needed time to sort herself out. Alone. To not have any pressures forcing her down a path she didn't want to take. So many people were pulling her in so many different directions that she wanted to scream.

"You're not getting any younger. You need to have kids now," her mother said as if she had any control over that. The woman had no idea that Adam had been the one to refuse children, said they weren't a part of his life plan. She'd blown nine years of her life with him and for what?

What a fucking waste.

Then there were all the changes at work. New systems coming in to the place—"modernization", they were calling it. A modernization that might just leave her out of work. Almost thirty, divorced, and maybe soon-to-be unemployed? Was the universe trying to force an early mid-life crisis on her?

None of these things were going to matter for at least one weekend. She was going to get away from it all and just be, without pressures, demands, or stresses. Without anyone nagging or criticizing. No exes, no tactless married friends. Just her and the woods. She was on her way to Rock Peak Lake, and she was going to enjoy herself. She was going to learn things that she'd never even thought about trying before. She would confront her inner fears and become a stronger woman. That was how it worked, right? Woman versus nature. Woman grows and comes out on top. Whatever. It didn't matter if she learned a goddamned thing. This was her weekend and there wasn't anything anyone was going to do to ruin it for her.

* * * *

"Come here, you," Candace said, pulling Ron in close. She kissed him on the lips, her tongue questing inside his mouth right away. She could taste the coffee he'd had earlier.

Ron pulled himself back and looked her in the eyes. "Whoa, slow down, baby, we just—"

"I don't care." She lunged in again.

At first Ron tried to hold off, but soon he relented. He moved his hands all over Candace's body. She plunged into his pants and took hold of him. He lifted her shirt over her head, then she did the same to him. Soon they were writhing on the bed, mixing bodily fluids, panting and heaving. When it was all over, she rolled off him and grinned.

He looked over at the naked body of his wife and marvelled at every curve and bare inch of her skin, unable to come to grips with his good fortune. She had married him. Her, Candace Mitchell, goddess of River City and the best tea store employee the world had ever seen, had married him, Ron Balor, boring old accountant and part-time marathon runner. It had only been a few weeks, but it still hadn't sunk in.

She ran her hand over his body, his chest, his stomach, then lower, grabbing hold again.

"A third time? I'm not a machine."

"That's not what this says," she said seductively.

God, she was an animal. Was this what marriage was going to be like all the time?

"Can we save some for the lake? As much as I'd like to

just spend all weekend here in bed with you, we did book a camping site. Besides, I think it'll be fun to make love under the stars, in the water, on the beach…"

"In the tent," she added. "Against a tree."

"On a cliff," he said. "Maybe in a cave?"

"On the highway," she offered.

"In the ranger's cabin?"

She pulled away. "If you think I'm sharing you with him, you've got another thing coming."

"That's not what I meant," Ron said, laughing.

"I'm sure we'll find lots of places to make love, but right now I want to do it again."

"You're insatiable," Ron said, shaking his head in awe at the woman he was blessed with.

"Just hurry up and get hard."

"Done and done."

* * * *

"Fired. Me. Fucking fired. What goddamn bullshit."

Sonny took a pull on his beer and threw the empty into the pile next to his shabby tent. There were already over a dozen stubbies laying strewn about the area and he had plans to have dozens more join them before this weekend was through.

"I don't understand it, baby," the pert blonde beside him said. Her feathered hair was held back with a bandana and she wore short jean shorts and a fringed, loose floral blouse. "You were playing so good, too."

"I know I was. Shit, the whole fucking arena knew I was. Mother fucking Alice Cooper was watching in the wings, scouting me. I could tell."

24

"Really? Alice Cooper?"

"Yeah. That was what I saw when I was hitting my solo. The man himself standing, watching me play. I heard he's in the market for a new guitarist. Shit. Could you imagine playing for a bigtime act like that? Touring the fucking world? It would beat the hell out of gigging clubs across western Canada."

"I'll bet he even hits eastern Canada," she said.

Sonny took another beer and popped the cap with his bottle opener necklace. He handed it to her then repeated the move and kept one for himself.

"Eastern Canada, the Maritimes, the West Coast, hell, America and Europe, too. I could see the world."

"I guess you didn't pass the audition then, right?"

He looked at the blonde and wondered how someone could be so dense. Then again, the kind of woman who waited backstage for the opening act of a show at the River City arena, then agreed to go camping with the now-fired lead guitarist of that act, might not have a bright future in rocket science. Still, she was good-looking, and clearly enamoured with the fact that he was a musician. Why else would she have sucked his dick in the car ride over here?

"Are we just gonna sit out here all night?" she asked.

"I brought a tent," he said, waving his hand dismissively at the collapsed fabric that he'd failed to set up. He dug into his pocket for his little box of cocaine. Inside was enough for a great weekend, even without the beer and company.

"Are you gonna finish putting it together?"

"I don't know how to do that outdoors stuff, baby," he said as he rolled a dollar bill.

"I can do it," she offered as she rose and wiggled her hips

over to the edge of the campsite.

"Really? Where'd you learn to do that?"

"I was in the girl scouts."

He hoped she wasn't still in the girl scouts. She did look awfully young. She knew her way around and had all the right parts, but IDs could be faked. His old boss Malcolm Barton always said, "If there's grass on the field, the boys can play," but Sonny hated Little League.

"Alright then," he said. "I nominate you to put the tent up while I get the coke ready."

NOW

"Case closed."

Frank Malone felt that immense sense of pride that came with another job well done. He grabbed the manilla file folder and opened the cover, writing in a line at the bottom of the yellow legal pad he'd been keeping his notes on. He put the date for the following Monday. Sometimes he amazed even himself with his detective skills.

He dropped the Bic and admired his penmanship. The writing was shakier than it used to be, some of the loops weren't quite so loopy, but then a lot of things were shakier with Frank Malone these days. His knees seemed to creak a little more, his back tended to get stuck if he bent over too far for too long, his aim wasn't quite as steady down at the firing range, and he had trouble reading without his glasses. He wasn't injured, concussed, or recovering, this was an ailment that there'd be no coming back from. Aging. It was one hell of a bitch.

But no matter what indignities Father Time was thrusting on him, the mind of Frank Malone was as sharp as a tack. A bag of tacks, in fact. One of those great big industrial sized ones they used for the huge tacking jobs, you know the ones. Extra sharp and extra deadly. At least with his wits intact, he could in some small way as the head of the Frank Malone Detective Agency still put his pointy crime solving brain to good use and help the fine people of River City. He might not be a cop anymore on paper and he might not be Detective Inspector Sergeant Frank Malone in the eyes of the mayor, the chief, and all the other officers that did the good work, day in and day out, but by God he was still the same man on the inside. The wrapper might have wrinkled, but the candy core was as solid as ever.

"Another satisfied customer, eh, Red?"

The desk calendar photo of Angie Everhart, next to the cream-coloured rotary phone, didn't answer, but then if it did he'd really have to start worrying about his wits. He'd picked it up in 1993 and had never quite been able to get rid of it. A woman who looked like that was timeless. Her photograph was mute, that red-haired angel just smiled at him, telling him that it was indeed another job well done.

It had been a simple open and shut case. Old man Ulster had lost his trailer. A family heirloom, used by the Ulsters to go on camping trips for a generation. He'd parked it one night and come back to find it gone. The police had been no help, so he'd turned to the one man who could get things done in this city. Frank Malone.

"You have to help me, sir," old man Ulster had pleaded. "It's going to be summer soon and what will I do with no trailer to take to the lake?"

"Don't worry, old man," Frank had replied. It was debatable which one of them was older, but then Ulster was coming to him for help, wasn't he?

"I won't let some degenerate criminal scum have a disorderly weekend with your property. I'll find that trailer and

I'll bring it home so you can get back to pitching your tent."

The old man had been relieved. He'd paid his advance plus expenses with no questions asked. "Oh, thank you, Mr. Malone, thank you. You're my only hope."

"I'm always here for my elders," Frank had said, patting the man on the shoulder as he'd led him out the door.

"We're probably the same age," the man had protested. "You might even be a little older. I'm seventy-seven, how about you?"

But Frank hadn't had time for chatting with possibly confused elderly gentlemen, he'd just pushed the man out the door and gotten to work. He was behind the eight ball already if the trailer had been missing for two weeks. So he'd hit the streets, checked out all the used trailer shops in town, only to find nothing, not even a faint trace of the thing. Then he'd had a brain fart. Old man Ulster had said he took his trailer to Rock Peak Lake in the Whiteshell. A place Frank knew well, but hadn't had the chance to go to for years. So he had taken his old car up to Rock Peak Lake, passed through the gate, been warned to watch for bears, then gone to the campground and made the rounds until he found what he was looking for. There, parked in a reserved spot, was old man Ulster's trailer. A little dusty and covered in mayflies, but there in its metallic flesh.

"The senile fool left it parked here all along."

Frank had been all set to tell the man the good news when he'd had an epiphany. "If the man thinks the trailer is gone, and it's right here where it's supposed to be, then what harm is it if I take a weekend sabbatical? I've certainly deserved a break for a long time."

As he walked around the antique, he remembered the good

29

old days of camping in the woods with a trailer just like this. A two-bed jalopy with canopy, truck hitch, propane tank, sliding windows, and off-yellow finish. It brought back memories he hadn't thought about in years. Him and his oldest friend, Derek, Russ, Fuller and the whole gang out in the woods hunting and fishing, drinking beers by the fire, laughing the night away. Why, it must have been over forty years since he'd last gone camping. Here was a chance to relive old times. And on salary, too.

Now, in his office, he closed the file folder and leaned back in his chair. He stared out the window at a city he was all set to leave behind for the weekend. "You'll have to do without me, River City, I've got plans. A little fishing and some R and R. No harm done. I'll tell Ulster where his trailer is on Monday." He could practically taste the fresh walleye and cold beer.

NOW

Another head exploded on screen as a demon died in a splash of blood and guts, crying out in anguish from being torn apart in the prime of his anti-life. Reloading, the space marine turned to the next creature in line and cut it in two with a double-barrelled shotgun blast at point-blank range. Soon, the grey-walled room was full of corpses. Blood soaked the walls and floor, gradually fading away into nothingness.

"Nice one, Matt," Josh said from beside him.

The world around him came back into focus as he realized that he'd let himself get completely immersed, ignorant of his surroundings or of the time of day. The annoying, shrill voice of his friend in the room snapped him out of it. He turned to the man who had broken his focus. Josh. Deeply tanned skin, black hair, pockmarked face. A small, beaded flower on his shirt pocket revealed his indigenous heritage. The man's heavy breaths betrayed the fact that he'd eaten McDonalds for breakfast even if there weren't crumpled up wrappers laying on the floor.

"Yeah."

Matt wondered why Josh was content to play spectator as he went through Doom for the millionth time. He knew all of the secret doors, where the demons were placed, the keycard locations, the route to the BFG; what was the appeal? But then it was obvious. Matt was simply the coolest person Josh knew. It was nice having a sycophant.

"You really fucked up that thing," Josh said.

"That's the point of the game, dipshit."

"Yeah, I know. But you did a good job of it. Clean headshot, pow."

Matt reached into a box and pulled out a beer. He cracked it open and took a drink. It was warm.

"I thought I told you to put this in the fridge."

"Not me, man, you must have told Beth that. Fact is, I'm pretty sure you did tell her to do it. I know I heard it. One hundred percent."

"Well, why didn't she then? Beth?" Matt shouted towards the bedroom. "Beth?"

"I don't think she's here, man," Josh said haltingly.

"Where the fuck did she go?"

"Uh, you guys broke up," Josh said.

Matt had to pause the game to think about that one.

"Broke up?"

"Yeah, don't you—"

He cut the man off with a raised hand. Beth had left him. It had come out of nowhere. He remembered them playing Resident Evil, then her going to bed, mumbling something about needing to sleep at regular human hours. He remembered stumbling in later, drunk and ready to fuck. She'd been all too eager if he was picturing things right. He'd passed out, but was sure he'd left her satisfied, like always. But then, it was all a little fuzzy.

"I'm…" He trailed off as he replayed those minutes in his

mind. Eyes opening. Sunlight. Burning urge to piss. Rising up to the can, spraying a solid minute's worth, mostly in the bowl. Then, after the nearly orgasmic release, he'd grabbed his phone and seen cryptic words from her.

"It's over. Don't call me."

"You think that's what she meant by her text?" he said to Josh.

"Is this a trick question?" Josh asked.

"What the fuck are you getting at?"

"No, it's just… I thought it was pretty clear and—"

"It was that stuck-up bitch, Ashley," Matt said. "She hates my guts and poisoned Beth against me."

"I dunno—"

"She hates your fucking guts, too, dipshit."

"Really? Why? What did I ever do to her?"

"She's been trying to get Beth to dump me for months," Matt said.

"But why does she hate you so much?"

"She's obviously jealous of what I have with Beth. It's probably been years since she's even sniffed a dick."

"That's a weird kink."

"It's a figure of speech, dumbass. It means she's not exactly going on a lot of dates."

"Maybe she's a closet dyke," Josh said, shrugging.

Matt could feel a vein pulsing in his forehead. He felt ready to pop. He turned and pointed at Josh, in no mood to explain himself, but doing so anyway. "She's mine. She should be home with me."

"But—"

"They've taken her somewhere, I just know it. I can find out." He opened his phone and scrolled through Facebook.

33

"Blocked? What the fuck?" he said.

"She blocked you? That's not a good sign."

He typed a name into the search bar and found one of her friend's accounts. She'd blocked him, too. So he kept trying until he found—

"There," Josh said, pointing to the screen. "Donna posted that she's going to a girls' weekend at the lake."

"She didn't block you?"

"Not Donna. She's a slut. She likes the attention. Beth must be with her."

"She didn't tag anyone else in the post," Josh said, looking over Matt's shoulder at the screen. "You don't know that for sure."

"It makes perfect sense. They're roommates. Of course they would go together."

"Maybe she has other friends?" Josh offered.

"Are you trying to cover for her now or something?" Matt said threateningly.

Josh blanched. "Of course not," he stammered. "But this doesn't tell us anything more than Donna is going to a lake. You could be jumping to conclusions."

"I'm not. It all adds up. But lake is too general. Where, specifically, would they be going? There's got to be a hundred lakes in this province."

"So there's no sense in going beyond this, right?" Josh said. "You said it yourself. You'll never narrow it down. No point getting worked up. She could be at Grand Beach or Patricia Beach or Victoria Beach or—"

"I get it," he said, waving his hand dismissively. "But there's got to be some trail. Can't you track her phone or something?"

"I'm not a spyware program."

"So hack it."

"Yeah, I'm not that either. I can barely use my own damn phone half the time."

"Are you're telling me I've lost Beth?"

A chill went through him. He felt almost faint. It was as if he was losing a piece of himself with only the thought of being apart. Did she really mean that much to him? Of course she did. She was his woman.

Josh paused and considered the situation for a moment, then nearly slapped himself on the forehead for missing the most obvious piece of the puzzle staring right at them both.

"No, you didn't lose her, man."

"But you said you can't track her or hack her."

"I don't have to do anything like that. Donna's profile is full public. She's such a narcissist that she's left it open for anyone to see. I can just deep dive into her account and look through her old posts. I'm sure somewhere in the past however many years she's been on Facebook she's mentioned going to the lake before. With any luck, she names it and bang. We've got a trail."

"Well, hurry up and do that then. I need to get some stuff ready for the trip. I want to be on the road as quickly as we can. We can't let them get too far ahead of us after all."

It took about half an hour of looking through a thousand dinner glamour shots, half-empty wine glasses, little black dresses, fancy cakes, puppies, cat memes, shared YouTube videos, and motivational pictures, but eventually Josh found what they were after. A post from six years ago, when Donna was still a teenager, talking about going to the family cabin at—

"Bingo," he shouted out and waved Matt over. "Found it,

dude. Rock Peak Lake. Her family has a campground there."

Matt leaned over his shoulder, breathing heavily. He was dressed in full camouflage. He felt something go wrong with his eyes. They were glazing over, seeing events ahead of him, picturing what was coming. A whisper in the back of his head told him a secret. "That's where they are."

"It's possibly where they are. Assuming 'they' is Ashley, Donna and—"

"Beth. She's there."

"Now, you sure none of the rest of them have ever mentioned a cabin or a lake or a campground or anything before?"

"It's there. That's the place." The voice confirmed it. Some kind of sixth sense speaking to him in his hour of need. They always told you to trust your intuition. He would do more than trust it.

"You really want to drive all the way out there without checking first?"

"If you're so fucking concerned about wasting gas, then deep dive their accounts, too, while I put on my face paint."

Matt turned and walked back towards the bathroom. He seemed to be really weirding out Josh. The guy squirmed like he had to go to the bathroom.

"You're painting your face, too?" he asked.

"It wouldn't be very good camouflage if I left my face uncovered, dipshit," Matt said coldly. He began drawing over his face slowly.

THEN

Hunger. Insatiable hunger. A driving need for blood and flesh to sustain the churning forces within. The forest was quiet, as if the trees themselves were anticipating what was to come.

The noises of those that knew to stay away had fallen silent as it moved through the night. Smells drifting on the wind told it of the promise of food nearby.

The rough bark of a tree dragged along its side as it passed, trying to orient itself in space to determine the best path to reach what it desired.

Perfectly still, the deer never realized the danger. Head down, it moved brazenly along the old trails. It realized its mistake too late.

Dead. Torn open rapidly. Entrails and gore spilling out onto the precious earth. This force was nothing more than a morsel. Hardly enough to quell the growing demand.

The great cycle was about to begin again. As it had countless times in the past. The role was familiar even if the player was not. The goal, though, was clear.

Feed.

Kill.

Devour.

Follow the wheel of destiny.

Rising from the corpse of the deer, it left the remnants to the carrion eaters. It must find better targets, feed on more deserving prey. They were out there, among the trees. Unaware. Soon to be their own cogs in the great everlasting machine of life.

* * * *

Frank pulled the car up to the park ranger station and rolled down the window. The burly man in the ill-fitting forest green uniform exited the tiny building. He leaned over the car and looked at the two of them inside with pale eyes.

"Welcome to the park," the man said. "You here for some camping this weekend?"

"You got that right," Derek replied from the passenger seat, raising his open beer in salute to the man in uniform.

"So it's camping and drinking then?"

"And fishing," Frank added.

"You boys have your licenses?"

"Damn straight," Derek said.

"Right here, Ranger Smith." Frank proffered the tiny white card he'd slipped out of his wallet as the man spoke. He always made sure to pick up a fishing license every year, even if he rarely had much time to use it.

"Nice to see you came prepared," the ranger said. "We sell them here, too, if you forgot."

"We didn't."

"Good on you."

"Get one every season," Derek said.

"It's the law," Frank added.

"Right," the ranger said. "It's the law."

"And we follow the law."

"Glad you do."

The ranger sized them up, checking the gear in the back seat. Derek took a sip of his beer. Frank waited for the man to do or say anything else, but he just stood there staring at them.

"So can we go now?" Frank asked.

"You look like a couple of experienced campers."

"Absolutely," Derek said.

"We had a bear attack last night. Seems an inexperienced camper was asleep up on the ridge. He didn't follow the rules, and it got him. It wasn't pretty."

"Wow. Black or grizzly?"

"Grizzly. Big one, too," the ranger said. "Of course we have signs up, but every now and again an inexperienced camper doesn't obey them and this is the unfortunate result. We have to share this beautiful place with God's creatures. But since you're experienced campers, you don't need to be reminded of that now, do you?"

"Sure don't," Derek said.

Frank turned to Derek and grinned, then looked back to the ranger.

"Say, it never hurts to have a refresher. What exactly attracts bears, Ranger Smith?" Frank asked.

"Oh, cooking smells, garbage, excrement. Experienced campers know. They're attracted to disruptions in the natural—"

"Say, Ranger Smith," Derek interrupted. "Was this man's food stored properly or improperly? Like perhaps in a picnic basket?"

"No, that's the problem," the ranger said. "He was an inexperienced camper, and it was all just left out in the open. He didn't—"

"So not in a picnic basket."

The ranger shook his head. "Nope. Right in the open. The smells would travel for kilometres. A bear could—"

"Unless the bear had already taken the picnic basket before you got to the scene," Derek added.

"I guess that's possible, but what kind of bear would—"

Derek finally burst out laughing and Frank couldn't help himself either.

"YO-GI!" they cried out in unison and crashed their beers together, splashing the bench seat of the old Caprice.

The ranger finally clued in to their inside joke. "Alright, alright, very funny. I get it. Yogi Bear. Picnic baskets. Park ranger. Ha ha. But let me tell you two so-called experienced camper goofballs something. Nature is harsh. A bear attack is nothing to sneeze at, so you just make sure you follow the rules. There's so much wild forest here, they might never find your bodies."

"Gotcha, Ranger Smith," Frank said. "But you don't have to worry about us. Like we said, we're experienced campers, and we can take care of ourselves."

"That remains to be seen," the ranger said as he backed away and waved them through.

NOW

The wind blew Beth's hair in her face. The streets passed by in a blur. When they crossed the perimeter highway and left the city behind, she was finally able to let herself relax. She looked over her shoulder. She didn't see any cars following her and let out a long sigh of relief.

"Why do you keep looking back?" Donna asked. "There's nobody out here but us."

"I know. I know," Beth said. "I just had this weird feeling, is all."

"Leave it behind," Donna said. "We're going to have a great time this weekend."

"I hope so."

"No negative energy allowed," Mandy said. "You don't want to jinx your chances."

"Yeah," Beth said. "You're right. No negative energy."

It felt good to be leaving town. But it felt even better to have finally left Matt. It hadn't gone the way she'd wanted—over the phone with a text—but she knew that there was no way Matt would let her go easily in person. It didn't matter what she might say, he'd claim that he needed her, flash his patented desolate look and make her feel so guilty that she'd relent and take it all back. Then all they'd end up doing was sitting in his living room the whole day while she watched him play video games. He'd get drunk, she'd go to bed early. He'd stumble in far too handsy and he'd…

No.

She couldn't do that again. She wouldn't do it ever again. She had to stay away from him. The first step was to experience a weekend on her own.

"What do you know about Percy's friends?" Mandy asked Donna.

"Roommates actually. They all live in his house."

"Hey, just like we all live in Ashley's," Mandy said happily. "That's something in common, right?"

"Hardly," Ashley said as she drove the convertible. "I'll bet they're all slobs and the place is falling apart."

"We're all slobs," Donna said. "What's your point?"

"My point is, don't get ahead of yourselves. These guys could be as big of assholes as Matt."

Beth caught Ashley looking at her in the rearview mirror. She chose not to take the bait for now. It wasn't that Matt was all bad. Despite what the others thought, he was actually a sweet guy when they were alone, and he wasn't drinking or focused on gaming. Maybe he wasn't the most motivated person, he never saw much point in going out and doing "things," but she wasn't much for clubbing or going to movies or out for dinner anyway. That world got old. It cost money. It took effort.

She could handle staying in. Sometimes she preferred it. The issue was that lately Matt's mood had darkened. He was drinking more and staying inside for longer stretches, sleeping through the day, staying up all night. "He's still getting over his night shift routine," she told herself and her friends. "He'll adjust eventually."

Sometimes he lost control.

"Why do you always have to point out how much you hate Matt?" Mandy asked.

"Because he's no good," Ashley said. "It was about time Beth dumped that waste."

Now Beth felt she had to speak up, even though she knew this was all a way for Ashley to dig the knife in deeper.

"You don't understand. They were shutting down his work. He was getting laid off. They called it delayed downsizing; making him do all the final clean up, shipping out parts, that sort of thing. He was going to be the last one left in the plant, packing it all up and turning out the lights. It's a lot to deal with."

"That's no excuse for the way he treated you."

Deep down, she knew Ashley had a point. That was what made it hard to defend the guy. Matt had hit her once. He'd been drinking and they'd been fighting. It had come out of nowhere. She'd done what she was supposed to do, walked out. He'd sobered up, apologized profusely, vowed never to do it again and he hadn't. There had been a few close calls, but he had kept his promise. But that didn't mean she didn't fear what could happen should he truly lose it.

"It was messing with his personality. He wasn't usually—"

"He's not the only guy out there," Ashley said curtly.

"I know, but you have to stand by people at their lowest," Beth persisted. "When they need the most help, you can—"

"Would he do that for you?"

It was a question she'd purposely avoided.

"I—"

"Look," Donna said, interrupting the debate. "You said it

yourself. He's not the only guy out there. In fact, you're about to meet three others who are most definitely not him."

"Exactly," Mandy said. "Think about it, three single guys, three single ladies."

"Me and Percy might not be super official," Donna said. "But that doesn't mean I haven't already called dibs."

"I know, I know, that's why I said three."

"Count me out of your attempts to play matchmaker, Donna," Ashley said as she drove. "I'm just here to make sure no one does anything stupid."

"Oh, come on, Ash," Donna said. "You might like one of them."

"Doubt it."

"Not with that attitude," Mandy chimed in.

"Nobody get ahead of yourselves," Ashley said. "They could all be pieces of shit. Like—"

"Matt," Mandy said. "We know, we know. Just think about how any of these guys should be a step up then."

"Hey," Beth said. "Can we not keep ragging on Matt, please? He's—"

"In the past," Ashley said. "Right, Beth?" She stared at her through the rearview mirror.

"Yup," Beth said tentatively. "Way in the past."

"Good, then if you'll stop, I'll stop, too. No more talking about Matt?"

She had to admit it felt good to be on the road. In a convertible with the top down, the sun shining, knowing she was getting away. The tension just blew away in the wind. She'd deal with the fallout when she got back. A part of her knew Matt would understand. He had to. And if not, she had her own place and three friends to help her through.

Ignore him. She would. She was going to enjoy being with her friends.

"No more talking about Matt," Beth said proudly.

"Great, then let's get back to figuring out who calls dibs on who," Mandy said.

* * * *

"They only have Blue here," Jack shouted from the beer fridge at the back of the small convenience store they'd stopped at on the highway. His voice carried in the nearly empty room.

"Just clear 'em out. I don't care what brand it is," Percy said back.

"But I hate Blue," John grumbled next to him at the counter. He plopped down an armful of chip bags in a precarious pile, shoving them away from the edge before they fell off the side.

The man looked half dead. They'd had a hell of a time waking him up and from his eyes, it wasn't clear they'd fully succeeded. He'd been drunk as usual and didn't want to move from his bed. A bucket of water in the face had jerked him right to life and probably cleaned his sheets more than he ever would.

"It's beer."

Dishevelled and awkward, John fumbled around with his towering pile of chips, catching bags that nearly fell to the floor until he finally just pushed the whole thing towards the clerk who stood watching with disdain. "I seriously hate that shit," John said.

"Who're you kidding?" Percy snorted. "You drink whatever's there. You'd probably drink your own piss if you thought it had some leftover liquor in it."

John had no retort because they all knew deep down that Percy was right.

"Fine," the man said, "but I want whiskey, too."

"If you're paying for it, then be my guest."

The woman at the counter looked at them impatiently. She took each bag of chips and rang them through the scanner before brusquely dropping them into a large brown paper bag. The cash register showed their total at almost fifty dollars already and that didn't even include the gas Aiden was pumping outside.

"Any more?" she asked when the chip mountain was depleted.

"Sure," Jack said, dropping down an entire rack full of beer. "Brewskis."

"For an army?" she asked.

"Camping."

"You need brew for camping. Otherwise, what's the point?" Percy said matter-of-factly.

She watched wide-eyed as Jack piled up the cases of beer to head height. John added two bottles of Jack Daniels. This was going to be one hell of a party.

"Jeez." The woman shook her head in disbelief and rang it all up. By the time she was done, they were at well over two hundred.

"You got the money to pay for all this?" she asked skeptically.

"Of course." Percy peeled off a couple of bills from his stack. "What are we, a bunch of degenerates?"

"Uhhh…" she started but thought better of it. She took the cash quickly. It was probably more than the place usually made in a week way out here in the middle of nowhere.

In no time they were back on the road bobbing their heads

to Tom Petty blaring on the radio. The sun shone high in the sky. The silver SUV, crammed with alcohol and camping supplies, roared through the prairie landscape and before the Full Moon Fever album had even finished, they were pulling into a campground spot at Rock Peak Lake.

"Alright, fuckers," Percy said. "Let's unload this stuff and get drinking."

"I think John already started," Jack said, pointing to the only one of them who hadn't exited the vehicle.

The man was in the back asleep. Snoring, with a bottle of Jack Daniels in his hand, a third empty already.

"Okay. Unload him, too. I don't want him pissing or puking in my car."

Working together, it didn't take that long. Sure, the tents might be a little crooked, the lawn chairs a little torn, and the beer a little warm, but they had the place ready to host a party in record time.

Aiden dropped into his chair with a beer. He had to admit that this was a nice break from streaming. It was peaceful out here in the woods. He didn't have to focus on constantly saying something amusing for the watchers at home, didn't have to worry about accidentally picking his nose or scratching somewhere awkward and having it meme'd the next day, and he certainly didn't have to check himself in front of these guys. The more they drank, the more offensive and politically incorrect everyone got. Aiden listened to his friends making fun of an entire religion just because they'd been stuck in traffic downtown for a few extra minutes. No one was spared.

Freed from the constraints of watching their words, they acted like old standup comedians.

Offensive, stupid, ignorant, it didn't matter. It was the guys, and he found himself laughing anyway. He blamed the booze.

"So, when do we meet these friends of your booty call?" Jack asked Percy.

"She said they were aiming to be at their site for three pm," Percy said, sipping from his beer, "so we've got time to pregame a little."

"You know anything about them?" Jack asked. "They hot or—"

"If they're anything like Donna, they'll be choice," Percy said.

"So what's the rule for tent hookups? Sock on the flap or—"

"You really think you're going to score that fast?" Aiden asked.

"Hey," Jack said, smirking. "Percy primed Donna, right? They have to be coming out here looking for a good time. What happens in Rock Peak Lake, stays in Rock Peak Lake."

"How about you just try to come across as not a completely desperate loser?" Percy said. "You'd be surprised at how well that works."

"Huh," Jack said, rubbing his chin. "You think?"

"I know."

"Well, there's always a first time," Jack said.

* * * *

"I don't get how this thing is supposed to go in." Greg fumbled with two aluminum rods that didn't seem to want to fit together.

The campsite was a disaster area. The van, parked backwards with the trunk open, seemed to have vomited out a boy scout group's worth of stuff; chairs, blankets, a cooler, toys, everything strewn about the ground like a tornado had passed through. Greg had their new tent out of the packaging, partly built but still looking like nothing more than a flat pile of fabric on the grass.

"It's supposed to be a four-person chalet-style luxury tent according to the box, but right now it doesn't look like anything more than an expensive mat."

The two rods he held didn't seem to want to fit together, despite the tiny drawings on the paper in his hand insisting they should. If the stick figures could do it, why couldn't he? What was he doing wrong?

"Just follow the instructions," Sally said as she tried to slather sunscreen on Max who desperately wanted to escape her grasp and go exploring.

"That's what I'm trying to do. But they don't make any sense."

"Maybe you aren't as fluid in French as you thought."

"Twelve years of immersion, I'm fine." He tried to re-read the steps on the previous page. "I'm just a little rusty. Besides, if you hadn't lost the English pages, we wouldn't be in this mess."

"Don't blame that on me, it came out of the box that way. You're the one who didn't want to go back to Canadian Tire to exchange the thing."

She was neglecting to mention that they'd already been on the road an hour when she'd cracked open the box to see how hard the building job was going to be. They would have lost precious time and then she'd have had to admit that not remembering to buy the tent before the day they were supposed to leave was a dumb mistake in and of itself. She'd never stoop to that.

"There's nothing wrong with the tent, okay?" he said.

"Just the manual is all wrong."

"Look, they're not going to take it back just because we whine about not knowing Canada's other official language."

"You could have damaged the thing first, used that as an excuse."

"I'm not going to vandalize a perfectly good bit of outdoor equipment just to return it. We're not Walmart shoppers, okay?"

Max tried to run off and Sally slathered some more lotion on his neck. He struggled fiercely and finally she just gave up and let go. She watched him run after his sister who was happily tossing seeds to a squirrel.

"Okay, Mr. Too Good For Wally-world. You're just so sophisticated. Only shopping at higher priced stores, I get it."

"It's not that. It's about making a political statement."

"If you think the Waltons give two shits about whether or not you find their store distasteful, you're more far gone than I thought. I mean, you are getting old, but usually senility doesn't kick in quite yet."

Greg stopped his attempted construction of the tent and looked at Sally, who just grinned at him. She knew exactly how to push his buttons, always staying on the edge of playfulness, but still saying just enough of what needed to be said to take the piss out of him. She'd always been like that, since their first date so many years ago. That was part of what had attracted her to him in the first place: her irreverence. But sometimes he wondered if the fact that she made the money and he lived a life as a starving artist had made her lose respect for him.

"Oh, did I hit too close to home?" She smirked and walked over and hugged him. Her loose dress and blouse gently swayed with her over-the-top movements. Despite it all, she was still the same girl he'd married so long ago, the one he'd fallen for pretty much from day one. The only one he'd put a ring on and the only one he ever would if the world cooperated. Sure, there might be a few stray grey hairs in her wild dirty-blonde mane, and she might have a few more curves left over from giving birth to two beautiful children, but he was just as in love with her as he'd always been. Even if she could be a real prick sometimes. Or maybe because of that. But did she still love him as much?

She leaned in and kissed him gently. "Let me see those instructions. Maybe my French holds up better than yours." She took the page and they got back to work together.

THEN

A lice perched on the rocky ridge and looked out over the vast expanse of the lake. It was calm and clear and stretched out as far as she could see. There'd be cabins somewhere on the other side, but unless she took a boat out, they were just little pricks of reflected light in the hazy distance.

This was peace. This was exactly what she wanted. Here she could just be and not worry about what anyone expected from her. Her small tent was fully constructed. She had her heavy-duty hiking shoes and she was ready to hit the trails. But first, there was something she had always wanted to do. She looked around, as if there might be someone watching, but trusting that she was as alone as she'd ever been, and stood up. She grinned to herself and quickly stripped down out of her clothes. Then, completely naked, she took a massive deep breath. She felt the sun on her bare skin and shouted out "I'm free!" to the vastness of nature.

No one replied but the animals and the wind. Then, as she stretched and let the warmth of the sunshine envelop her bare skin, she thought she heard a man's cry distantly across the water. She paused, waited, felt the grass between her toes. She listened to the chirping of insects and gentleness of the silence. It must have been her imagination. She took a few more deep breaths then carefully put her clothes back on and grabbed her trail map, ready to set off on an adventure.

* * * *

"You think this spot is secluded enough?" Ron asked Candace. The clearing wasn't big, but carrying all of this gear was beginning to wear him down. It looked as good a place as any to set up, with towering spruce trees providing shelter and cover.

She looked around at the woods on all sides of them and grinned. "Sure looks like it." She walked up to him and grabbed his crotch.

"Whoa, hey, let me put this stuff down first."

He almost fell over backwards as she pressed in faster, knocking him off balance.

"Sorry, I want some now." She unzipped his fly and reached inside.

He was already hard.

"What if someone's around?"

"Then they get a free show," she said.

He collapsed to the ground with a grunt as she frantically started in on him. Any thoughts of not being alone were gone in a flash.

* * * *

"I still don't think you're supposed to park there," his companion said as Sonny shut the door of his Bel Aire.

"Look, it's my fucking car, I paid good money for it, and I

53

don't see any goddamn lines on the ground telling me where to park, do you?"

"No, but it's partly in the bush and—"

"Sorry if it's not driving test approved. I was a little busy." He snorted the dangling bits of cocaine in his nostrils and joined her over at the clearing where she was finishing setting up their tent.

"Are you going to help?" she asked. "This would go a lot faster if you—"

"Babe," Sonny said. "I am helping."

He unfolded two lawn chairs and plopped down in one. He reached into a brown bag and pulled out a dark brown bottle.

"See? I set up the chairs and I got the whiskey from the car. What more do you want from me?"

"But I meant the—"

"Hurry up before I go and drink all the booze," he said.

She sighed and went back to assembling the tent.

"Oh, and when you're done with that, don't forget we're going to need a fire."

"You can do that. Just put some sticks in the firepit and light them. You've got a lighter, right?"

"Look, uh…" Sonny trailed off. He suddenly realized that he didn't actually know this groupie's name. It felt weird to ask now, after she'd already sucked his dick, but he may have to use it at some point, so he should probably get it over with. "Did you say your name was Chrissy?"

She stopped working on the tent and looked at him with a raised eyebrow. "All that coke fry your brain already?"

"Could be. Or it could be a test. To see if you remember the name you told me back at the arena."

"Janet. I told you my name was Janet."

"Good. Then you passed the test," he said and unscrewed the bottle. "Now the next part is getting that tent finished and a fire going."

She shook her head, but went back to work.

* * * *

The bus disappeared down a bend in the highway, travelling off further into the woods of Whiteshell Provincial Park. Two thousand, seven hundred, and twenty-one square kilometres of forest, lake, rock and beach that spanned the westernmost part of Manitoba where it met the easternmost part of Ontario. A vast natural wilderness to get lost in. Manfred pulled his pack over his shoulder, watching the faint wisps of the greyhound's exhaust trail gradually fade away. The cooking pans he'd strapped to the bag rattled at the bottom with a hollow clang. The weight on his back was a refreshing sensation after being cooped up in the bus for so long. He took a deep breath of the fresh forest air and turned to the path off the gravel road. It was a half hour or so walk to the campground. He had to get moving if he was to have time to set up before dark.

Alone with the sounds of nature around him, his feet crunched along the crushed gravel. His stomach growled again, and he cursed himself for not taking out that jerky before slinging his backpack on. *Plenty of time to eat once I make camp.*

There were no cars on the road. The silence was omnipresent, as if he'd been covered in a blanket of peace, but it was beautiful after being trapped in River City for so long. Working downtown every day, surrounded by people and cars and the noise of construction; horns, catcalls, panhandlers, buskers. It would be wonderful to just have a chance to think and reacquaint himself into his own headspace. It wasn't that he didn't like his job or his city, but there was only so much a man could take before he needed a break from both.

An hour later, his tent was pitched and set up. His campsite was a short trek from the lake and the beach. He could see the water through the trees; calm, clear, reflecting the night sky like a giant mirror. He'd finished just in time to catch the remnants of a gorgeous sunset. He had a fire going and was cooking some hotdogs on a spit, his mouth watering at the aroma of the meat.

"This feels right," he said aloud, knowing that there was no one around. "Like what a man should be doing with his life. Alone. Eating meat in the woods. Primal. Natural. You hear that world? This is what we should all be doing."

He shouted once, a piercing cry up to the sky that drifted away on the wind, then sank back down, relaxed. He could have sworn he heard a woman's shout echoing across the lake, but it was so faint that it could have been a loon for all he knew.

What a feeling, being alone like this, a part of a larger state of being. He ate and cleaned up, letting the fire run down before climbing inside the tent.

NOW

"**R**esidents have noticed an increase in bear sightings lately, but park officials have dismissed them as—"

Frank switched off the radio and dialed the telephone number on the page of notes in his file folder. Someone answered on the third ring.

"Hello?"

"Old man Ulster?" he asked.

"Who is this?"

"It's Malone, from the Frank Malone Detective Agency. Specifically, Frank Malone. I just wanted to call to let you know that I, uh, have a lead on your missing trailer. I'm just leaving for the weekend in, uh, pursuit. But I'll make you a rock solid guarantee that I'll have the location of your missing bit of home away from home for you when I get back. In fact, if I don't, I'll refund your money."

"Oh, thank you so much, Mr—"

Click.

Giggling to himself, Frank hung up the receiver. "It's the perfect, well, not a crime, let's just call it a delayed measure of justice. A weekend at the lake with some fishing and a case of Labatt's. What could be better?"

He closed the manila file folder with his pre-emptive 'case

closed' markings and slid it over to the side of his desk. He rose and made ready to go, but paused at the door. He had that nagging feeling that something was missing.

"I'm forgetting something here."

He looked around the room at his photos and desk, wondering what it could be. His keys? A change of socks? Then it hit him. Going camping wasn't a solitary occupation. He'd always gone with—

"Derek."

His oldest friend. The man he'd known since the days when River City was still a sprout. They'd lived in the old North End by the river, on small farms adjacent to each other, separated only by a frog-filled creek. That had all been before the land swindle, their university days, his sojourns overseas with Go-Team and before he'd spent a lifetime pounding the beat. It seemed like only yesterday that they'd been ankle deep in pig shit, chasing down loose sows out raising hell in the neighbours' fields.

"Shit, how long has it been?"

Frank moved from the doorway to an old faded black and white picture of the two of them on the office wall. Derek in a white shirt and suspenders, with thick dark glasses and the small patch of reddish blond hair on top. The man had been huge, linebacker size, a real mountain. A killer on the football field and with the ladies. There was Frank beside him, in a red windbreaker, with his dark hair and moustache, before the grey, the wrinkles and the stoop had taken over. They looked like a million dollars, adjusted for inflation.

"You're probably not getting out much these days, eh, old buddy?"

Derek was his last connection to his childhood. With his

parents and Bacon long dead, the man was the only one who remembered how things were. But Derek was in a care home now. He suffered from vascular dementia. The brain didn't get the blood it needed and things went all haywire. The poor guy had trouble remembering who he was, let alone the olden days. The man's family had locked him away and washed their hands of him.

"Who am I kidding? You probably don't even remember me."

Frank had barely visited him. It was hard to watch as his oldest friend wasted away when there wasn't a thing anyone could do about it. Who do you shoot to reverse time?

Frank checked his watch. It was still early.

"Alright, old buddy. I'll drop in on my way to the lake and say hi. Hopefully you'll be happy to see me."

It wouldn't affect his plans. He'd stop in and check up on the old man. He knew he should have been doing it a lot more than he had been. But it wasn't too late. At least not today.

* * * *

"Not much of a room here, is there, old buddy?" Frank said as he looked around the tiny white and beige cube they called a suite in the Pine Hollow assisted living facility. Sleeping area, a small bathroom with more handles and railings than an Escher staircase and a closet with an assortment of tracksuits and sweatpants hanging inside. The only furniture was a bed, controllable to raise and lower as needed, a dresser upon which sat a couple of old family photos, and a television silently playing a rerun of Bumper Stumpers propped on a nightstand.

"At least it's not the old Occidental Hotel downtown, though."

Frank sat in a hard wooden chair with a crushed, faded grey fabric backing next to the bed. He'd had to drag it into the room when he saw nowhere for him to sit. He leaned an arm on the small nightstand. Inches from the television were an alarm clock and a half-empty glass of apple juice with a straw in it. Derek lay upright on the bed, wearing a navy housecoat and grey sweatpants. He stared absentmindedly at the screen. His mouth hung partly open. He didn't seem to be fully cognizant of what was going on around him.

"Remember the bar in that place? Used to be so tough. Idiots would come from miles around to—"

The images in Frank's mind played like they'd only happened yesterday, but Derek just sat there, as if lost in a stupor. Frank could swear there was a tiny trickle of drool slowly oozing from the corner of the man's mouth.

Frank snapped his fingers. "Hear me?"

Derek slowly turned to look at him and Frank waited for him to speak. He couldn't get over the change in him in the time since he'd last visited. The man seemed to have deflated. From the old photo on Frank's wall to seeing him now in the flesh, it was like seeing a plump grape become a tiny raisin. Derek had lost lots of weight. His posture slouched. The thin reddish hair on the top of his wrinkled head had thinned and turned totally white. He wore the same huge framed black glasses, but they were almost comically out of place on the shrivelled-up man who formerly had been an imposing giant. They were as thick as coke bottles, too.

"Did you bring the TV guide?" he said to Frank.

"The what? The TV guide? No, why would I bring that? I

didn't even know you wanted one."

"You forgot to change the channel."

"Okay," Frank said, confused. "But to what?"

"Don't know what's on unless you've got the TV guide," Derek said and turned back to the screen.

"I can get you one next time if that's what you want. I'm surprised they don't have them here for you already. That seems like the kind of thing they'd—"

Derek didn't even seem to have heard him. He was lost in the dancing images of excited contestants on screen.

"You know they've got a channel now that tells you what's on. Here, let me see that remote. Maybe I can find it."

Frank grabbed the television remote control and looked for the right button to press. There were so many of them that he was as lost as if he was reading a map in Spanish. What happened to on/off and zero through nine?

"Last. Mute. Page up. Page down. Shit, no wonder you want the TV guide."

Frank tapped a button and the channel changed to the local news. A reporter was talking to a park ranger. The volume was so low that Frank couldn't hear a thing. He cranked it up.

"—would a bear like this be dangerous?"

"Oh no, no," the ranger said. "Bears stay away from humans. It's garbage and food that attracts them so—"

"He's back, Frankie."

"Huh?" He turned to Derek. The man was staring intently at the screen. Frank looked back but the man talking to the reporter didn't look familiar at all. And the reporter was a woman he didn't know either.

"Who's back?"

"Maybe's it's a different guy, but I figured he'd come back

eventually."

"Who? Who's come back?"

"A rerun. Part of the cycle."

"You want me to put Bumper Stumpers back on?"

Derek turned to him and frowned. "You still haven't told me who you are or why you're in my room."

There was something missing in the man. He wasn't in any obvious distress, but he didn't seem to be fully there either. Whatever train of thought he was following had already left the station. Maybe he could pull him back out.

"It's your old friend, Frank. I just stopped in on my way to Rock Peak Lake for the weekend. Going to do some fishing like the old days. Got a trailer set up and everything. The whole idea made me think of you. That's why I stopped in."

"Take me with you."

"Oh geez, I don't think you're allowed out on day passes and—"

"The time has come again. I've got to answer the challenge and—"

"Derek, you're not making any sense here. I can't just spring you. They'd notice, right? There's staff here and—"

"Did you hear about Bacon? He moved away. Said he died in—"

"That was thirty years ago, Derek. I know all about it. I was there. Let's call it an incident, but it's dead and buried, trust me."

"You ever sort out that business with your wife and Sully?"

"That was the seventies, buddy. More ancient history."

"We thought it was, but it's back. It's the cycle. Happens over and over again. Preordained, you know. Nothing we can do about that. But now it's time. Again. See?"

Frank sighed. The man was making less and less sense the more he spoke. "You know what they say," Frank said. "Neither one of us is getting any younger. You especially."

It was shocking how old and enfeebled Derek seemed. And to think they were the same age.

"Time's running out. I can still fix it," Derek said. "Someone has to."

"Fix what?"

"The forest."

"The forest? You were an accountant, not a…"

That was when Frank realized that the man wasn't ever going to understand what he was saying. He probably didn't even realize what he was saying himself. The ranger on the news must have put him into some kind of loop and his mind was just too scrambled to get out.

"Don't worry," Frank said. "I'm on my way there right now. I'll make sure it's fixed."

Derek's eyes never wavered from the screen, so Frank gently patted him on the knee and headed to the door. He stopped to take one more look at his oldest friend, sure that this was probably the last time he was going to visit. Deciding that it should be. It was just too painful. He'd rather remember the old Derek than this poor shell with one foot in the grave.

He was all set to leave when a thin voice stopped him.

"I'm serious, Frankie, you have to take me with you."

"Derek, I—"

"It's important. I have work to do, and I can't do it here."

Frank walked back to the man and looked at him in confusion. He hadn't moved, showed no indication of having spoken either, but he was sure that he'd just been talking.

"Work to do? At Rock Peak Lake?"

"The cycle. The return. The endless battle. I can't stay here," he said. His eyes never left the screen. "It's my responsibility to make things right."

"Make what right?"

"Do you really not remember?" The man turned to look at him, as if he was surprised he was even there.

"Do you know who I am?"

"Do you remember who I am?"

"I'm not the one locked up in an old folk's home," Frank said.

"I want to go fishing. I haven't been fishing in months."

Frank raised an eyebrow. Derek had been in here for almost two years now. There was no way he could have gone fishing in that time.

"The nurses—"

Derek grabbed his arm tightly. "They steal my money."

"I'd be shocked if they didn't."

"If you go without me, you'll die. You need me."

"I'd like to bring you, but how would—"

"Fuck that," Derek said, getting to his feet. "Let's just leave. Mom won't be home for two hours. We can leave her a note."

Frank watched as the man took off his housecoat and grabbed a sweater and a tracksuit jacket from his closet. He came back over to Frank and patted his chest. "You've got your gun, right?"

"Of course. I never leave home without it." Frank reached into his coat and pulled out his Magnum. It glistened in the harsh florescent light.

Derek admired the sheen and pointed at his reflection in confusion. "Who's that fucker?"

"That's you."

"Don't recognize the bastard." Derek zipped up his tracksuit top. It hung on him loosely, so it must have been from before his massive weight loss.

"Neither do I," Frank said, still trying to wrap his head around how much his friend had aged.

"Let's not let that stop us. It's important we go."

"Look, I—"

"Pitstop for fried chicken. At that place on the highway and—"

It was clear that the man was deadly serious, but Frank didn't see how sneaking him out would work.

"Listen. The longer you delay, the more powerful he gets. I have to be there to stop him, or the forest is screwed."

"Who? What are you talking about?"

"Going camping," Derek said. "Keep up, old man."

"I—"

Suddenly, Derek appeared to lose his energy. He blinked a few times, seemed to not know where he was. He held onto the wall for a moment, as if he was worried he would fall over. His vacant stare gave Frank the chills.

"Maybe you should lie down and—"

"It's one more adventure," Derek said. "Can't you give an old man even that?"

"I can." Frank patted him on the shoulder. "It's the least I can do for an old friend. I'll figure out what to tell the nurses later."

"Good, then let's blow this shit hole."

* * * *

Frank drove down the flat prairie highway exactly eight

65

kilometres over the speed limit. The window was down, and the breeze blew through his white hair. Frankie Lane blared from the cassette he couldn't remove from the old stereo in crackling glory and there was nothing around them but the vastness of the great province they called home.

"Is this the way to Dairy Queen?" Derek asked.

"I'll bet those nurses won't even notice you're gone. You're probably one of those patients they barely check in on, aren't you? The way we just walked out the door makes me think they hardly even know who's in that place."

As the music played and the landscape blew by, he knew he'd made the right choice. Even if the old man was barely coherent, he'd at least have a great weekend. They'd do all of their usual things; fish, drink beer, roast marshmallows and relive old times. It would be just what they both needed.

"This was a good idea, Derek," Frank said. "Forget about the forced retirement, patchwork men, mummies, werewolves, mafiosos, those guys who refused to keep their pants on right... We can take a little time to get back to nature. Just be the old Frank Malone."

"Who?"

Frank laughed. "You know, they thought I was slipping."

"Where are we going?"

"Rock Peak Lake. Just like you wanted. Betcha haven't thought about that place in ages, eh?"

Derek sat staring vacantly off into space. Frank wondered if he'd thought of much at all in ages.

"Maybe the memories'll flood back when we get there. The good ones, at least."

A couple of days away from it all would be good for the both of them. Maybe the best thing to happen to Derek in years. If not, he'd bring him back and just play dumb. He was a master at that.

"I don't know if you realize what you're walking into," Derek said.

Frankie Lane sang of outlaws making their last stand at the OK Corral as Frank looked from the road to his friend.

"The past," Frank said. "Where we both belong."

"It's all a cycle," Derek said.

"Then we're going to close the loop."

"I'm thirsty," Derek said.

"Hang on to that thought. We're almost there. I can practically taste the Labatt."

NOW

"Come on, Matt, what do you need that for?" Josh asked.

Matt held a massive bowie knife in front of his face, inspecting the serrated blade for any imperfections. Satisfied it was perfect, he began to look at himself in the reflection on the metal. He seemed lost in the weapon, almost hypnotized. The clerk watched with bored bemusement at the man dressed in camouflage fatigues with his face painted, examining a knife straight out of Rambo.

"A knife like that has many uses," the clerk said. "Hunting, fishing, cutting rope—"

"I'll take it," Matt said. "But I'll need a leg holster, too."

"Of course. We sell those for ten percent off with any blade purchase. Would you like that pre-sharpened?"

"Absolutely," Matt said.

The man took the blade into the back area of the store.

Matt took out his wallet and grabbed his credit card, ready to pay. Josh nervously watched him for some sign that he was slipping. Truth be told, he did look a little crazy being out in public like this in full outdoor survivalist regalia, but no one else in the hunting and wilderness supply store seemed to much mind. In a strange way, he almost fit in.

"So?" Josh asked. "Please tell me you need that thing for hunting, fishing, or cutting rope. And not for doing something awful to your ex-girlfriend or her friends."

"Relax," Matt said as he tried on a leg holster for the knife. He practiced pulling out an imaginary weapon and waggling it in front of him a few times. He was a little too rehearsed at the movement. "I'm just going to scare them a little."

"You're scaring me a little."

Matt mimed stabbing him in the neck and twisting an invisible blade. "Do you hear the call? I can."

"Okay, you're scaring me a lot actually."

"There's nothing to be scared of," Matt said. "It's nature."

"Right. Maybe I should—"

"You want a knife, too? My treat?"

"I, uh… think I'm good."

He watched as Matt carved up invisible targets with his phantom blade and suddenly wondered if coming along had been a good idea. The man seemed to pick up on his doubts and re-holstered the non-blade he held.

"I said I'm just going to scare them a little."

"And I said you're scaring me a little."

"Boo." He jerked forward and Josh stumbled backwards into a spiral rack of maps.

The man snorted derisively. "As long as you're with me, you've got nothing to be afraid of."

"I'm not so sure of that," Josh said mutely as Matt returned to his shadow blade work.

THEN

"Oh yeah, put it in me. Right there. Harder, faster. Again!"

Ron pressed Candace forcefully back against the tree and rammed her with all the strength he had in his pelvis. He felt her insides enveloping him. He focused on trying to map out where he was within her, how deep, how far. He was pressed all the way that he could be, nudging upwards. He could hardly contain himself.

"This is so fucking hot," he said into her ear. The darkness and chill air combined to make everything feel that much more present. With his other senses dulled, it had never felt like this before. "I'm so hard right now."

"Shut up and fuck me," Candace moaned.

"I am. I—"

She rammed her thumb in his mouth and screamed to the sky. It only made him push even harder.

* * * *

"That was the smooth stylings of the Miles Davis quintet with his composition *Circle* on KJAZ, your late-night destination for relaxation and romance. More soft jams to lay your head on coming right up."

Alice stared into the fire with a mug of warm hot chocolate in her hands. She watched the dancing sparks as they tumbled through the air like acrobats. The portable radio was playing the soft jazz that calmed her mind. It was quiet and peaceful stuff that seemed to float on the night air. It might have been Lawrence Welk for all she cared, but it was soothing, and she just let the moment overtake her. Her hike had been invigorating, but now she just wanted to sit and relax in solitude.

The radio crackled away from the melodic jam to the voice of a man. "We interrupt our regularly scheduled broadcast with a special announcement. Authorities report increased bear sightings in the Whiteshell provincial—"

* * * *

The radio had stopped playing elevator music and someone was talking. Sonny turned up the dial to hear what it was the man was saying.

"Repeat, very dangerous. Park authorities caution against approaching. If sighted, call 9-1-1 and stay indoors. Repeat, stay indoors. It's believed to be traveling east but—"

"Can't even keep the tunes playing for our bonfire." Sonny changed to another station. "Just give me something rockin'," he said, finding only static until the velvet voice of Burton Cummings came over the airwaves.

"I bet he'd hire me for his backing band. He doesn't seem like as big a prick as Malcolm Barton."

"I don't know," Janet said. "I heard he's pretty demanding."

Sonny took another snort of the coke he'd brought. "Demanding I can take. Unreasonable I'll stick up Malcolm Barton's ass."

With the tent set up, they were drinking and getting high while he complained about how Malcolm Barton had fired him after their poorly received set before the Alice Cooper show.

"I was the goddamned glue of the Who's That," he spat. "Sure, Malcolm wrote the lyrics, but who do you think came up with the riff for European Woman? Or Clap For Frankenstein's Car? Or—"

"Was it you?" she asked, rubbing her hand along his shoulder.

"No, it was Buddy, but I'm the guy who had to play those riffs each and every night."

"Wow. That must be hard, remembering all those notes."

"You have no idea, Nancy," Sonny said.

"It's Janet."

"Right, right. Janet. You have no idea how hard it can be to remember notes. To play them in the right order, to stay in time with the drumming of a real shithead like Boom-Boom."

"Who's that?"

"Yeah, that's the band. That's what we were called."

"But who was Boom-Boom?"

"The drummer. He fucking sucks, too."

"Dicks? Is he queer?" She seemed really interested in his answer.

"Maybe. I don't know. Doesn't matter. I mean he's a shitty drummer. But I'm the guy Barton fires."

"Why'd he fire you?"

"My solos are apparently 'no good'," he said, making air quotes. "I'm always 'high'." He repeated the motion. "I 'drink all the beer' and 'snort all the coke' and 'keep getting the clap.' I'm 'not contributing to the band' and 'have no future in the industry'." With each air quote he made, repeating the diatribe Malcolm Barton had subjected him to, he grew more and more furious. He really should have punched him out.

"You know what I should do?"

"What?"

"Start my own band. Yeah, fuck Barton and the Who's That. I'll get my own group. I'll call it the Who're We. Then I'll solo as shitty as I want and sing what I want and—"

A rustling in the bush stopped him. Janet turned towards the sound.

"What was that?"

"Probably a deer or something," he said.

"You think so?"

"We're in the woods, ain't we? That's where deer fucking live."

She seemed to accept that logic and, with no further rustling, relaxed. Sonny stood up, feeling the effects of the eight beers hit him all at once. He started to stumble towards the tent, then stopped.

"Fuck, I gotta piss."

He staggered away from the tent, reaching into his tight leather pants to pull out his cock.

"Ewwww, don't do it here," Janet said. "I don't want to see that."

"You were sucking this thing a few minutes ago," he said, flapping his loose dick in her direction.

"That's different. That's—"

He waved her off. "Bah, fine. I'll piss in the bush like the deer."

He staggered forward, away from the tent, into the brush, feeling the tall grass scratching his dangling dick and balls. The piss seemed to bunch at the tip, threatening to burst out at any minute. Finally, feeling like he was far enough away from the girl, he stopped and took hold, letting the stream fly. It was a big one and was going to take a while. He felt a near orgasmic pleasure at the release.

Janet shouted behind him.

"What's that, baby?" he called.

But she never replied. So he just kept pissing, flooding the forest with as much diluted beer as he'd ingested over the past few hours. Something rustled behind him. Still in mid piss, he started to turn.

"Changed your mind, eh? Wanted to see how a man does it?"

But it wasn't Janet he found himself facing. One swipe of the claw and his pissing seemed to expand midstream. He looked down, saw a great bloody gore where his dick should be. A spray of blood shot out, mixed with piss coming from the wound, all over his fancy boots he'd just bought before the Alice Cooper show.

"What the—"

But the question went unasked when a second swipe took the front of his face clean off, leaving him to forever wonder what might have been if he'd only started that band.

* * * *

It was a calm night, with hardly any mosquitos. The only sounds came from the loons down at the water. Then, just as he was about to drift off to sleep, Manfred heard a branch snap as if from underfoot.

"Hello?" he called out, wondering if someone had stumbled on to his campsite.

He crawled out of the tent and looked around. It was pitch black under the tree canopy. He could hardly see a thing, only the few fading embers from the fire.

"Someone there?"

Nothing. No response, just the gentle sound of the leaves rustling in the faint breeze. Shrugging, he was all set to go back inside the tent when he heard another snapping branch. Now he was sure something was out there and nearby.

"Hello?" he said again. "You may as well come on in and say hi. We can share some jerky, maybe a beer or two. The more the merrier, I always say."

Manfred could take care of himself. He'd been living in the North End for years after all, but the solitude of the moment made the hair on the back of his neck stand on end. He suddenly felt like he should get the knife he had in his pack, just in case. He bent over and reached inside, grabbing the hilt just as a breeze sent a fallen leaf fluttering by his head. He swung around quickly, knife at the ready, but saw nothing. When he realized what had happened, he felt silly. Still, it was so dark that he could barely see anything at all and that was making him strangely nervous. The stars above were huge and crystal clear, yet offered no help.

"Why don't we talk about this face to face?" he said curtly. "There's no need for all this running around."

He wondered if he were even talking to a person. Maybe it was a bear. They were known to roam these woods. Perhaps it had smelled the hotdogs and wandered over, curious. What was the rule for a bear? Play dead? Run up a tree? Shit, why couldn't he remember?

A drop of sweat fell down his neck and he shook once. Maybe this whole alone in the woods thing wasn't such a good idea.

"I've got a knife, you know," he said, knowing that if it was indeed a bear, threatening it was useless.

Another crunch of a branch and he turned towards the sound, knife aloft, expecting an animal to leap out at him.

But there was only a wall of nothing again.

He stood in the darkness for a long time. Breathing, looking, waiting for his eyes to fully adjust to the night and wondering why they were taking their sweet time to do it. After what felt like an eternity, he could finally see more than just outlines and began to relax. There didn't seem to be anything there. Maybe he was just overreacting to the normal noises of the woods. After so long in the big city, he'd forgotten what the bush was like. He shook his head at his own foolishness and turned back to the tent. He'd hunched down about halfway when he felt something poke him in the stomach.

He looked down. His eyes took a moment to understand what was going on. He hadn't been hit, something had pushed itself through him in one clean go. He stared in confusion as a dark liquid poured down his front. He coughed once, something slick coming up his throat. He touched the object in his gut. Sharp?

Then the realization hit him. That liquid was blood. His blood.

He coughed again as the thing inside of him was yanked out in a sudden pull. He felt something heavy sliding out of his stomach. He reached down and touched a heavy viscous oozing mass, warm to his fingers with the texture of slimy rubber. Tubes? Sausages? No, they were his intestines. They weren't supposed to be on the outside of his body, what was going on? His thoughts clouded, and he tried to figure out how something like this could happen when a breeze flew past him. He coughed again, then dropped to his knees. He felt his neck give way, releasing its hold on his body in a clean break. Now he knew that wasn't supposed to happen.

His body fell one way, his head the other, but before he could put these strange occurrences into perspective, he landed facedown in the dirt and grass. The darkness swelled around him as his vision faded. The last thing he knew was the distant sound of the calling loons.

* * * *

Alice lay in the tent staring at the orange canvas roof. Despite the peaceful quiet, she couldn't sleep. She should be able to let herself go, but for some reason, she just could not get comfortable. It wasn't the sleeping bag or the pillow or her flannel pyjamas. It wasn't too hot or too cold. She wasn't hungry or thirsty or over-caffeinated. The problem was the nagging feeling that she wasn't alone out here, which was crazy because she most assuredly was. There wasn't a soul around for kilometres as far as she knew. So then why couldn't she sleep?

She heard a noise outside the tent. It sounded like shuffling.

She froze. Was that a bear? There were bears around here, she'd read that in the park brochure before deciding on the spot and the radio had just warned of recent bear sightings in the area. While it hadn't specified Rock Peak Lake, it had said bears often came towards campsites, curious about the new smells.

The announcer had said that the trick was not to panic. Prepared campers knew not to leave anything out that might attract bears, and she'd followed the rules laid out on paper before the radio had reminded her. She'd also come prepared. She reached into her bag and took out the can of bear spray she'd brought from Canadian Tire. She took off the cap. She heard the sound again. Closer this time.

It was dark, but the light of the moon gave her just enough to see by. There was definitely a shadow outside her tent.

It's just the trees, dumbass, don't panic.

But then it moved. It wasn't just the trees. There was definitely something out there. What should she do? Stay in or go and spray the thing? Run away? Scream? Call for help? Wait it out? She had a car parked in the parking lot. She could make a mad dash to it, get to a phone and call the ranger office. Or maybe she could—

You have the spray, use it.

That was a better idea. Make the thing run away. Send it to another section of the park. Then she could move her campsite in the morning if she had to.

Okay. That's what I'll do. On three. One.

She started to unzip the door of the tent as the shadow seemed to move closer.

Two.

She gently touched her finger to the spray nozzle.

Three!

NOW

"Oh no, you're burning it," Donna said as Percy stared at his blazing marshmallow on a skewer. He pulled it away from the flames, blew it out and took the whole thing in one bite.

"Just the way I like 'em," he said proudly.

Towering spruce trees surrounded the clearing where the girls had set up their tents and lawn chairs. A raging fire in the centre, encircled by the eight of them, provided warmth and a prime spot to roast marshmallows.

"You have to cook them like a man," Jack said as he put a stick loaded with five over the fire.

"What exactly makes that a man's way of cooking?" Ashley asked.

"You know, because of the quantity," Jack said.

"Oh, a woman can't stack multiple marshmallows?"

"No, it's just—"

"She's messing with you," Donna said, shooting Ashley a death glare. "She's still not exactly in the party mood."

"This is only night one," Ashley said sarcastically. "There's no sense in partying ourselves out all at once."

"Tell that to John." Aiden reached over and poked their friend. "I think he's blacked out."

"What else is new?" Percy said, finishing a beer. He tossed the can into a bin at the edge of the camp.

"Just try to enjoy the weekend," Mandy said quietly to Beth. She wasn't participating in the conversation, instead staring into the campfire as if hypnotized. Her eyes made her seem like she was somewhere far away. "There's lots of people here to talk to. You don't have to shut yourself off."

"I know, I know," Beth whispered. "But I can't stop thinking about what Matt might do if he reacts to my text the wrong way. If he's been drinking all day with Josh, he could do something... stupid."

"Like what?"

"Pick a fight with the wrong person, drive drunk, overspend on some old video game on eBay... all the kinds of things I used to stop from happening."

"You're not his mom," Donna said. "You're not even his girlfriend anymore."

"If he wants to kill himself or waste his money on stupid stuff, that's on him," Mandy said.

"Who wants to kill themselves?" Aiden asked.

"Her ex, hopefully," Ashley said.

"He wasn't that bad really, alcohol just clouds his judgment and—"

"It clouds everyone's judgment," Mandy said. "That's the point."

"Look at John," Jack said. "He barely lasted an hour before blacking out."

John sat slumped in his chair, head dangling precariously to the right. An empty beer rested between his legs and a moth had perched on his ear. He snorted as he slept, drool slowly soaking his shirt collar.

"Is that normal for him?" Donna asked.

"Dude's just dealing with some shit," Percy said.

"Truthfully, I think he's an alcoholic," Aiden chimed in.

"What are you, his mom?" Percy said. "He's a grown up. If he wants to piss away his life getting blasted, that's his decision."

"Don't you care about him? Or his liver?" Ashley asked.

"Of course I do. He's my bud," Percy said. "But there are plenty of fuck-ups in the world. Some people just aren't equipped to deal with it all. He has to come to the conclusion that he needs help himself otherwise it'll never click."

"Yeah, he needs to hit rock bottom first," Jack chimed in. "My uncle did that. Went to meetings and everything. He had to come and apologize to all of us for being an asshole at Christmas one year. I was just a kid, so I had no idea what the fuck was going on."

"Wait," Aiden asked, "the uncle that died a few years back?"

"Yeah, that's the one. Liver disease. Cirrhosis."

"They used to call that consumption," Mandy said.

"So, what, the meetings didn't stick?" Aiden asked.

"Nope."

"Was your ex going to meetings?" Jack asked Beth.

She looked up as if she was going to answer, but Ashley cut her off.

"Fuck Matt," Ashley spat with finality. "I don't want to hear about him again, from any of you, alright?"

Her tone was that of a kindergarten teacher scolding her class and they all felt suitably chastened.

"Uh, we don't even know the guy," Jack said.

"Consider yourselves lucky then."

Nobody spoke for a while, withering under Ashley's bitter

gaze. The crackling of the fire and gentle calls of birds were the only sounds until Donna finally broke the deadlock by reaching into a nearby case of hard lemonade.

"Look, it sure seems to me like no one here is drinking enough for a party." Donna started handing out bottles of the neon yellow alcohol. "Ignoring your friend, of course."

Beth reluctantly took one and unscrewed the cap. She took a sip and pulled the fleece blanket around her body tighter. The fire wasn't keeping her warm enough, no matter how close she sat to the flames. For some reason, she was wracked with full body chills and nothing she did could keep them away. Was it just the cooling night air or was it her nerves?

"He'll get a second wind at some point," Percy said.

"He's sleeping it off and—"

"Not here, he isn't," Ashley said curtly.

"You sure they can't just set their tents up here with us?" Donna asked. "It seems kind of silly to make them go two sites over and—"

"We don't know them," Ashley said.

"That's what the party is for," Jack said.

"We went over all this before. I'm not going to let four random guys around me when I'm sleeping."

"You are such a stick in the mud."

"No, I'm careful. And you should be more careful, too, Donna."

"Thanks, Mom," Donna said.

"Look, it's no problem really," Percy said. "We already set up our stuff at the other campsite. It's not that far of a walk."

"Well, maybe for John."

"Oh shit, are we gonna have to carry him?"

"I'll bet Percy could do it all by himself." Donna pounded

the rest of her bottle and tossed it into another plastic bin they'd set up for the empties. The glass crashed inside with the others. She grabbed a second one and popped the top with a keychain bottle opener.

"Yeah," the big man said. "It wouldn't be the first time."

"There, Ash, see?" Donna said. "Percy's a good guy. I'm sure his friends are, too."

"Remains to be seen."

"I am," Jack said. "You are, too, right, Aiden?"

"Last time I checked."

"The frigid bitch routine will melt, I promise," Donna said. "We'll all have a great time this weekend, right?"

Ashley shot her a death glare, and the forest went silent once more. The fire popped. Off in the distance, a loon called mournfully. Jack took a careful bite of his marshmallow stack. Was the woman going to explode on them all again?

"I know, let's play truth or dare," Mandy chimed in, interrupting the waiting game. "That's always a fun icebreaker."

Jack rolled his eyes. "That's kid's stuff."

"No, it's fun, come on," Donna said.

"Doesn't bother me," Percy said, opening another beer.

"Great, I'll start," Mandy said. "What do you want me to do, truth or dare?"

"Truth," Aiden said.

"Ask me anything." Mandy gestured wildly with her hands. "I won't hold back."

"Who was the first guy you went down on?" Donna asked.

Aiden spit some beer all over the ground. "Whoa."

"That didn't take long." Jack leaned forward, suddenly interested.

"You know that already," Mandy said. "Bobby in eleventh

grade."

"Any of you guys know Bobby?" Jack asked.

"Ewwww," Beth said. "Him? I didn't know that."

Mandy shrugged. "Whatever. It was no big deal."

"Did you at least make him go down on you first?"

"That's another question," Mandy said. "You only get one at a time."

"Inquiring minds want to know," Jack said, grinning.

"Sounds like someone volunteered to go next," Donna said. "So, what'll it be? Truth or dare?"

"Uh, dare."

"Chicken," Aiden said, laughing.

"I dare you to, uh—" Donna dug into the cooler and came up with a hotdog. "Eat this uncooked wiener."

"Sure," Jack said, taking it from her. He finished the thing in three bites.

"Gross," Mandy said.

"They're already cooked once," Jack said. "It's not that bad."

"My turn," Donna said. "I choose truth."

"What's your body count?" Percy asked.

"Before or after you?"

"Wouldn't that only be one different?" Jack asked.

After a brief stare down with Percy, Donna broke out laughing. "Six, okay? Now with you it's seven. That's not that bad."

"Six?" Mandy said. "I thought you—"

Donna elbowed her in the ribs and she shut up.

"Which one of you guys is next?" she said.

"To be with her?" Jack asked.

"No, in the game, dumbass," Percy said, backhand slapping him on the shoulder.

"I'll go." Aiden put his hand up. "I choose truth, too."

"Do you go down on a woman before expecting her to go down on you?" Donna asked.

"Jesus, Don," Ashley said. "You're just going right into it with everyone."

"What? It's a valid question."

Aiden took another sip of lemonade. "Of course. It wouldn't be fair, right?"

"Okay, see how easy that was? Now, who's next?" Donna asked.

"How about big sis?" Mandy said.

"Ugh, fine." Ashley rolled her eyes.

"Truth or dare?" Donna asked.

"Truth."

"What happened and with what guy made you hate men so much?" Mandy asked.

"What do you mean?"

"Obviously there was something or some incident or just some jerk that made you start to hammer home to me that all men were pigs. I even remember when it started. You were fourteen. I just assumed some guy broke your heart, but I never did ask you the full story."

"I don't really want to talk about it," Ashley said. "Not with this company or any company."

"Oh, come on, you can't back out now. You picked truth," Donna added.

"Yeah," Jack said. "No one here's going to spread it around. We're not even Facebook friends."

"I'll pinky swear if it helps," Aiden offered.

"Yeah, come on, sis. What made you hate all men?"

Ashley sighed. "I really don't want to."

"Then I dare you to streak down to the beach," Donna said.

"I'm not doing that."

"Then you know what you have to do."

"Ugh, fine."

Ashley stared into the fire for a moment before taking another drink and looking them over in turn. Her face darkened. The dancing red of the flames cast an otherworldly glow on her severe features. "You really want to know? Fine. But it's not a pretty story."

* * * *

"I think they're finally asleep." Sally crept out of the tent on tiptoes. She gently closed the flap and came over to sit next to Greg at the fire.

"Christ, it took long enough," he said with a sigh.

"It's the strange surroundings," she replied. "That's pretty normal. But they'll sleep well after all that excitement today."

"You think they'll sleep in?"

"God, I hope so."

They sat in silence for a moment, enjoying the warmth of the fire and lack of children peppering them with questions and demands.

"So now what?" Greg finally asked.

Sally took her drink and slumped further back into the chair, looking at the night sky, at the fire, at the man she'd been married to for so long, trying to find an answer to his question. They were usually so busy, with no time to themselves. The demands of parenthood were stressing the bonds of their marriage. Everything he did was starting to annoy her. Her job, their only real source of income until Greg's art started to pay off, kept pulling her away from her family. Life was getting so hard, and she felt just about at the breakdown point. So, what to do right now? Clean up? Look over tomorrow's itinerary? Work through some shit with Greg? She decided that she didn't particularly want to do anything at the moment, just sit and enjoy the rare slice of quiet.

"Nothing," she said simply.

"Nothing?" Greg asked.

"Nothing."

"I don't know when the last time was that we had the chance to do nothing."

"Exactly."

* * * *

"I was at a party," Ashley said haltingly. "Mom didn't know. I told her I was with friends, but I was actually out with Rod."

"Who was that?" Aiden asked.

"He was on the football team. Seventeen. A real hunk. I couldn't believe he was even talking to me since I was a junior."

"What school?" Jack asked.

"Not important."

"Maybe I know the guy?"

"If you do, you're going to have bigger problems than sleeping two campsites over."

"I'm pretty sure I don't," Jack said, trying to avoid setting her off anymore. "What about you guys, you know any Rods?"

"Nope."

"Nope."

"I think I can speak for John, too. So none of us know the guy."

Ashely shook her head in frustration. "You were right, I was fourteen," she said to Mandy. "But he invited me to go. My friends all told me to go, too."

"And?" Donna asked.

"I'm getting to that part." She took another sip of her drink, as if she was trying to summon the courage to continue. "It was a football party. The whole team was there. He brought me in and I was so nervous. These were all seniors and I felt like a little kid."

"You were a little kid compared to them," Mandy said.

"I know. I know. In retrospect that should have been obvious to me, but I was so blinded by this big hot football guy asking me out that I didn't catch the warning signs."

"Uh oh," Beth said.

"Yeah. Major uh oh."

"So what—" Jack started but Percy stopped him with a glare.

"What happened?" Donna asked eagerly.

"There was a lot of beer going around. I'd never tried it before. I didn't know what it did, let alone how much to have. I don't remember everything about what led up to it, but I woke up and he was—"

* * * *

Frank pounded back another Labatt's and threw the can into the pile he'd accumulated at his feet. Derek was still nursing his first one, but from the looks of him, he may have, in fact, forgotten what he was supposed to be doing with the bottle.

"Ready for another beer yet, Derek?"

Frank popped a new one and looked at the man sitting in his chair, lost.

"You hear the forest people?"

Frank shifted in his seat and stared around the campground. The trailer parked at the edge, the trees surrounding the small clearing with a firepit in the middle and an old wooden sign reading 'CAMP SITE 11' stuck in the dirt. They were alone as far as he could tell, but the raging fire did little to illuminate anything beyond the tree line.

"Hearing aid picking up someone's radio, old buddy?"

"They said hello," Derek said.

"Alright then. I guess if you see them, tell them I said hello back."

"They already know."

Frank took a sip from his beer and watched his friend by the firelight. The flickering light cast shadows that made him look even older than he already did. He'd been fairly quiet since they'd arrived and set up, letting Frank do all the work. Now, he seemed to be trapped in his own mind.

"The sights and smells of this place triggering anything in that noggin of yours?" he asked.

"You looking to get married again?" Derek asked.

"Hell no. I'm too old for that."

"Not me," Derek said. "I think I'm gonna ask Ellie to marry me when I finish my courses."

"She died almost ten—" Frank trailed off, seeing the look in his friend's eyes that told him there was no point in trying to bring him back to the present. He was probably happier where he was. "Yeah, yeah, she's a great gal."

"The best."

Frank dug into his pack and pulled out a three quarters full brown bottle. He unscrewed the lid and took a sniff of the Jack, as if he needed to smell it first to know he wanted some.

89

He took a sip, then passed it to Derek. "Here you go, see if this does anything for you."

"You swipe this from your pops?" Derek asked.

"He'll never notice. He's been dead for over fifty years."

Derek drank one huge gulp. Then he stood up suddenly.

"I think I've been here before."

"We both have. Plenty of times," Frank said.

Derek sat back down as quickly as he'd risen.

"There's something I need to do."

"There's a public washroom about a click down the road. You—"

But he didn't need to finish as the man had abruptly fallen asleep. Frank took another sip of his beer and watched the fire tell stories from his own memories.

* * * *

"Oh God," Mandy said when Ashley was done telling them her story. "I never knew."

Ashley simply stared into the fire, lost in thought. She'd gone cold, her voice dropping to a barely audible murmur. A tear dripped from her left eye. It was obviously still painful to relive what had gone on all those years ago.

"I don't know how many of them there were or what happened, but I know it was something. I overheard them laughing about it. I'm sure there was a video, but I never did find out."

"Fucking pricks," Beth said.

"Totally," Donna said.

"A fourteen-year-old girl," Aiden said softly.

"I don't know what to say," Jack said.

"Why didn't you tell someone?" Mandy asked.

"What could I say? I had no idea what even happened."

"You could have gone to the police," Aiden said.

"Yeah, gotten one of those rape kit things," Jack added.

"Do you have any idea how those work?"

"Uh, no. But wouldn't a doctor have been able to tell that you weren't a virgin anymore, that someone had—"

"I wasn't a virgin before that," Ashley said.

"What?" Mandy said in shock, nearly dropping her drink.

"Wow," Percy said.

"That's a twist," Jack said.

"I told you Rod was a hunk. I'd already, you know. Been with him."

"So the guy was a paedo."

"You were fourteen."

"That was consensual."

"This is out of my wheelhouse."

"The party wasn't."

"So what happens if I get checked out? Mom finds out I've been sleeping with an older boy and goes bananas. People accuse me of wearing the wrong thing or asking for it. Or maybe the school covers it up for the champion football team. Maybe I get them all expelled or put in jail, and everyone hates me. Maybe nothing happened and I get accused of lying. Or maybe it all happened, then they put the video out there and I see the whole thing online, find out just how disgusting it all was and have to see that forever. Maybe it goes viral and spreads and the whole city or country sees it. Maybe it follows me around everywhere I go. That's even more trauma. I just... stayed silent and dealt with it."

"You shouldn't have had to," Mandy said.

"That's heavy shit," Jack said.

"But I did. And now you know the story. All of you do. No one else does. And it stays that way."

"God," Donna said. "I don't know how you could handle that on your own so well."

"Who says I really have?"

"Fuck," Mandy said in disbelief.

"Right, uh…" Aiden stammered.

"My brother, he—"

"Don't," Percy said to Jack and cut him off.

"Maybe we should have some more drinks," Donna said. "Skip the rest of the game and just get drunk."

"I'm all for that," Beth said and finished her bottle.

"I think it's about time we carted this guy back." Percy pointed to the dozing John. "We can pick all this up in the morning."

"I'll, uh, help them," Donna said, rising.

Ashley grabbed her hand and shook her head, but she slid out and moved over to help Percy lift the unconscious man up and out of his lawn chair.

"See you girls tomorrow? Bright and early for some breakfast?"

Ashley said nothing. Beth slumped back in her chair. Only Mandy smiled to the guys. "Sure thing."

And with that, Percy slung John over his shoulder, and he and Donna led the others down the path towards the other campsite.

NOW

S omething woke John from his contented slumber. He'd been having a dream about going to a closing down sale at an old department store and being there just in time for them to put out a dusty old box from the back. The clerk had no idea what was inside, but John had just known it was going to be something ultra valuable still priced with 1980s labels. But exactly as it was being opened, he woke up.

A pain in his groin told him that he had to piss. Really badly. He knew if he didn't move, he'd piss himself. It had happened before. He had to get to a bathroom.

He rolled off his bed, but found that it wasn't his bed at all. He was trapped in his sheets.

Where am I?

Was this still a part of the dream? Then he remembered. They'd gone camping. He was in a sleeping bag in the woods. He had no idea where the bathroom was. Should he just let it go?

Don't be stupid.

It was all fine and good to piss yourself back in the house where he could change, shower and wash the sheets without anyone knowing. But out here he'd wreck the tent, stink all day and they'd all find out.

Fuck, I'd better get up.

He rolled over and escaped the sleeping bag. He crawled out of the tent, leaving his things behind.

Where do I go? It's the woods, stupid. Go anywhere. Just not here.

He stumbled through the darkness, away from the campsite and the few smouldering embers of their fire. His head was spinning, his feet unsteady. He braced himself on trees to avoid falling over. He was having trouble picturing coming here in the first place. Just how much had he drank? He didn't even remember starting. He couldn't seem to focus on the ground in front of him or his feet underneath him. They seemed to move of their own accord.

He found himself surrounded by tall trees and long grass. He had to be far enough away from the others by now. He stopped. Or his feet did and he just let them. Swaying, he took out his dick and aimed it up and away from him.

Here we go.

He pissed in a high arc, letting it all flow out in a powerful stream that almost curled his toes. He could feel it shooting through him in waves and when it was all done, he shoved his dick back inside his pants and turned around to walk back to the tent.

That was when he realized that he had no idea where he was. Where was the tent? How far had he actually gone into the woods? Had he pissed in his tent and this was another dream?

A loon called in the distance. The woods were silent. The moon above shone through the trees.

"I'm pretty sure it was that way," he slurred and started to move forward, but after a few meters of walking, he realized that nothing looked familiar. It was all just trees and more trees. He needed a landmark, or maybe a trail of breadcrumbs.

"Maybe that way?" He walked in a different direction. But nothing this way was familiar either. He tried a third direction After what seemed like an eternity of walking through thick brush, he began to wonder if he should go back the first way.

A branch snapped behind him.

"That you, Percy?"

No one answered. He didn't see anyone there. The world spun and he had a hard time focusing on one spot.

"Must be a rabbit or something."

He felt like he was going to throw up. He sat down for a moment. Something brushed past him, but by the time he turned to look, whatever it was had gone.

"Jack?"

Still no answer.

He reached into his fleece pants for his phone, but realized it was back at the tent hooked up to the portable charging block they'd brought. At least, he thought it was. He tried to shout but his voice was garbled. It was so dark that a person could be two feet from him and he'd not know.

"Wait until morning…" he muttered.

He leaned up against a tree trunk and took a deep breath. He felt his eyes grow heavy. Soon he was back in that old department store waiting for the clerk to open the box.

* * * *

Blood. Life. The energy from one provides not only for another, but for all.

The hunt was simple. This one had understood its place in the natural order of things and made a sacrifice of itself.

Stopping and waiting to see if it tried to escape again, it watched the contented victim succumbing to its fate.

Soft. Tender. Full of vitality. This one would offer much.

So it feasted.

THEN

"So you're just paddling your way through to Atikaki? By yourself?" Alice asked incredulously.

"That's the plan," David said.

"Isn't that super far?"

"I've got maps and plenty of food packed in the canoe. The whole trip is set to take six weeks there and back."

"Wow, six weeks on your own. Here I thought I was doing something big taking a weekend solo."

"I didn't start out doing trips like this. I worked my way up from a lone weekend, just like you."

Alice watched the shirtless man working at the remnants of the breakfast he'd made them. He scooped up the cooked eggs with his metal spoon and chewed happily. David Ashern. Heavily tanned, hairy and wiry, the man had the beginnings of a thick beard and long hair held back in a tie. His brown eyes nearly matched the colour of his skin. The shorts he wore looked well used.

"And did someone surprise you out of your tent in the middle of the night when you started, too?" she asked playfully.

"Sure. But I didn't mace them."

His bloodshot eyes revealed the after-effects of her overzealous use of her protection when she'd heard the noises outside her tent the previous night. She'd sprayed before knowing what exactly was waiting for her. Luckily, he'd been a few meters away or he might have needed more immediate medical attention instead of just a dunk in the water.

"I'm sorry about that. I thought you might be a bear."

"You'd have smelled me a lot sooner if I'd been a bear. And while I have been alone for a week so far, I don't think I have that much of a musk yet." He sniffed his armpits, just in case.

"No, no, of course not. You smell fine. Like a normal sweaty man."

"Thanks. I think?"

She nearly cursed herself for her awkwardness, but this whole situation had come out of nowhere. A strange, gorgeous man stumbles into her camp as she's trying to go to sleep. She sprays him. He screams in pain, and she feels so bad she helps him wash out his eyes in the lake. She apologizes. He insists it was his fault for scaring her. He asks if he can stay at her fire for a while until he can see straight again. She agrees. They get to talking and connect immediately. She learns all about him and he her. He says he'll sleep in his canoe to make her feel more comfortable and promises to make her breakfast in the morning before he heads out again. She secretly hopes he comes to her in the middle of the night, but he stays the perfect gentleman. Then, in the morning, he cooks up the eggs she'd brought and makes her an incredible simple hash that used something he found in the woods as garnish. Now here they were, chatting while she tried to find the right words to say to him to make him want to stay a little longer.

"I'm sure I smell, too," she said. "If only from the nerves of doing all this on my own."

"You seemed to have done alright," he said. "And thanks for sharing the eggs. Not something I could bring on my solo trip easily."

"No, no, I guess not. I had a cooler..."

You're blowing this, Alice.

He finished his plate and stood up, wiping a few crumbs off his shorts. She eyed his bare skin eagerly. He looked like someone who knew his way around a lot of things, not just the woods.

"I'll get these cleaned up and then I guess I'll get out of your hair. You probably have a lot planned and I should get back on the route."

He started to carry his plate to the water.

"Wait," she called out.

"Yeah?" He turned back.

"Think you could teach a girl how to canoe?"

* * * *

Ron watched as Candace bent over and took out a bottle of water from their cooler. She gave him a great view of everything she had. But then it'd be hard not to when all she was wearing was a short skirt that left little to the imagination even when she had underwear on, which she didn't right now.

He was feeling great after the night they'd had. Exhausted, but great. They'd indulged themselves many times under the night sky, tried out some positions from a book Candace had found in a used bookstore, then fallen asleep under the stars in each other's arms. Neither one was a nudist, but here alone in the woods, it didn't seem that important to get dressed.

Especially since they were too busy getting undressed anyway. Somehow, the bug repellent they'd used hadn't sweated off in their numerous liaisons and neither were the victims of the dreaded Whiteshell mosquito. But now, he saw them beginning to swarm and wondered how long the stuff was supposed to last.

Candace stood up and popped the cap off the water. She took a long drink and stretched out. Just looking at her pert breasts made him amazed that she'd ended up with him. What a body. What a woman. What a—

"What are you smiling at?" she said, finally noticing him watching her.

"You," he said.

"Oh yeah? Why?"

"I think you know."

"Well, it is a new day." She walked over and straddled him on the chair. He leaned in and kissed her breasts. She pressed her lips to his forehead. He started to move his hands to her skirt, but she held his wrists. "We did it here already. I want a new experience."

"Like what?"

She kissed him again. "Let's go exploring and find out."

* * * *

"You're doing great," David said behind her.

"This is actually pretty relaxing," Alice said.

She switched the paddle to the other side of the canoe, gently dipping it into the water, feeling the motion dragging slightly as she pressed it through. On either side of the river, the wall of trees passed by, silently judging her progress.

"Now you can see why I'm on a six-week trip."

"Six weeks of quiet. I could really use it. Life has just been—
"

"Life," David said in understanding.

"Yeah."

"I get it. I work for a computer supply firm, small, but we handle a few big clients in River City. The field is really set to explode, you know. Evolving rapidly. But it's a challenge. Working with machines, parts and circuits and things that are only going to speed up all our lives once they become more readily adopted. It's… hectic. And why I need the peace and quiet of this trip to refocus and centre myself."

The gleaming metal canoe was packed with gear, but it still had room enough for the two of them. As she paddled on one side, David would do the other, following her awkward newbie rhythm, ensuring they stayed straight and in the middle of the brown water.

"Computers, wow. That all seems so futuristic."

"Not really. They've been around for a while. It's just every year they get a little smaller and a little more powerful. Used to be a computer took up an entire floor of an office building and cost a fortune, now they're just about ready to be affordable enough to fit on your desktop. As things progress, you're going to see them doing a lot more common applications, spreading everywhere, even in the average home."

"The average home?"

"Sure. Everywhere. That's the next phase, trust me. Personal computers. Everyone'll want one and you'll use them for all kinds of things." He started laughing. "Look at me, going on about my work. I was supposed to be away from all that. You were, too."

"I'm sorry, I'm ruining your solo trip, aren't I?"

"Of course not. The trip was always about having an adventure. Meeting a new person on the way is just—"

"Look at that," Alice said, resting her paddle on the edge of the canoe, letting them glide for a moment. In the distance, a bear stood at the edge of the brush, watching them with dark eyes.

"That's a big one," David said. "Grizzly. You don't normally see them around these parts. I've run into a few, but none that size. Must be almost nine hundred pounds."

"Is that big?"

"Let's just say it's not the one you'd want to run across in the woods."

Alice shivered as they passed the thing. Its gaze followed them.

"Can they, uh, swim?"

"Oh, sure. But there's no reason it would come after us. They're wanderers. He's probably just here for a drink. He'll go back to his travels soon."

She looked over her shoulder to see the bear still watching. It began walking along the shore in the same direction they were.

"Uh, he's wandering this way."

David turned to see the bear slowly moving behind them. "Sure seems like it. But don't worry. We'll be moving much faster than him. He's probably just curious about us. He'll get bored and move on once we get too far away."

"Right. Sure. Okay."

The way the bear was looking at her gave her pause, but David seemed completely unconcerned about the whole thing, so she turned back and resumed paddling.

"Now this river was used by the voyageurs hundreds of years ago to bring beaver pelts back East and—"

NOW

"How'd you guys sleep?" Mandy asked as Aiden, Percy, and Jack walked into the campsite clearing, carrying coolers and lawn chairs.

"I've got a splitting headache, my throat feels like I swallowed a cat and only half of it went down, and I'm covered in mosquito bites," Aiden said.

"Welcome to camping." Donna smiled as Percy set up his lawn chair next to her.

"I must have forgotten to close the tent when I collapsed. I'm going to pay for that mistake all weekend."

"I might have some lotion." Mandy ducked into her tent.

"Well, I slept like a baby," Jack said proudly.

"Crying and covered in your own shit?" Percy laughed.

Ashley poked at the small fire, then tossed in a few more logs. "It was peaceful here, in case any of you care."

"I, uh…" Jack stammered, unsure what to say.

"Anyone know why I brought this?" Mandy emerged from her tent brandishing an electric razor.

"I think you can plug it into a tree I saw back there," Donna said.

Percy opened the coolers and set up a skillet. He began laying down strips of bacon. As the pan grew hotter, the smell of the cooking bacon wafted through the campsite. Jack opened another cooler and grabbed a beer.

"Breakfast of champions," he said, at Ashley's raised eyebrow.

"Where's your friend John?" Beth asked.

"Still sleeping," Aiden said.

"He's going to have one hell of a hangover," Jack added.

"Did you guys check on him?" Ashley asked.

"No, he was still sleeping. The tent was closed. Why?"

"Uh, I don't know, to make sure he didn't die in the middle of the night."

"The dude does this all the time," Percy said. "He can handle it."

"And none of you think that's a problem?"

"I can go back and check," Aiden said.

"After breakfast," Percy said. "He's not going anywhere."

"But—"

"Relax, eat first."

"Some friends you guys are," Ashley said.

"Ash."

"I'll go," Aiden said. "It'll only take a second."

"Dude, fresh bacon." Percy held out the skillet as if that should end the discussion.

"I'm not saving you any either," Jack added.

"I guess it can wait ten minutes."

Aiden sat back down in his lawn chair. Ashley seemed unimpressed with them, but the others showed no signs of caring either way. As Percy cooked, chatting with Donna and only half paying attention to the sizzling bacon, Aiden just watched him. The guy made Aiden feel completely inadequate. While Aiden was slender and lanky, Percy was thick and muscular. While Aiden made his living performing a lifestyle online, Percy lived it. Percy had women practically throwing themselves at him everywhere he went. He owned the house they all lived in, he had the nice clothes and expensive watches that Aiden borrowed for his fictional existence. Percy was the one who went on vacations to exotic resorts and brought back photos and souvenirs that Aiden pretended were his. Percy was the real deal and Aiden was a fake. It was enough to make a guy jealous. And yet, imitating him was his meal ticket. It was almost as complicated as the sycophantic relationship Percy and Jack had. Jack did his best to imitate the man, too, but offline. Neither of them were successful on their own.

"Any of you ladies feeling it this morning?" Jack asked.

"Yeah," Mandy said, holding her head. "Kind of lost count last night."

"Everyone did," Ashley said curtly.

"You don't seem too worse for wear."

"I'm the responsible one."

"Remind me not to drink that lemonade again," Beth said.

"We've got beer," Jack offered.

"Uh no, I've got water."

"Suit yourself," he said and took a pull from the bottle.

"That sure smells good," Donna said as Percy flipped the bacon.

"Plenty here," he said. "I brought five packs."

"There's something about fire-cooked bacon that just tastes better," Donna said.

"John's really missing out," Jack said.

With the bacon cooking, bread was mounted above the heat on a spinner and Donna rotated it around. The chatting continued until Percy began dishing out the dripping meat onto paper plates.

"Thanks for cooking," Mandy said as they all dug in. "This is great."

Percy just shrugged.

"So, what's the plan for today?" Mandy asked.

"Well, it's only a short walk down to the beach, I just assumed we'd all go swimming," Donna said.

"You just want to show off your new bikini," Mandy added.

Jack's eyebrow raised in interest.

"We left our suits back at the camp," Aiden said.

"Then after breakfast, you can go get them and check on your friend at the same time," Ashley said.

"That works."

"Then it's settled. We clean up and meet down at the lake in thirty minutes," Donna said, grinning.

* * * *

"I'll check on him." Aiden walked over to John's tent as they returned to their site.

"You just can't stop talking about dicks," he heard Percy say to Jack behind him.

"What? I do not," Jack retorted.

"That's always the first place you go."

"Is not."

"Is, too."

Aiden ignored their bickering and lifted the flap of John's tent as the two of them kept arguing like kids. Sleeping bag, pillow, pile of clothes spilling out of a backpack, empty bottle of Jack Daniels—

"Is not."

"Do you not want to make a good impression with any of Donna's friends?"

"I think that Mandy has the hots for me," Jack said.

"LOL, keep dreaming."

"Guys, shut up." Aiden patted the sleeping bag, found a damp spot, but no sign of the man. "He's gone."

"What do you mean, he's gone?" Jack asked.

"I mean his tent's empty and he's not in it."

"Well, where the fuck is he?"

"He must have wandered off."

"Recently or in the middle of the night."

"Did either of you check when you woke up?" Aiden asked.

"No, did you?"

"No."

"Shit. Should we go and look for him?"

"John," Percy shouted.

"Of course we should go and look for him. He could be lost in the fucking woods," Aiden said.

"If he gets lost it's his own dumb fault," Jack said, but even as the words escaped his lips, he seemed to know they were wrong. "No, he could be wandering for days out here and never find anyone. We should go look."

"He's probably just passed out somewhere like a sack of shit," Percy said.

"When we find him, I'm going to beat his ass for taking away my chance to see Donna's new bikini," Jack said.

Percy coughed angrily. Jack spun to see the man shooting him a cold look.

"What, a guy can look, can't he?"

"Just get looking for John, dipshit."

* * * *

"The guys are missing out," Donna said. "The water feels great." She floated on her back, shutting her eyes as the sun shone down on her. The warmth from above overtook the cool lake beneath.

"It's a little cold," Mandy replied, shivering.

"Oh, come on, it's fine. Just enjoy it and shut up," Donna said.

"Is this the water with that bacteria where you're supposed to take a shower immediately after going in?" Beth asked, still refusing to wade in more than knee deep.

"Why would you have to shower right after swimming?" Mandy asked, suddenly moving back towards the shore.

"It's some kind of algae or bacteria or maybe a worm. I'm not sure. But that's Clear Lake, not here," Donna said.

"I remember going there as a kid and my mom being super paranoid about the whole place," Beth said.

"But you're sure that it's not this lake," Mandy said.

"Yes. This is nothing more than cool, clean, natural Whiteshell water."

"Cold, clean, natural Whiteshell water, you mean," Mandy said.

"Obviously you've never done the Polar Plunge," Donna said derisively.

"Hey, Ash, are you gonna come in here and join us or what?" Beth called out to Ashley, who remained on the beach, laying on a towel. She wore a large yellow sun hat and had a book in hand.

"I'm fine here," she shouted back, not even looking up.

"What's with your sister?" Donna asked Mandy. "Why's she

staying on the shore instead of enjoying the lake?"

"You think she's waiting for the guys?"

"I don't know. She's been acting weird all morning."

"You think she regrets telling us about… that?" Beth asked.

"Maybe, she's hard to read."

"Or did she not bring a bathing suit?" Beth asked as if that was a scenario no one had thought to bring up.

"Why should that matter? There are no kids here. We could all swim naked if we wanted," Donna said.

"Please don't." Mandy dove underwater and popped back up.

"Why not? The guy's aren't here yet. What're you scared of?" Donna asked, grinning.

"What about those people way on the other side of the lake?"

"They couldn't possibly see anything."

"We've all seen you naked enough already," Beth said. "At this point seeing you with your clothes on is a shock."

"You're only young once, girls. You may as well flaunt it. Speaking of, do you think Percy will like my new bikini?" Donna rolled onto her stomach and gently paddled in place. She wore a small, yellow and blue polka dotted two-piece that left little to the imagination.

"He's already seen what you've got underneath."

"Yeah, so?"

"Did you really get another new bathing suit? How many do you own?" Beth asked.

"I thought I'd seen that one before," Mandy said.

"Nope, I got this one especially for the trip."

"Which makes it number…?"

"I lost count at fifty."

"Fifty, Jesus Christ," Mandy said. "Why do you need fifty

bikinis?"

"Options. Comfort. Who cares? Now who wants to race to the other side?" She waved her arm and splashed Mandy in the face, giggling as she kicked away.

"Hey," Mandy shouted and started chasing after her.

* * * *

Greg tried desperately to stay awake, but was losing the battle. With the sun blazing down in the sky overhead and the gentle breeze coming from the lake, it was a gorgeous twenty-three degrees Celsius, perfect for napping. The kids were building a sandcastle on the beach. Sophia carried buckets of water over to the structure that Max carefully shaped. She poured it around the trench he'd dug as a moat. The two of them were carrying on some kind of sprawling narrative about wizards and Minecraft monsters, clearly having a good time without anyone's interference. They didn't need him hovering over them like a helicopter parent.

Sally was out in the lake swimming. He'd lost sight of her, but knew she was out there somewhere. He would have been in the water with her, but he had a foot fungus and was told specifically not to immerse it in public water. The doctor had most likely meant a pool or hot tub, but as far as he was concerned, a lake was pretty damn public. Sally said he was being crazy, but he'd still rather not take the chance. Besides, there was another group way across the lake. She wasn't swimming alone. It gave him a perfect excuse to just lay on his blanket in the sun.

Fighting the pull of sleep, he'd propped up a towel underneath his head so he could watch the kids from his prone

111

position. He held a book he'd taken out from the library in his hands. The pages were warm from the sun. He'd fully intended to read it but the more he scanned over the sentences, the less coherent they seemed. His eyes grew heavier with every passing moment. It was just too warm, too peaceful.

He blinked once. Twice. The third time Sally appeared standing over him.

"Where are the kids?" When had she left the water and walked up beside him?

He shook his head once and looked towards the sandcastle. "They're right… ummm."

"You fell asleep," she said angrily. "I was counting on you to watch them."

"I was. I mean, I wasn't. I mean, I was watching them, I wasn't asleep."

"Then where are they?"

"Calm down." Greg scanned the beach. "They couldn't have gone far. I wasn't even asleep. I just blinked."

"There are bears in these woods, Greg," Sally said, pulling a shirt over her wet body. "Bears that could eat the fucking kids, you asshole."

"Hey, relax. Where would they go? They know not to run off on us."

"Really? Do they? Because from where I'm standing, they most certainly seemed to have run off on us."

"Sophia? Max?" he called out as he stood up and looked around. The beach was deserted. The people way across the lake were gone, too. "Kids, this isn't funny."

"I'm freaking out here, Greg," Sally said.

"Just breathe. I'll go and look where they were playing. There's bound to be tracks. We'll just follow them and find them in no time."

He walked over to the sandcastle. The kids had left it nearly finished. The moat wasn't quite full, but the turret was packed down solid.

"Maybe those people saw," he started but trailed off. There was no sense in bringing up anyone who was as gone as the kids were.

He examined the area around the castle and saw some indentations in the sand that had to be footprints. At least, he hoped they were. He wasn't any kind of tracker, let alone someone who even knew much about the woods. But he had to act like he knew what he was doing, if only to keep Sally from totally losing it.

"See, here. What'd I tell you?" He pointed to the tracks as Sally came over. "Matching sets of footprints. Leading off to—"

"To the fucking woods, Greg. The kids have wandered off into the woods."

"Then let's go after them, before they get too far."

He ran through the sand towards the tree line, where the markings that he hoped were actually footprints headed.

* * * *

"Suit yourself Miss Anti-social, stay on dry land, we're having fun." Mandy splashed once as she swam away from shore, waving derisively.

Ashley was sweating, but didn't want to take off her shirt. She didn't feel up to it just yet. It covered up the embarrassing facts beneath. She hadn't worn this bathing suit in a few years, and had assumed that it would still fit, but she'd apparently put on a couple of pounds in the interim. When she'd slipped it on the night before they were leaving, she'd been aghast at the changes. Not only did the suit barely cover her chest, but it was so tight that it pushed things around in ways that made her feel even worse about herself than she already did.

She pulled on the suit straps under the shirt. She could feel herself ready to pop out. She didn't need that humiliation even if the guys weren't here. Instead, she'd just sit here and suffer in the heat. It was the lesser of two evils.

But it was so hot. The beach was deserted. The guys hadn't shown up yet, and the only other people on the lake were way off on the opposite shore. The girls were in the middle of the water splashing each other. She was alone. What would be the harm in just getting a little sun? She was looking a little pale and the other day had seen an ad on her phone extolling the virtues of vitamin D. She could always cover up when the guys finally showed up.

"Fine, sun, you win," she said softly. "Here goes nothing."

She slipped the shirt over her head.

"Hello," a man's voice rang out.

She cried out, became tangled in her shirt, felt her boob slip out of her too-small swimsuit, panicked, and pulled the shirt back down. She knew she was beet red when she saw Jack, Percy, and Aiden smiling at her knowingly. They all wore tank tops. Percy's barely fit and made him look like a lifeguard. Jack seemed like he was trying to be his smaller avatar only with dark hair and less muscle mass, while Aiden was even lankier and wore sunglasses. She wondered how much skin she'd just flashed.

"Didn't realize it was that kind of beach," Jack said. "Do we just drop our trunks now?"

So they had gotten an eyeful.

"I've got a rape whistle," she said.

Percy laughed, which might have been meant to put her at ease, but instead just put her more on guard. "We'd be the only ones to come running to your rescue out here," he said.

"There's a ranger," she retorted.

"Sure, back at the gate."

"And there's a station up on the ridge. I saw it."

"Where?" Jack said, scanning the horizon.

"I'm serious. It's right here in my bag." She reached over to grab her rape whistle, hoping they'd get the message.

"We're not here to rape you," Aiden said.

"That sounds like something a rapist would say to catch his victim off guard."

Jack laughed.

"Okay, okay, we get it. We shouldn't have snuck up on you."

"Then why did you?"

"You knew we were coming," Percy said.

"What took you so long?"

He looked out to the water, seemingly counting the bodies. "So he's not here either?"

"Who?"

"John. We're looking for him," Percy said. "He wasn't in his tent when we went back and we didn't find him around the campsite. We thought maybe he came down here instead."

"I haven't seen him."

"She hasn't seen him," Aiden said. "So we need to keep looking."

"Shit," Percy said. "We're going to have to postpone beach day. We can't leave John out there alone. This is a pretty big park."

"And there are bears around," Aiden added. "The ranger at the gate told us to keep an eye out."

"Us, too."

"He could have fallen into a ravine or wandered too far into the bush and gotten lost. Are you sure you haven't seen or heard anything?" Percy asked.

"Nope."

"What's going on?" came the voice of Donna.

She and the other girls had noticed the commotion and swum back. They came walking out of the water to join Ashley at her blanket. She saw Jack eyeing up Donna like a slab of meat.

"Hello, ladies," Jack said.

"What took you guys so long?" Mandy asked.

"They've been looking for their drunk friend."

"Have any of you seen our friend John?" Percy asked.

Mandy snorted.

"What's so funny?" Jack asked.

"That just reminds me of a song."

"Has anybody here,

Seen my old friend John,

Can you tell me where he's gone?" Aiden sang the words softly, then trailed off when everyone turned to stare at him in disbelief.

"What the fuck, dude?" Jack said.

But then Mandy chimed in: *"He freed a lot of people,*

But it seems the good die young,

I just looked around

and he was gone."

"You, too?" Donna said in shock. "What's going on here."

"It's a song," Mandy said. "Some old folk song from the—"

116

"And how the hell do you know it?" Donna asked.

Both Mandy and Aiden said in unison: "Mr. Spock."

Jack tossed up his hands in frustration. "Oh, great. Another one who knows what the hell he's talking about."

"Dude. It's a song from this album of Kirk and Spock songs. Well, not actually Kirk and Spock. It was Nimoy and Shatner singing, but anyway, that's not important at all really."

"Don't tell me you have that album, too," Donna said to Mandy.

"Downloaded, sure."

"Why?"

"It's kitch."

"Sounds more like shit," Jack retorted.

"We can argue over the merits of the Nimoy and Shatner album or we can keep looking for John," Aiden interrupted with annoyance. "That is what we were doing, after all."

"We'll help you look," Donna said.

Ashley shot her a death glare. "We'll what?"

Donna arched her back to stick out her chest a little and Ashley saw Jack ogle her. But it was clear that Donna was vying for the attention of Percy. "Sure. We can help. We're not really doing anything that important. And besides, the guy could be in trouble."

"This isn't our problem," Ashley said.

"We'll team up and go in different directions. We'll cover more ground that way."

"He couldn't have gotten that far," Beth said.

"Yeah, there are trails all over the place. Signs telling you where to go. The highway's back that way, so between all of us, someone's bound to find him. I'll go with Percy; Ashley, you and Beth go with Mandy; and Jack, you go with Aiden."

"No way I'm splitting up with someone who sings Spock songs," Jack said. "I'll go with Percy and you."

Ashley stood up. "No way I'm letting two girls go with one guy. I'll go with you, too."

"Then I guess that leaves Mandy, Beth, and Aiden as the other group?" Donna said.

"Hey, no fair," Jack said. "That's two girls to one guy."

"This is starting to look a lot like we're just pairing off into two big groups. Wouldn't it be more efficient to go in pairs?" Aiden said. "We could cover even more ground that way."

"He's right," Mandy said. "If we each went in one compass direction, there'd be a better chance of finding something."

"There's not enough of us to do that," Ashley said. "And besides, the lake is this way. So unless he was drunk and swam across, there's no point walking east."

"If he was that drunk to try, he probably drowned," Beth said.

"How deep is the water?"

"I don't know."

"Anyone have a diving suit?"

"Of course not. We'll just have to hope he didn't drown," Mandy said.

"But what if he comes by here later?" Beth said.

"She's right," Mandy said, nodding. "Someone should stay here. Like a base camp, just in case."

"Who's going to do that?" Donna said. "I hate just standing still."

"I'll do it," Beth said. "I'd rather not be wandering in the woods if there are bears around."

"You getting any signal out here?" Percy asked, holding his phone and aiming it in different directions. "I don't seem to be."

"We only have one phone, in the car. This was supposed to be a phone-free weekend."

"Better get it so Beth has something to keep in touch with."

"Okay, wait here, I'll be right back."

"What are the teams again? I'm confused," Jack asked.

"I'll go with Percy, you go with Ashley," Donna began.

"And the nerds can sing their nerd songs alone then," Jack finished for her.

In a few minutes, Ashley was back with not only a cellphone but also some cans. "There's no signal, but maybe it'll kick in with the right wind." She handed out the cans. "Now each of us is carrying bear spray and knows how to use it." She pointed threateningly to each of the guys in turn.

"I don't know how to use it," Mandy said meekly.

"Point and shoot."

"This isn't some prank," Percy said. "We just want to find John. Safe and sound. Any luck he'll just be asleep against a tree somewhere and we can all come back and still have time to swim. Then beers and bonfire on us, alright?"

"Great," Donna said. "Let's find him quick so we can all get drunk."

NOW

The gravel crunched underfoot as they walked. With the sun shining above and the fresh forest air all around them, it could have been a nice hike through the woods, but Matt was walking with purpose that made it akin to a forced march.

"Come on, Matt, we drove around the place for hours. I don't think they came here," Josh said from two feet behind the man.

Matt was barely listening—he was totally focused on the path ahead, in his own world. They'd been up all night and it was starting to wear on Josh. They hadn't even arrived at the park until almost dusk, then had driven around the entire area three times, slowing down at each campsite and lake they found, looking for Ashley's convertible, but at each stop, they hadn't found any sign of it. Even when it was pitch black and almost impossible to read the signs on the side of the road, Matt had refused to stop looking. He'd simply put on the high beams and done another circuit.

"Maybe we got it wrong when we figured out where the girls were. It's a possibility, right?"

Matt wasn't answering. He was following his own internal monologue, just like when he'd suddenly decided to start walking the trails deeper in the woods. After driving around all night and finding nothing, he'd abruptly stopped the car and gotten out.

"What're you doing?" Josh had asked him.

"They must be deeper in the park. On one of the sites near the lake. Let's go."

That was over an hour ago. They'd been walking ever since. At this point Josh just wanted to pitch a tent and lay down. He was exhausted. He'd been too nervous to sleep while Matt had been driving and now it was all catching up to him. His eyes struggled to stay open.

"What if we take a break? Sleep for a few hours?"

Matt just kept moving, refusing to slow down and reconsider what he was doing. He looked like he was about to snap. At the start of the march, he'd taken some kind of small, white pill and since then, he'd been subsisting on the energy drinks they'd brought from home.

Matt took another sip from the neon printed can he'd been pounding back every few minutes. Josh had lost count of how many he'd had when they were driving. The back seat was littered with empties when they'd left the car. The combination of that pill he'd taken and the energy drinks had wired him like a powder keg.

A mournful loon called off in the distance.

Suddenly, Matt stopped in the middle of the trail as if he smelled something. He began fingering the large knife from the supply store in the holster at his leg. That thing made Josh nervous.

"What is it?"

"Shhh."

"You hear something?"

He slid the knife an inch out of the holster as he listened for whatever it was that had stopped him.

"I still don't get what you need that for," Josh said.

"Bears. Other shit in the woods. You want to be prepared."

"You're really going to take on a bear with—"

"Shut up."

Josh wasn't sure what Matt was planning to do with that weapon. He didn't want to think about what he might try all amped up like this. The massive serrated gleaming blade made him nervous. If they did find the girls, could he stop him from whatever he might try?

"You hear the voices?" Matt asked.

Josh held his breath, trying to focus on the slightest noise, but all he could hear was the breeze blowing the leaves of the towering trees that surrounded them on the path. A bee flew past his face.

"No, I don't hear a thing, man."

"Just listen."

"I am."

"Not with your ears. They're in your head."

"What the hell are you talking about?"

"I understand," Matt said, then began to move again, this time off the main path onto a much thinner strip of flattened brush that might have been a little-used trail or perhaps an animal's migration route, pressed down by years of instinctual roaming.

Josh followed him. "Are you even sure you know where you're going?"

Matt pressed through the wooded path, pursuing some invisible trail. Branches clawed at their faces as any semblance of human passage seemed to disappear. Suddenly the man stopped again and held up a finger. Josh froze.

"Shh," Matt said calmly.

"The voices? Are they back?"

Matt shot him a death glare and Josh stopped talking, focusing instead on the noises of the forest. Birds, the rustling of leaves, bugs… then he heard it. A faint laugh. It was a girl's.

"There. You hear it," Matt said.

"The laugh?"

"They're laughing?"

"That's what I hear."

Matt stared into the brush without blinking. Josh heard the laughter again, but it was so faint he still couldn't be sure he wasn't just imagining it.

"There's no guarantee that's them," Josh said.

Matt popped another pill. He offered one to Josh.

"No way, man."

"Your loss." He bolted off the path, hopping through the brush like he was Rambo.

"Hey, wait!"

Josh knew he had to stay with the guy, if only to keep him from doing something incredibly stupid. He ran after him as fast as he could.

* * * *

"Did you even go to bed?" Frank emerged from his old army surplus tent to see Derek still sitting in the same position he'd been in before they'd finally called it a night.

"What time's *Let's Make a Deal* come on?" Derek asked.

"Monty Hall is dead."

"Well, fuck."

"That's what I said, too. There's no point getting pissed off about it. How's about the two of us go and catch some fish? If I remember my Rock Peak Lake layout, and there's no reason to think the place has changed much, then there's a great spot about twenty minutes' hike from here."

Frank helped Derek to his feet and led him down the trail towards one of the rivers that wound their way through the park. In no time, they were both set up and standing in the middle of a bubbling stream in black hip waders.

The brown water flowed gently over rocks polished by time. A clear blue sky and bright shining sun canopied the trees on either side of the water. Frank's fishing line was far out in the centre of the water drifting along with the current. He reeled it in every few moments, dragging it backwards to try to fool any fish that found his bait. Derek stood nearby in the water. He looked out of it, barely holding his rod steady.

"Isn't this the life?" Frank said. "Two old friends out in God's country catching God's snack food, underneath God's heat lamp, wearing God's waterproof pants. Doesn't get any better than this."

"Huh? Whose what now?" Derek said.

"You got a bite yet, old buddy?" Frank asked, although he wondered if he did, that he might not even know it.

"I left my teeth back at the office."

"You still have your teeth. At least, as far as I know. You do still have your teeth, right?"

Derek reached into his mouth and checked. "Sure do."

"That makes two of us then."

"Then what did I leave back at the office?" the man asked, confused.

"You retired seventeen years ago. How would I know?

Maybe a pen or a stapler."

"No. I'm pretty sure it was my teeth."

"You still have your teeth, you just checked."

"I did?"

"Check again if you don't believe me."

Derek reached into his mouth a second time and felt his teeth. "Whaddya know?"

"Told you so. You didn't leave them at the office."

"I've been looking for my teeth all day. I must have left them at the office."

"Look, I'm telling you it wasn't them you left there, alright?"

Derek looked into Frank's eyes to try to gauge his sincerity. Squinting, as if reading things that weren't there, he stared so awkwardly that all Frank could do was match the man's look and stare right back. After what seemed to take forever, the test was passed and Derek slowly nodded. "I'll trust you this time."

"Glad we can finally move on. Now you got any nibbles yet?"

"Not yet, Frankie."

Frank relaxed his grip on his rod and looked at his friend standing in the middle of the stream. This was the first time the man had said his name since he'd been to see him in the care home. In fact, there'd been few real signals of recognition since that brief flicker of life just before they'd busted out. He'd begun to question if this had all been worth the trip, but now, he could see that, in some small way, it was.

"You are still in there, Derek."

"Where the fuck else would I be?"

"Now, what was it you were saying earlier about needing to be here? I—"

125

Frank stammered. He didn't know what to say. He didn't want to blow this rare moment of lucidity. Derek was a shell of his old self, but some of who he was might still come to the surface. Even fractions of his mind were enough. They might be all he could truly hope for.

"This is some flood, eh, Frankie?"

Frank looked around at the stream in confusion. It didn't seem any higher than usual, but then it had been a long time since they'd last been here, so maybe he was the one with the memory problem.

"What do you mean?"

Derek looked at him like he was an idiot, waved at the water with his free hand. "You're telling me the creek being high enough to walk in is normal? Fishing ain't no regular occurrence in city limits. You must've hit your head harder than I thought when you fell off that fence."

"Hit my head? What the hell are you talking about?"

"Now I know you did. You fell off old man Miller's fence not ten minutes ago. Reaching for apples. Did a total one eighty and landed right on your noggin. Thought you were dead for a minute. You sure you ain't dead, Frankie?"

Frank stared at his friend, trying to figure out what he was talking about. What murky aspect of their collective past was he reliving? Then it hit him, he was talking about their childhood almost seventy years ago. The man was remembering something he himself had completely forgotten.

"What year do you think it is?"

"I ain't the one that busted my noggin. I know what year it is."

"Maybe I don't. So tell me, okay?"

"Maybe we should call old Doc Wilson to come take a look

at you."

"Indulge me, okay?"

"Indulge?" Derek said sarcastically. "What big words you're using. What, are you listening to the *CBC Wednesday Night* now? *The Happy Gang* not good enough?"

"Just tell me the year."

"Nineteen-fifty, what the hell year you think it is?"

"That's not important right now."

Nineteen-fifty. Derek thought they were back in the year of the great flood. One of the defining moments of River City's first century. Frank hadn't thought about that disaster in decades. River City had been under water. The creek near the farm had swelled up to the size of a river. It all flashed through his mind in an instant, despite the passing of time. They'd gone fishing, actually caught a few strays that had wandered through the now connected waterways. One of the pigs had drowned. They'd called it the biggest natural disaster in city history. The flood, not the drowned pig.

He looked at his old friend with a scrambled mind and remembered those days for the first time in decades. What must it be like to be reliving them now? Maybe Derek's disease wasn't as bad as he thought. Maybe he was just getting the chance to experience his life all over again, from the start.

"What do you want to do after we catch some fish?" he asked.

"What do you mean, what do I want to do? I want to fucking fry 'em up and steal some of Pa's beer. Jesus, Frankie, we already planned this."

"Right, right, sorry. I guess I really did hit my head harder than I thought."

Derek nodded as if that was explanation enough. He held

his rod a little straighter. Frank smiled, wondering what other of their childhood adventures the man would get to replay next.

"Hey, Frankie," Derek said, breaking the silence of the moment.

"Yeah?"

"I'm got to go find the little forest people."

"You what?"

"I said, I can hear nature calling. It needs me."

"There's an outhouse up the trail."

"Gotcha. This won't take but a minute."

Derek waded to the shore and climbed out of the water. He walked up the trail leaving Frank alone with his rod and the ripple of the flowing stream.

THEN

"What kind of sick and deranged mind could do this?"

The cabin looked like an abattoir. The furniture had been stripped out completely. Hooks dangled from the ceiling on iron chains. Hunks of flesh pierced onto the ends swayed slowly. They dripped blood onto the floor to pool beneath each rotting piece of meat in ever growing puddles of crimson gore. A rat licked up a few droplets then scurried away when it realized it wasn't alone in the room.

Frank took in the whole horrific sight. It was worse than the old slaughterhouse his dad kept out back when they used to raise pigs. Worse because this was people.

"Jogger found the place like this when he got lost," the park ranger said. "He was looking for directions back to the lake."

"Instead he found the route to hell."

"Uh, yeah, sure," the ranger said. "Also the stuff in here."

"It's a good thing you brought me here, Ranger Smith. This kind of thing is my specialty," Frank said.

"It's Johnson, not Smith," the man said. "That's the other—"

"That someone could be out here, right under our noses doing something like this. It boggles the mind. My good buddy Derek and I were enjoying a wife-free weekend fishing just a few clicks away while this was all happening."

"This is some kind of fucked-up," Derek said in awe at the grotesquerie.

"It's galling, is what it is. What is the world coming to when you can't even take time off from your jobs and wives without someone out redecorating a cabin in Satan chic?"

"Right, so now that you're here," Ranger Johnson said, "I really should get back to the short wave. I put the word out to the other rangers to keep an eye open for bears wandering around the woods. Who knows where this big fella is at? They oughta double check their repellant and—"

"I know where he isn't," Frank said. "Here. But he sure left his handiwork."

Frank paced around and examined more of the room. He took in the meat on hooks with interest, trying to figure out how it had all happened. Then it hit him—the ranger's story didn't add up. "Tell me something, Ranger Smith, you ever see a bear do something this bad before?"

The man rubbed his chin in thought. "One time I saw a bear get into the garbage down behind Gertie's bait shop. That was some kind of mess but—"

"Me either," Frank said, cutting him off. "That's because this ain't no bear's handiwork. This is that of man's greatest enemy."

"You think it's a mountain lion?"

"No. I meant man. Man's greatest enemy is man."

The ranger frowned. "Then you ain't ever seen what a mountain lion can do to someone. Why, this one time—and this is years ago, mind you—before my—"

"The boy scout camp?" Derek asked.

"That's right. Used to be just down the bend. Let me tell

you something, the old timers around here still talk about how there were short pants and tiny limbs as far as the eye could see."

"How the heck did you know about that?" Frank asked Derek.

"My cousin Hank told me the story when I was a kid. He was trying to scare the crap out of me before I went to—"

"And you still remembered it? Jesus, I can barely remember what my wife told me two days ago."

"What can I say? It's a gift."

"It happened back in the twenties," the ranger said. "It was a major news story in all the papers. They had to call in—"

Frank wasn't paying attention anymore. His cop instincts were going haywire. He was sure there was more to this situation than just a confused ranger and possible rampaging wildlife. This was serious. He took out his gun and checked the load. "Don't worry, Smith. Despite what our killer might think of himself, I'm also man's greatest enemy. But only the criminal man. And this guy's clearly a criminal, which means I'm coming for him."

"Why do you have a gun when you're just out here fishing?" the ranger asked.

"Don't tell me how to fish," Frank said dismissively. "Just get on that radio and tell the other rangers to keep their eyes open for more than just bears or mountain lions. They need to watch for the real killer. If my cop nose tells me anything, it's that he's not done. And I aim to stop him."

"Aren't you jumping the gun just a little bit? There's no proof that this wasn't a bear. There's bear tracks outside, I showed 'em to you."

"Did the bear hang up the meat?"

"You'd be surprised what those things can do with their paws. They can dig around in bee hives and—"

"That's Pooh—" Derek started but Frank cut him off. "It's bullshit, is what is is. This work requires the fine motor skills of a deranged mind. Well, the hands of said mind."

"Believe what you want. I'm still not convinced that there's not some simple explanation for all of this. We don't even know that this is people meat yet and—"

"Either Yogi has moved on from picnic baskets to people baskets, or we've got a psycho killer on the loose. Human. So step back and let the experts take the case."

"I'm an accountant, Frankie."

"Yeah, I'm the wildlife expert here," Ranger Johnson said. "I got a degree in natural resource management and—"

"Does that thing let you carry a gun, Smith?"

"I've got a rifle in the truck."

"A gun in the hand is worth two in the truck," Frank said.

"I got some bear spray in there, too," the man said.

"Got an extra can?" Derek asked.

* * * *

"There." Candace pointed. "Right there."

Ron followed the line of her finger to a small clearing in the woods. Just visible inside was a crimson Bel Air, semi parked in the brush.

"You want to do it in someone else's car?" he said incredulously.

"I've never fucked in the back seat of a Bel Air before."

"But that thing's not ours." He looked around the area but didn't see anyone else nearby. "The owner could be back any second."

She pulled him by the hand and led him over. His resistance quickly fell away as she looked through the windows. The back seats were empty, and there didn't seem to be anyone sleeping on the back floor either. She looked in the front seat, which was also clear. She checked the door and it was unlocked, so she pulled it open slowly.

"Looks usable to me," she said and teasingly ran her fingers over his chest.

"But they could come back."

"Put the blanket down."

Ron looked inside again, unsure, but before he could argue, she pulled the blanket away and laid it on the back seat. She climbed inside, slid her skirt up and leaned back. She spread her legs, flashing him a pink stare that he was very familiar with by now.

"Dive in."

"I, uh—" he stammered, still not feeling it.

"Imagine we're at the drive-in. Maybe there are shocked people watching."

"No kidding they'd be shocked to see you doing that."

"Roleplay. We're the crazy couple that lives life on the edge. No one wants to call the cops because they've never seen anyone making love in real life like this."

She began touching herself, gently playing with her slit while shooting him hungry eyes. This woman was insatiable.

"You like people watching you?"

"It's turning them on, too. Some of them are touching themselves in their cars."

"Please don't tell me we're going to start doing it in public now."

"They can all see us," she said, lifting her shirt and playing with one of her exposed nipples. "Hurry up before someone else comes over and fucks me first."

"I just want to get a feel for what I'm supposed to—"

She rammed her foot into his crotch, massaging him as she got herself ready.

"Just hurry up and fuck me."

"I, uh, I can handle that." He looked around, seeing only the forest, still unable to imagine the scenario she'd laid out.

"Someone in the car next to us just whipped out his cock. His woman's sucking him dry. Behind us two girls are getting it on. There's another couple wondering if they can join in. The concession stand guy has a huge erection. A couple of teenagers with binoculars can see everything from a rooftop blocks away."

"Oh jeez. This is getting elaborate and—"

"Oh God, I can't wait anymore. Just take it out and stick it in me."

He still needed more to get himself in the mood. "What, uh, movie are we watching?" he said as he undid his pants.

NOW

"I wanted to come back to your tent last night," Donna said to Percy as they picked their way through the thick forest, following a mostly grown-over path that wound deeper through the trees.

"Why didn't you?" he asked.

"Ashley would have freaked out."

"So? She's not your mom."

"No, but I do live in her house. I can't afford to piss her off."

"Why would she care what you do? Or who?"

"She's got this thing against men. I used to think she was just a bitch, but then—"

"Her story."

"Yeah. I mean, I get it. That's fucking traumatizing, but you can't live in the past forever. I was hoping she might like one of your friends and—"

"Jack's a good guy. Maybe he'll win her over."

"Sure, sure. You think?"

She was only half paying attention as she eyed up his muscles as he walked. The tight shirt, the thick legs, the broad back and shoulders; he was exactly her type. The second she'd seen Percy at the gym, she'd known she wanted him. He'd been almost comically oblivious. Usually guys like him were all over her. They'd want to talk about their crypto holdings, fantasy football, or protein requirements and she'd want to vomit. Percy was on another level. He had his shit together and didn't seem to find it necessary to chase her at all. That only made her want him more. She didn't even care if he was simply playing his own kind of game; the guy was a stud.

"—but I do know other guys. I could ask around."

"Oh yeah, do that."

Then he stopped. It was so sudden she bumped into his hard back, her hand hitting his ass accidentally. She left it there. He didn't seem to mind.

"What's the matter?"

"There's a cabin up ahead," he said. "Maybe we should check it out."

She slid her hand into his shorts pocket and brushed his dick.

"Sounds good to me."

* * * *

"Do you think we've gone far enough?" Mandy asked Aiden. They'd pressed deeper into the woods on what looked like a forgotten hiking trail. She didn't remember the last time they'd seen any route markers, or even signs of human passage. "It feels like we've been walking forever."

Aiden sat on a tree stump and rubbed his leg. "Tell me about it. I'm not used to this much hiking."

"I'm not even sure this is an actual path."

"It was at first, but it seems to have died out. Now I'm worried we're way past where we should be."

Mandy leaned up against a tree and wiped her sweaty brow.

136

"You getting a signal?"

Aiden checked his phone—miraculously, he had one bar signal strength. "Yeah, actually I am. Must be a tower nearby that I'm somehow connecting to." He looked up at the top of the trees, as if that was somehow going to do anything. He felt stupid for even trying.

"What model phone is that?"

"The nine."

"You've got a nine? Let me see that." Mandy sat beside him against the tree and took the phone from his hands. She smelled faintly of sunscreen and lake water. She immediately started swiping the screen and looking at all of his apps.

"You're on Tinder?"

He stammered, "Occasionally."

"You like it?"

"Do you mean have I met anyone on it? Then the answer is no. I either swipe and get no response or they stop talking to me after they see my other pics."

"What? Why? There's nothing wrong with you. You're a perfectly normal looking guy."

"Thanks? I think."

"Come on, it's not an insult. Plenty of girls would be happy to swipe with a guy like you."

"Then where are they?"

"See, here's your problem," she said, looking at his dating profile. "You're using bland pictures from unflattering angles. Bathroom selfie? Come on, everyone uses that one. You need something more unique to stand out. What do you do for a living?"

"Influencing. Vlogging, stuff like that."

"Really?" she said, surprised. "How many followers do you

have?"

"Depends on the video. Sometimes a few hundred, others a few thousand. If it's something hot I might get twenty thousand plus."

"You're like a minor internet celebrity."

"Hardly."

"I've never known an internet celebrity before."

"Not much call for that in the bush," he said, motioning to the silently judging trees. "If only I had some skills to fall back on."

"So you don't make any money influencing?" She kept looking through his phone, scanning the other pictures. She seemed very curious at what he had in there and was in no hurry to give it back. "You seem to be able to afford nice clothes and take vacations."

"Those are Percy's clothes and his vacation snapshots. I'm more one of those fake it till you make it bullshit artists."

"Oh," she said, still scrolling, sounding disappointed. "It's still more interesting than my life of working at Shoppers Drug Mart. I spend most of my time making sure people don't steal the makeup."

"At least you're providing a service to someone. I'm just a phony."

"How often do you, uh, influence?"

"Every day. But I'm on temporary hiatus for this weekend."

She handed him back his phone. "Better conserve battery. We don't know if we're gonna need it later."

He slid the phone back in his pocket. "Heck, we might need it now. If we're as lost as I think we are."

"I guess neither one of us is very good at this," she said. She brushed her hand against a tree and flinched, bringing it back up to her face and examining a red blotch on the back of her hand.

"What is it?" Aiden asked.

"Something red. I think it's dried liquid," she said as she looked closer. "Could it be blood?"

"Is it animal?" Aiden asked.

"I don't think vegetables or minerals bleed." She stepped around the tree. "There's something back here."

"More trees?"

She put her hand to her mouth. "Oh my God."

"Let me see." He moved beside her and saw, tangled in the brush, a bit of fabric from a flannel shirt. Like the kind John had been wearing last night.

"It's just a bit of—"

"Not that, look," she said.

She pointed to a mangled hunk of red and flesh a few meters deeper into the bush. Mostly hairless, it didn't seem like it belonged to a forest animal. Flies buzzed around the edges. The skin looked like it had been pecked at by crows. The foul smell coming from the hunk of meat was enough to make him feel like throwing up.

"Do you think that's John's?" he asked as he tried to keep his composure.

"A bear or something must have got him," she said haltingly. "The ranger warned us on the way in."

He kept staring at the hunk of flesh, trying to figure out if it was his friend. The bit of ripped shirt being so close was more than circumstantial.

"We need to get back," Mandy said nervously. "It could still be around. We should get the others. Call somebody for help."

"Right," Aiden said. He took out his phone and swiped it on

only to find it useless. "So much for the one-bar signal. I'm dead again."

"At least get a picture."

He snapped three at various angles. "Not sure how much help they'll be."

"Better than nothing. Now let's go. I'm getting scared just standing near that," Mandy said, clutching her bear spray tightly. "Whatever did that could come back."

"Yeah, I think you're right."

She slid her arm into his and pulled him along, back the way they'd come.

* * * *

"So, uh, you guys are all roommates, right?" Jack asked Ashley as they picked their way through the partially overgrown trail in the woods.

"Yes," she said curtly.

"And you own the house?"

"Yes."

He ignored the coldness in her voice as he watched her ass swivel in her shorts as she moved along the path slightly ahead of him. He had to admit that it was pretty good, even if her attitude wasn't. He understood why she'd be a little distant with her past, but he had nothing to do with any of that, so why should she take it out on him?

"You ever been out here before?"

"Nope," she said.

He wasn't getting very far with her, but he wasn't about to give up so easily. He'd been striking out so much no matter what he did or how hard he tried with everyone he met. It didn't make any sense. He worked out, dressed nice, went to clubs, even joined a hot yoga class for the express purpose of meeting women, but so far had failed everywhere.

"I came up here once when I was a kid," he said. "Friend of mine's parents have a cabin closer to Falcon Lake and—"

"I'm not really that interested, I promise."

He wasn't going to let her get to him. He'd just be Mr. Nice Guy until she finally started talking to him like a human being.

"You know, before we decided to come up here, I googled the place. Turns out there was a whole bunch of crazy stuff that—"

She froze and spun on him, wagging her finger in his face. "How the fuck did you find out?"

"I told you," he said, confused. "I was googling and—"

"She was my aunt, okay?"

"Wait, what are you—"

"The missing person, presumed murder victim. You must have been reading about—"

"I saw stories, I had no idea that—"

"Bullshit."

"No, I swear. I just googled Rock Peak Lake and found some old River City Free Press stories about what happened here. A scout troop mauling, rumoured cannibal, some hunting accidents, and yeah, a missing person. The cursed woods, they call it. It's actually kind of cool that we have a place like this here. But I had no idea you were in any way connected to—"

"I'm not. Not to most of those, or any really. Things happen in places. Animals attack. Hunters fuck up because they're drunk and stupid. And yeah, my aunt was here camping a long time ago and went missing. It's hardly unique. Maybe she just ran away, maybe not. Nobody knows. They never found a body, even though they've found plenty of others here. I've read all the stories over the years."

"Shit. I don't know what to say and—"

"You don't say anything. It's ancient history. It's not relevant to us coming here. None of the girls know anything about the stories, let alone my aunt's. Donna's so caught up in her own world I don't think she'd realize that we were coming to the very same place unless I told her. If she had read any of those old articles, she certainly never mentioned it."

"You really have quite the past."

"Drama," she said flatly. "That's what you mean, right? Baggage?"

"No, I—" He paused, trying to find the best words to navigate this awkwardness.

"I know what you're doing. You're trying to be Mr. Nice Guy. Non-threatening. Melt my cold, cold heart. Well, it's not happening. I can see right through you, so let's just keep looking for your drunk friend and get back to our vacations."

She spun back around and marched forward. He had to jog to catch up.

"John didn't used to be like this. Ever since his ex dumped him, he sort of fell off the deep end."

She said nothing, just kept walking.

"At first it was just endless whining and pining over her. Facebook stalking, going through his photos, playing old Cure records. But when she started posting pictures with her new boyfriend, something snapped. He started drinking. Sure, we all drink occasionally, but this was like he was trying to kill something inside of him. Night. Day. Didn't matter. He'd spend all his time locked in his room. He's somehow managed to keep his job, but even that's on a thread. He—"

Ashley suddenly stopped again and turned around, shooting him a disgusted look.

"Did any of you stop to think that taking an alcoholic out for a party weekend," she said, making air quotes as she talked, "might not have been the best idea?"

"Uh, not really."

She rolled her eyes and turned back around, continuing down the trail.

He rushed to catch up, sensing his small talk had backfired. He had to recover before he blew it completely.

"Okay, you're right. We're idiots. It's our fault he wandered off. But this whole search party thing wasn't a part of our weekend plans either. So I'm sorry we fucked up, okay?"

Ashley never even looked at him. "I'm already wasting a precious sunny day helping you dickheads find your lost friend. I really don't want to turn this into a whole thing where we start to talk and then you think you can play your cards right and get into my pants."

"Whoa, hey, I never said that."

"No, but you were thinking it. All men do."

How had she seen right through him like that?

"I was just talking, trying to have a conversation. There wasn't some ulterior motive."

But there actually was an ulterior motive. There always was. But there was no way he was going to give her the satisfaction of hearing him say that.

"I wasn't born yesterday," she said. "I know how it works. Mr. Nice Guy leads to Mr. Buys You a Drink Laced With Something leads to Mr. Slips His Hands Up My Shirt. Then Mr. Pressuring Into Sex ignores my drunkenness and Mr.

Films it for his Friends spreads a video around. I've seen it all before, okay, and I'm not interested."

He blanched. He wasn't so sure he could recover here.

"Small talk is to, I don't know, make this whole hike less awkward. Mr. Nice Guy doesn't have to be an act. It could be…" He could tell that Ashley saw through any and all bullshit. Maybe he should just try to be genuine. He took out his phone, opened the photos app and scrolled through until he found one of John and Stacey. He turned it to her.

"That's John. That's his ex. The reason he's drinking himself stupid. I didn't tell you the whole story. They were engaged and he found out she'd cheated on him with her jiu jitsu instructor. It was a pretty big scandal. They joined the club together. She had her work schedule changed and started going to an early morning class. She hooked up with the instructor, right under everyone's noses. They were both forced to leave the school. So not only was John cuckolded, but it was done in front of the entire gym. So he's still fucking broken and clearly a danger to himself. We need to find him before something even shittier happens."

She sighed. "Okay. I'm sorry. I'm not being fair. But you have to admit that this is a fucked-up situation. Alone in the woods with no cell reception and no one around to hear you calling for help."

"You said you've got bear spray and last time I checked I'm a lot smaller than a bear."

"Then let's hope I don't have to use it."

"What about on someone else?"

"You're saying you wouldn't protect me?"

"Would you let me?"

"I'm cautious, not an idiot."

"I'll take that as you warming up to me."

"Don't get ahead of yourself. Now let's keep going."

"I'll take what I can get," Jack said.

They looked at each other in silence for a moment. She was reappraising him and he didn't want to mess with that. Finally, she turned back to the path and continued moving. After a few minutes they came to a clearing where a natural ridge gave them a view of the entire lake.

"We have a great view from up here," she said, admiring the clear, reflective surface of the calm water. The forest stretched beyond to the horizon.

He could see the beach and traced the way they'd come. But Ashley was more interesting. The way the sun caught her face made her seem to glow. Her figure was outlined in shadow as she looked out over the landscape. Ample bosom, curving thighs, strong legs and arms, smooth hair. She was a looker. The fact that he was still so focused on that instead of John should have made him feel like shit, but he couldn't help himself.

"You see anything?" he asked as he turned away from admiring her to check out the lake view.

"You can't even see the cabins on the other side of the lake from here. It makes you feel so small. Like an insignificant speck in the landscape. Out on the ocean there's just nothing but empty sky and blue water, while here it's all a sea of green. We're intruders. We don't belong. Can't you feel it?"

"You're losing me," he said matter-of-factly.

"They might never find your body. A bear or wolf would eat it and nobody'd ever know. That's what they think happened to my aunt. It's like she never even existed."

"This is a really upbeat conversation."

145

"Comes with the territory."

"I'll keep that in mind."

"Hey," Ashley said as she pointed to something orange on the ridge down the slope from them. "What's that?"

Jack followed her finger and squinted in the sun to see what it was. "It looks like a tent."

"Could be another camper," she said. "Maybe they've seen your friend. Let's go ask."

They headed down through the trees towards the orange structure in the distance.

* * * *

"Max?"

"Sophia?"

Sally was growing more frantic with each passing moment that they found no sign of either the kids or their passing. They'd been following the main path from the beach where the tracks had ended. She could feel her heart pounding in her chest.

"Max?"

"Sophia?"

"This isn't working," Sally said. "They could have gone anywhere. They could *be* anywhere."

"Maybe they didn't come this way," Greg said. "Maybe they're back at the beach and all we've done is walk away from them."

"I'm about ready to walk away from you right now."

"That won't solve anything."

She wanted to slug him in his overly calm face. Why wasn't he as scared as she was? How could he not be when their two kids were missing in a huge forest full of bears and other dangerous animals?

"You should start thinking about lawyering up."

"I said I'm sorry, I didn't mean for this to happen."

"This whole fucking trip was a terrible idea. I should never have let you talk me into it."

"You were the one who said you wanted them to experience nature more, not—"

"Fuck you," she interrupted him. "Don't put this on me. I said I wanted them to enjoy nature, like the fucking park. You're the one who has to take things too far all the time. We could have just gone on a day trip, but no. You had to be Mr. Rustic."

"You were a part of this decision making, too," Greg said in frustration.

"Just shut up," she spat back, a part of her happy that he'd finally shown some emotion. "Don't say another word unless it's shouting out the names of our kids that you may have let get eaten by a bear."

"Oh, come on, don't catastrophize. There's no reason to believe anything bad has happened to them. They're just playing hide and seek or—"

"You'd better fucking hope so."

"I know so—"

"Max?" she cried out. "Sophia?"

Just then Greg spotted something on the trail. He froze in place, blocking Sally from seeing it. She took three steps before realizing that he'd stopped.

"The kids were wearing bathing suits, right?"

"Why?"

"I was trying to remember—"

147

"What is it?" she said behind him, trying to see over his shoulder.

"Maybe nothing. It might not even belong to—"

"What do you mean, nothing? Goddamn tell me."

He moved to the side and pointed to a torn bit of flannel shirt pierced on the end of a jagged branch. Sally moved in closer and pulled it off. "They weren't wearing this. For fuck's sake, don't you even know your own kids?"

"I don't—"

"Yeah, you don't. You don't get to ever again when this is over." She took out her phone and scrolled to a photo of the kids. She turned it and held it to his face threateningly. "These are your kids. You know them, right?"

"Of course I do, I—"

"Then get focused."

She walked away from him, shouting again: "Sophia? Max?"

He stayed a few paces back, maybe finally starting to take this seriously. Then, ahead, an arrow sign with the words "RANGER STATION" was planted at a fork in the trail. It led off down another path in the woods.

"Greg, get over here," Sally called. He ran to catch up. Looking in both directions, she realized that they'd gone through bush to return to one of the trails.

"What?" Greg said breathlessly. "Did you find them?"

"No, but look at that."

He noticed the sign and seemed confused.

"Okay, we found the ranger station," he said. "I thought we were looking for our kids."

"And it's clear that we need expert help." She headed down the path to the right, in the direction of the station.

* * * *

Beth sat alone on a dark green towel on the beach. It was getting late in the afternoon. The others had been gone for a while without any word. She decided that she didn't like being the one left behind. It was strangely eerie sitting here in the open on a deserted lakeside. If she'd thought they were going to be gone for so long, she never would have agreed to be the one to stay here with their stuff.

She pulled out the only cellphone they'd brought to see if anyone had texted her, but of course there was nothing. She hadn't missed any chime, checking it was just a habit. The cell service out here was sporadic. Deeper into the wilderness, she doubted it would even be that. The phone display icon simply read NO SERVICE. Even if they were frantically trying to let her know something, she'd have no idea.

At least it was something to kill time with. Mandy had told her the password. She opened up the photos folder and idly scrolled through her pictures. Most of them were selfies from a million different angles. There were shots of the girls, dinners out, saved memes, but then she found a few of her and Matt. They looked so happy frozen in digital time. She was smiling, holding on to his arm in a restaurant patio in the downtown exchange distract. There was even one of him in a funny hat that made her laugh.

They'd gone into a vintage clothing store on a whim. She'd made him try on this bizarre old jacket with epaulettes and tassels, then added a wide-brimmed hat with a feather in it. She must have sent the picture to Mandy because of how funny he looked. He'd attempted to stop her from taking the photo, but she'd won out. He looked cute in his embarrassment.

"You put on this front of being a big tough strong man, but underneath it all, you're actually pretty self-conscious."

She looked up, half expecting to find them all listening to her talking to herself, ready to hear them tease her about losing her mind, even ready to have Ashley berate her for defending the guy. But nobody was there. The beach was just as deserted as it had been a half hour ago.

Breaking up. The nagging voice at the back of her head had finally won out. The countless PSAs, the endless talks in school, her friend's lectures about his abusive behaviour. The signs had been there, but she'd refused to notice. Until he'd forced the issue. These photos only served to remind her of who he really was.

She deleted each one she found, clearing Mandy's phone of any record of their relationship. It was a good start. She'd do it again on her own phone when this was all over.

She had the strange sense that someone was watching her. She put the phone down and looked around the beach, but could see nothing but the clear sky, light brown sand, and slowly rippling lake water. A hawk soared lazily overhead. She felt alone and shivered. Then, almost across the lake, something padded out of the brush and stared at her. It was hard to make out from so far away, but it seemed to be—

"A bear?"

It was looking right at her, but not moving towards her. She picked up Ashley's dropped book and started reading. She looked up a moment later and the thing was gone. She relaxed and let herself breathe again. She was only two pages in when she heard the screams.

NOW

"There, see? What'd I tell you?" Matt peered through the trees at the old crimson Bel Air partially hidden in the small clearing.

A pair of woman's legs were sticking out from the back seat. A man mounted on top of her was thrusting wildly. His hairy backside bobbed up and down as the woman screamed in ecstasy. Her voice rose higher and higher as he worked away. It was impossible to actually see inside the car from where they crouched in the bushes, the angle was all wrong. It was clear what was going on, but not who was currently doing it.

"I don't know, man," Josh said. "How do you know it's her?"

"They told me she was here."

"Who?"

"I recognize the 'o' sounds. I heard them every time we fucked. You saying I can't make her fucking cum?"

Josh backed away from Matt's outburst. He was legitimately concerned that Matt was going to hit him. His eyes were wild and he was practically frothing at the mouth. The paint he'd applied to his face was starting to run, the green and black bleeding together into a mess of darkness. With his full camouflage attire and huge knife, he looked like some kind of crazed survivalist. The pills he'd taken had pushed him to the edge and he seemed just about ready to snap.

"No, no. Of course I believe you." He held his hands up in surrender to try to calm Matt. "I just— I can't see her doing that out here in an old car."

"Why else would she come out here if not to cheat on me? She knows she can't get away with that shit in town. What happens in Rock Peak Lake, stays in Rock Peak Lake." Matt started pacing back and forth in front of him, fingering the knife as he worked out some equation in his head. "Fuck," he suddenly spat angrily. "They're right. How could I have been so stupid? Some asshole with a classic car. All this time, right under my nose. The fucking cunt."

"Who're—"

Matt stormed off out of the bush towards the car and the two people going at it inside.

"Hey, wait, Matt." Josh ran after him. He tried to grab him by the shoulder, but Matt shrugged him off. He grabbed him a second time and Matt spun, raised the knife and brandished it in Josh's face threateningly. His startled reflection in the blade was crystal clear. Matt stared at him with dead eyes. The man had completely lost his mind. But what could Josh do when he had such a big fucking knife?

"Don't get in our way," Matt said calmly.

Our?

"What are you going to do?"

"Like they said. I need to make sure she knows she can't do this to me."

"Don't do whatever you're or they're thinking or telling you to," Josh said, suddenly picturing the worst. "You can't—"

"Of course I can," Matt interrupted. "It's the fucking Napoleonic Code."

"I don't think that means what you think it does."

"I'm not about to let that bitch make a fool of me."

"Just put the knife away. You don't want to go to jail over this."

Matt was breathing heavily, seemingly looking right though him. His lips were moving in silent conversation with an unseen second. But there must have been something in Josh's eyes that sold him on the idea of listening to his advice. He slid the knife back into the holster slowly.

Josh breathed a sigh of relief.

"You coming or not?" Matt asked.

"Let's just go. You saw what you came here for. Confront her when she gets back."

"If you're not going to help, you're a part of the problem. Stay out of our way."

He pushed Josh backwards. He tripped over an exposed tree root and landed hard on his ass, leaving him helpless as Matt ran towards the car. Josh didn't get up to chase him. If he followed, he'd be an accessory. Instead, sitting here in the dirt, he was simply a coward.

It was like watching a movie unfold. None of it seemed real. He wanted to yell, but his throat constricted. Helpless, he saw Matt run to the car screaming. He grabbed the man in mid-thrust by the leg and pulled him out of the car. He had feathered hair and wore nineteen-seventies clothes. An open shirt, peace necklace, tight pants around his ankles. Matt punched him once in the face with a bestial snarl. Josh didn't recognize the man and the guy didn't seem to have any idea what was happening. Caught totally off guard, he didn't even try to block the punches. His tan pants were down around his ankles. His erect penis vibrated and glistened moistly in the light. With an astonished expression, mouth hanging open wide, he tried to speak when Matt swung again. This time the blow broke the man's nose with one shot. Blood splattered on the old window with a sick plop.

The confused man bellowed in pain. The woman screamed as she leaned up. Matt grabbed the guy's face and rammed it into the glass of the open passenger side door, shattering it clean through. He then pulled the man's head out and it was cut in a thousand places. Blood poured out of a patchwork of jigsaw-like wounds, sliding down his bare chest. He coughed and blood bubbled from his ruined mouth. He started to go limp, but Matt refused to let go. He rammed the man's head into the car door six times in rapid succession, bending it right off the hinges. Holding the nearly comatose naked man, he kneed him in the stomach four times, then chopped down on his neck. This had gone too far. It was past assault and had become a complete mauling.

The poor guy fell limply to his knees, coughing again, spitting a glob of blood all over Matt's pants. With a final shout, Matt kicked him in the ribs and let go of his grip on his hair. The man collapsed face first into the dirt, landing flat. He lay prone. Matt kicked him again and again and again, screaming inhumanly as he continued.

"Jesus, Matt stop," Josh said meekly, but he was frozen in place. He could only watch the car wreck in front of him.

The woman shrieked again as Matt raised his foot up. He brought the huge military boots down on the unknown man's wrist. A sick cracking reverberated through the clearing as it landed. The man screamed, arching his head back, his hand bent the wrong way. Matt kicked him in the raised face, knocking teeth loose, denting his entire jaw inwards like a broken mannequin.

Josh felt like he was going to throw up at the sight of the shattered skull. The poor guy was being turned into hamburger.

The man collapsed back to the dirt and finally fell still. He must have slipped into unconsciousness. Unfortunately Matt wasn't done. He kicked the prone body again, huffing and puffing in undiminished rage. The makeup oozing off his skin, his face underneath had turned beet red. He looked like he was going to have a heart attack. The woman shrieked louder and slunk back into the car, trying to get away from the lunatic who'd come out of nowhere.

Josh just stayed frozen in place, as if he was glued to the earthen floor. He couldn't budge as he watched the brutal beating finally stop. Matt began to reach for the knife. Finally Josh rose and ran forward. He grabbed Matt's hand and shouted. "Stop. Enough. You've proved your point."

Matt's vacant glare made him think for a moment that he would lash out at him, too, but whatever switch had been flipped seemed to flip back. He seemed to finally realize he'd done what he came for and began to calm down. He nodded slowly.

He turned away from Josh and leaned into the car. "Come on out, you cheating cunt," he said. He grabbed the woman's leg and yanked her out to the ground. She landed hard with her skirt up over her hips. She wasn't wearing a shirt or underwear. Her skin was covered in sweat and globs of splashed blood. Slender, with small breasts and well defined abs, her hair was dark, just like Beth's, but feathered and huge. Josh realized in horror that it wasn't Beth.

"Who the fuck are you?" Matt asked in confusion.

She just screamed in primal terror. She looked down at the man that had only recently been on top of her laying, possibly dead, on the ground and screamed again.

"It's not her," Josh said.

"I know it's not fucking her," Matt said. "I can see that. But who the hell is this?"

She began to sob unintelligibly.

"And who the fuck was that?" Matt looked at the unmoving man that he might have just killed. Matt looked from the man, to the woman, back to the man, and back to the woman again. "I don't understand. They said… Who are these people? Why are they dressed like that? Where's Beth?"

"Please. I don't know who you're talking about," the woman pleaded through body-wracking sobs.

"We have to get this guy to a hospital." Josh crouched down and found the man's breathing raspy and shallow. Blood bubbled out of his mouth with each weak exhale. He touched his good wrist and tried to find a pulse. It was faint, but present. "He could be in serious trouble. Let her go and we—"

"I won't say a thing, I swear," the woman said, sobbing.

"You heard her," Josh said.

"Not good enough. I don't know you. I can't trust you."

"You can, you can."

"Listen to her, she's—"

"She could be just like Beth. A fucking liar."

"I'm not. I promise."

"Just let her go, man," Josh said, trying to appeal to Matt's faint lingering humanity. "Let them both go. This was all a misunderstanding. It doesn't have to get worse."

"I can't do that." Matt grabbed the girl by the hair and pulled her to her feet. "They warned me."

The woman cried out in panic and tried to squirm away, but Matt held her tightly. He bent her neck backwards, watching as the blood on her chest began to slide down between her breasts, meeting her exposed belly button. He looked at her like a butcher looks at a slab of tenderloin. With his free hand, he reached to his leg for his knife.

* * * *

"I think we're lost," Sophia said to Max as he pushed his way through the trees and long grass. Deep in the woods here it was almost up to their noses and the trees above seemed like giants blocking the sky.

"Are not," he said. He was taking them into the bush off the gravel path, but then he'd done that plenty of times at the playground by their house. There were lots of interesting things that lived in the bushes. Squirrels, raccoons, one time he even saw a skunk. She might not think so, but he knew what he was doing.

"I want to go back to Mommy," his sister whined again.

"We're going to find the leprechaun first," Max said. "You saw him, too, right?"

His sister paused and he turned back to look at her. She hesitated for a moment, but saw the look on his face and slowly nodded. "Yeah, I think so," she said.

"Me, too. And we know they live in the forest, so if we find him, then we can get him to tell us where his gold is. You remember the story Dad told us, right?"

"Yes. But I'm really hungry."

"If we find his gold, we could buy all the candy we wanted."

"Really?"

"Of course. Gold is just as good as money. Maybe even better."

"Okay, but how much more do we have to walk?"

His sister was always complaining like this. It didn't seem to matter how little they walked or for how long, it was always too much. "It can't be that much further, I'm sure," he said. "Leprechauns don't have long legs."

"That makes sense," she said.

"So follow me." He turned and kept pushing through the trees. He didn't really know how long they'd been exploring, he didn't have a watch or a phone. It certainly seemed like this bush was a whole lot bigger than the one near the playground by their house. When he and Sophia went in there, they eventually came to a wooden fence and couldn't go any further. Then they could turn back and find the sandbox all over again. He didn't know if there was a fence here. All they'd seen so far was the trees. Trees didn't worry him, he knew all about them. They even had some in their backyard.

They pressed in deeper until something strange appeared. A man standing in the woods ahead of them. He was an older man and looked a little like Grandpa. His face was all wrinkly and he had grey hair. He just stood there looking at them. He wasn't scary—the man smiled at the two of them. Did he know them?

"Hello," Max said as they came closer. "We're out hunting leprechauns. Have you seen any?"

The man grinned, showing glistening teeth as his skin stretched outward.

* * * *

Frank drifted into a meditative state, barely cognizant of his surroundings. He had become one with the rod and reel. He could feel every slight tug caused by the flow of the current and the testing nibbles of curious fish looking for an easy bite. His hands moved without thought as he stood in the water. This must be what they called nirvana.

It had been so long since he'd been out on a lake like this. He'd let himself grow too accustomed to city life and had lost touch with his roots. But everything had come back to him over the course of the day. It really was like riding a bicycle. Three good-sized walleye waited to be fried up for lunch as soon as Derek came back.

With his mind almost empty of all thought, one suddenly forced its way through; he had no idea how long Derek had been gone. It seemed like only a moment ago that he'd walked off to find the bathroom, but Frank had been existing outside of time, so it could have actually been quite a while since the man had left. He looked up at the sun and realized that it was already late afternoon. That meant the man had been gone much longer than he should have. Maybe it hadn't been such a good idea to let someone with vascular dementia wander off on his own to find a bathroom. It was clear that Frank had a lot to learn about dealing with the elderly.

"Shit, I'd better go look for him," he cursed and propped his rod against some rocks.

THEN

"This is an amazing spot," Alice said as she leaned back against a tree and stared at the setting sun.

"I promised you, didn't I?" David said as he finished starting the fire.

"It's worth not going back to my tent, that's for sure," she said.

"I swear this wasn't my plan. I had every intention of having you back, but then I remembered this spot and… You can use my tent, and I'll sleep outside if it makes you more comfortable."

She watched him spark the kindling, admiring his tanned skin, and felt like it wasn't really a problem that they'd paddled out so far they had to make camp here. Old Alice might have been upset, accused him of purposely getting her away from civilization so he could have a chance to take advantage of her, but new, free Alice was excited at the opportunity. She hadn't been with any man since Adam. This could be a magical experience.

"Well, let's play it by ear, okay?"

He looked up at her with a raised eyebrow but didn't say anything to ruin it. He was already a step up over Adam in that respect.

In a few moments he had the fire raging, and they were roasting hotdogs from her cooler on skewers.

"I sure didn't think I'd be having any fresh buns for a while," David said as he took a bite.

"I guess sometimes you just get lucky out here, eh?"

He grinned again.

As the sun finally set, they finished up and sat next to each other against the tree talking, just letting the fire's glow be the centre of their shared world.

"—so the next step was divorce," she said.

"I'm sorry."

"I'm not. Some things just reach their end point and there's no reason to fight for them when one side has no interest in doing so."

"If it makes you feel any better," he said, "I can't imagine why he wouldn't have fought harder."

"A nineteen-year-old secretary with big tits."

"Ouch."

"The joke's on her. He's a piece of shit. She can have him."

A loon called out in the darkness. The fire crackled. Alice leaned her head on David's strong shoulder. He put his arm around her. The moment was almost too perfect. She tilted her head. He gently touched her chin, lifted her face up to his.

This is it.

Their lips met in a magical explosion. She unleashed all of her pent-up emotions. The hurt, the pain, the longing, the desire she'd suppressed. He met it all perfectly. Time lost all meaning as they lay under the stars and the fire warmed them. She turned her head as he took her and looked out at the lake, feeling him inside, enjoying him connecting with her.

Each movement sent shudders through her body and she

writhed with pleasure. And yet, as she looked out at the water, she saw the strangest thing. A bear, wandering in from the river's edge, towards them. It had to be a trick of the light. And yet, it couldn't be.

"David," she moaned.

"Alice."

"What's that?"

"What's—"

He leaned up and paused his rhythm, saw her looking towards the water and turned his head.

"Oh, fuck," he shouted and slid off and out of her.

She didn't know what to do. She lay on the ground as David, nude and glistening with sweat, reached for a log from the fire and pulled it out. Brandishing it like a flaming torch, he waved it in front of him and charged the bear.

"Back. Go back," he screamed.

The thing was huge. It looked like a very old grizzly, with the scars of countless battles written on its fur and snout. The fire seemingly had no effect. David waved threateningly but it simply stopped and regarded him like a curious insect.

"Leave. Away. Go."

Alice sat up, unable to do anything but watch.

"Alice, get another log and—"

But David didn't get to finish his request. The bear swatted out with its massive paw, knocked him flying towards the water. The flaming log fell from his grip and landed on the forest floor.

"David!"

Finally, her body caught up to her mind and she snapped into action. She darted for the torch, had it up and in the bear's face, swaying towards him.

"David, are you okay?"

She couldn't see where he fell. The bear watched her from the other side of the flame dispassionately.

"Leave us alone. Go find a deer or something. Leave."

Then it took a step forward. She thrust the flame into its face. It cried out and recoiled in pain.

"I warned you."

Its great paws came to its face and patted out the singed fur. Blackened, it turned to her with fiercely burning brown eyes that shone with far too much intelligence for a simple animal. Even the stamping out of its own fur seemed too advanced for the thing.

She moved to stick the log in again, but it twisted its face and clamped down on her hand with its massive jaws. She screamed out in agony as the teeth shredded her skin and she lost all feeling in her fingers.

It pulled back and her hand went, too. She pulled the pumping stump and stared dumbfounded at the mangled arm. Looking back to the bear, she didn't even have time to scream again before it lunged forward and wrapped its massive mouth around her face.

* * * *

"Alright, men. There's a killer in these woods and I aim to find him. He may be a man. He may be a bear. He may be some kind of man that turns into a bear or a bear that turns into a man or perhaps even some other animal that turns into a bear. Or maybe a person that turns into another animal and has learned how to also turn into a bear. That I'm not sure of."

The amassed crowd of rangers and campers looked at each other in confusion as Frank spoke to them.

"What I do know is, this killer has killed and will kill again unless we stop him or her or it or whatever. So we're going to spread out in an orderly fashion with our guns, and turn over every goddamned leaf in this forest until we find the bastard. Then, we will bring him or her or it or whatever in for the law to take care of. The law in this case represented by me."

"Shouldn't the RCMP have jurisdiction?"

"Not according to this," Frank said, holding up his gun.

Another one of the rangers held up his hand. "Can we shoot him or her or it or whatever?"

Frank turned to the man in his crisp green uniform with his rifle slung over his shoulder and almost scoffed. He looked like a boy scout leader, not a soldier. But you took what you could get in times of war.

"If you're left with no other options," Frank said. "But I'm not authorized to deputize anyone here, nor can I promise that the local municipality won't frown on vigilante justice. If this were River City I'd say go ahead and shoot the bastard, but for now, aim for the balls or legs or arms or tail. Taking him or her or it alive is what's most important."

The crowd of rangers talked amongst themselves. There were a few grumblings and disgruntled comments, but no one spoke up. Frank counted heads again. Twenty. There wasn't enough of a posse here to really comb the entire woods, the Whiteshell was far too vast, but it would have to do. Ranger Smith had put the word out for backup and this was all who had shown up. Maybe for nothing if the killer had already fled the park, but Frank had a feeling that the sicko was still out there in the trees, maybe even watching them right now.

This was a real head case. Someone who could do to a person what that monster had done to those poor people back in the cabin was probably either insane, or right on the edge. Either way, they had to be stopped.

"If there's no further questions, spread out. Stay in touch with the walkie-talkies, and let's find us a killer."

The crowd began to disperse in pairs. Frank approached Derek, who waited for him near the line of parked ranger jeeps.

"You ready to do some hunting, good buddy?" he said.

"Sure. It's why we came up here, isn't it?"

"I'll bet you thought we'd be after a little less dangerous game."

"Could still be a bear or a rabid moose."

"Or one of those crazed hippies hopped up on powder and pills."

"Either way. As long as I get to shoot something."

"That's the spirit. Now let's get moving before one of those glorified scout leaders accidentally catches the perp and we miss all the fun."

NOW

"There's no one around," Jack said to Ashley as he looked over the abandoned campsite.

"But all their stuff is still here," she said, confused. "Like they plan on coming back any minute."

The fire had been extinguished, but other than that, it seemed like the camper had just stepped away for a moment. Everything was left exactly as it would have been had someone still intended to keep using the site. Tent, gear, clothes, cooler of food, and yet, nobody was around.

"Do we wait? Maybe they just went for a hike?" he said.

"We could leave them a note. Saying to come find us if they've seen your friend."

"Do you have a pen?" he asked.

"No. You?"

"Me either. Maybe there's something we could use inside the tent." Jack got onto his hands and knees and opened the flap. "Holy shit, look at all this stuff."

"What is it?" Ashley asked and moved forward to look inside with him.

He held out a package of Duracell batteries to her. "These things are vintage. Did they have them sitting in their basement for forty years and just now decided to use them?"

"Wow." She took the black and copper coloured cardboard package and flipped it over in her hands. "I've never seen batteries this old. You think they'd still work?"

"The package is in mint condition. I'll bet there's someone out there who'd pay good money for that on eBay."

"What else did you find?"

He started rummaging through the backpack in the tent, pulling out clothes. "Everything in here is super old. This camper has a serious seventies fetish."

"Maybe they're just using old gear."

"Doubt it. This shit is all super new. Some even still have their price tag on 'em. Look at this, Woolco. How long since that place existed?"

"Not since I was a kid," Ashley said.

She climbed the rest of the way inside the tent with him and looked over the vintage collection of whoever had left it here. Everything screamed out of date.

"You're not kidding. You could have a retro party with all of—"

"Found a wallet," Jack suddenly said, pulling out a brown folded leather wallet from the side pouch of the backpack.

"Whose?"

He fished around inside, pulled out some one-dollar bills. "Someone who's got some seriously old currency."

"This has to be a movie set or something," Ashley said. "Nobody's this retro."

"Apparently Alice McCormick is," Jack said, reading over the driver's license he found.

Ashley blanched. "Say that again."

"Apparently Alice McCormick is."

"Give me that." She snatched the paper card and stared at

it for a long time, recognizing the face in the picture from old photographs in her grandmother's albums. The feathered hair, the brown eyes, the large smile. "This isn't possible."

"Why? You don't think Alice McCormick passed her driver's test?"

"This is my aunt. The one who went missing forty years ago. The one whose body they never found."

"What? Are you saying—"

"We just stumbled on her campsite, yeah. Shit, maybe there's some clue as to what happened to her. Maybe—"

"Ashley, think about this for a minute. How the hell would your missing aunt's campsite still be up forty years later? How would all of her things still be perfectly pristine and not, I dunno, decomposed or covered in dirt or chewed on by animals. And that fire looked fresh. There's got to be another explanation."

"How could the RCMP have missed this? It wasn't that hard to find." Ashley replaced the license in the wallet.

"Because this isn't her campsite. It's got to be some kind of prank. It—"

Ashley pocketed the wallet and climbed out of the tent. She stood up and started scanning the river's edge in both directions. Jack joined her.

"What are you doing?"

"Looking for someone around. Anyone who—"

"You don't think she's coming back, do you?"

"Uh, no, it's been forty years. If she'd been hiding out in the bush here all this time someone would have run across her. I'm checking for hidden cameras or a film crew. Maybe someone's making a true crime show about her disappearance and—"

She trailed off as she spotted a canoe drifting down the river. Metal, splattered with red, it lazily bobbed on the current towards them.

"Oh my God," she said. "Look."

"Someone's boat, so?"

"So what's all over it?"

"Paint?"

"We need to get it," she said.

"You mean I need to."

"If you're going to offer," she said, shrugging.

He sighed and waded out into the water, grabbing the edge of the canoe and dragging it back to shore. He pulled it up on the grass and wiped his hands.

"You need to see this," he gasped.

Ashley ran over but he blocked her from seeing inside. Up close, it was clear that the canoe *was* splattered with red marks, but they weren't paint. Either someone had done a terrible job of decorating it or it was blood.

"Well, what?"

"I think he's dead."

He finally moved and let her peer over the edge of the canoe. Someone lay on the bottom. Completely naked, with tanned skin riveted with deep gouges in his side. He'd been badly slashed by something sharp. It wasn't clear if he was alive.

"You sure?" she asked.

"I'm not a doctor, but—"

"Animal attack?"

"Looks that way."

"What the heck do you think did it?"

"Wolf, maybe," he said. "Or a bear."

"You think this was his campsite?"

"Could be why he came back."

"But he's naked."

"Maybe he's a naturalist."

"And he was attacked while out canoeing in the nude?"

"The ranger did say to watch out for bears," he said.

"I've never seen a bear attack before."

"It's not pretty."

"We have to go tell someone," she said "The ranger or whoever. Someone who'll know what to do."

He checked his phone and found it had no service. "Not happening."

"Wait, why would he have all of my missing aunt's things?"

"I don't know if he can answer that."

Then, a low moan came from the man.

"He's not dead."

"What do we do?"

"Maybe there's medical supplies with the gear."

Jack crawled back inside the orange tent, returning with a small first aid kit and a towel.

"You know anything about wound care?"

"Not really, but we should get him out of the canoe," she said. "Grab his legs and help."

* * * *

"Did you hear something?" Donna pulled away from Percy's embrace and looked out the dirty cabin window.

"I'm not paying attention to anything but you right now," he said, his eyes never leaving hers. He really hadn't heard anything anyway, but he knew that letting her know how focused he was on her needs would be a big turn on.

It was.

She smiled and moved in to kiss him again. Her lips were soft against his. She plunged inside his mouth, gently moving her hands along his back, and he held her as firmly as he could, pulling her up close. He wanted to feel her tight form against his.

"There," she said, pulling away. "I heard it again."

"There's nobody in the cabin but us, babe," he said.

She pushed away and looked around the strange room. "You really think it's safe to do this in here? It seems like it might be a museum."

Percy let go for a moment. "Some museum," he said. "It's just a ranger shack. See?" He started walking around the room. "Maps." He tapped a map of the park on the wall. "Radio." He pointed to the old HAM radio set up on a desk in the corner. He walked around to the small sleeping area. "Dresser, closet, and… bed." He grinned and waved her to him. "Just a regular old ranger station."

"But it's all so retro."

"You know how government works. They're still using seventies tech. No budget for upgrades. The guy probably has to walk to town to use the phone."

"You think so?"

"I know so. He's out on patrol. Doing his job. We're in here all alone."

"But what if he comes back?"

"Then he'll get a bit of a show, won't he?"

He pulled her wrist and jerked her into his arms. He made a show of stumbling backwards onto the bed, gently rolling her over and pressing her down flat. He leaned in with a kiss.

"Oh, you're bad."

171

"Someone's got to get some use out of this bed." He began to slide her shirt up and over her head. He could practically feel her melt under his touch.

She dug her hands into the back of his shorts, and he pulled off her bikini top. He could smell how wet she was right now. His quickly forming erection had to be obvious to her, too.

"This is fucking hot," she whispered.

"Totally," he said.

She slid his shorts back. He dove his hand between the waistband of hers, feeling for her bikini bottoms. He pulled the string. There was no stopping what came next. They plunged together. He grunted with exertion, she moaned in passion. Then, she swung on top, pushed him back and slid down his body. She grabbed him by the shaft, regarded it like a lollipop, then plunged it inside her mouth.

"Whoa," he said as he leaned back.

Her rhythmic head movements pushed any thoughts of finding John out of his mind—they were pushing pretty much all thoughts out of his mind.

A creak. From the door or maybe from the old bed, but he couldn't focus on spatial awareness when she was working him like a pro.

"You like that?" she asked as she pulled away.

"Oh yeah," he panted.

He tried to pull her up to mount him again, but instead she shrugged him off and went back to work. He shut his eyes and focused on her tongue, her grip, her other hand massaging his balls. It was all just too much.

"Oh god, here it comes," he said to warn her.

He grabbed her hair. She didn't pull away. She just stopped moving. Her hands went slack as he exploded in her mouth.

When it was all over, he opened his eyes and saw her still on her knees, latched on tight to his quickly softening cock.

"Donna?"

Something was wrong. Her head wasn't attached to anything. He watched as it sat perched on his crotch. He sat up and it fell from his now flaccid dick in his hands. Holding her by the hair, there was nothing below the neck. Blood and semen poured from a ripped gash at the base of her skull. He lifted the decapitated head up, staring at the impossible sight, unable to process what he was seeing. Her crumpled body lay at his feet on the floor of the cabin. Red ooze drained from the gash between the shoulders, coating the wooden floor in gore.

He wanted to scream, but couldn't. He could only gargle unintelligibly. Nothing escaped his mouth at all. Something dripped on his chest. It had come from his neck. It burned. He touched it and his hand came away covered in blood. He touched it again and found that his fingers pierced right through where his skin should have been and went inside his throat. He could feel rubbery tubing inside.

What's going on?

He understood now that his throat had been slashed open. He looked back down to the cabin floor and Donna's body. That was when he realized that his dick was gone. He reached down to his crotch, but met only air. Where was it? It couldn't be gone. Why didn't it hurt? The head. Her mouth. It was stuck inside Donna's mouth. He watched as a chunk of flesh slid out the bottom of her torn neck and landed flat on the wood with a splat. The crimson sausage was all too familiar.

None of this made sense. The cabin door was open. The sunlight poured in. A shape blocked the light. He gargled again as more blood oozed from his torn throat. The shape grabbed him by the shoulder and a sudden tearing in his stomach area jerked him back against the cabin wall. Digging, claws buried deep in his body. He couldn't make out the details of what was doing it, just felt his abdomen lightening as meat was pulled free in lengths. He saw the faint images of his guts falling out, unspooling at his feet. The pain was short-lived. Gravity took over. He was hoisted up. Some kind of hook plunged into his back. The thing that had come inside the cabin began to drape his intestines around the room like a Christmas garland. His eyes drifted back to the door and the sunlight. He wondered how long he could look at it before he went blind, but that thought was lost as what remained of his sense of self merged with that red ball in the sky and flared away to oblivion.

* * * *

"It's so isolated out here," Aiden said. "John could be ten feet away and we'd never know."

"You think the others have found him?" Mandy asked.

"I hope so," Aiden said.

Little sunlight made it through the thick canopy of trees above them. The grasping branches struck their faces as they pushed along overgrown trails that seemed to abruptly stop then begin again meters away. Insects buzzed around their heads and the tall grasses brushed their bare legs as they walked. Phantom ticks crawled along their skin and mosquitos landed for brief moments before being swatted flat by increasingly agitated hands.

"Then whose, uh, part was that we found?" Mandy asked.

"I'll leave that to the authorities to figure out."

"What if it was him? How do you think they're going to handle the news?"

"I'm not sure how I will. Nobody deserves to end up like that."

"Do you think it hurt?" she asked tentatively.

"Getting eaten by a bear? Absolutely."

She slid her arm into his and looked around the woods with a newfound worry. "I'd really like to get back to the others. I don't like it out here anymore."

"Me either, honestly. I keep feeling like someone's watching us and—"

The sound of a branch snapping came from behind them.

"I think we should run," he said. Grabbing her hand, he began running down the thinning path, leading her along frantically. Behind them, he could hear the sound of something in pursuit.

"What's that?" Mandy asked, panicked.

"Just keep moving."

A loud thunderclap erupted in the air, and something struck him in the shoulder. A jolt of pain shot through his arm. He lost his grip on her hand and stumbled to the ground, scraping his face along the dirt. A jagged branch clawed a long line into his leg. Mandy skidded to a stop.

"Aiden. What—"

His shoulder throbbed. There was something lodged inside the skin. He reached with his other hand and felt a pit. He couldn't move his arm. His fingers went numb. Mandy tried to help him up.

"You're bleeding. You—"

Another thunderclap. Something whizzed by her head, just

missing her face by a few inches. She turned to see a piece of the trunk of a tree blasted out, exposing the soft wood beneath the bark.

"That's no bear," she said. "Someone's shooting at us."

"Run. Get help," he said, wincing in pain.

"I'm not leaving you," she said, trying to help him up.

Not even thinking about what she was doing, she slid her arm under his and yanked him to his feet with more strength than either expected. A wave of excruciating pain shot through his numb arm, but he didn't cry out. He could feel blood slowly trickling through his leg hair from the deep scrape.

"Into the bush," he said. "We're too exposed on the trail."

They plunged through the tree line and ran, leaping over downed trees. More branches scraped along their faces as they put as much distance between them and whoever had shot at them as they could.

"Where'd he go?" someone shouted.

"Thattaway," another voice called out.

They never looked back, they just kept running, even as Aiden lost all feeling in his hand. He tried to wiggle his fingers, but they responded on a second delay. His leg started burning and he limped as he ran.

"Are they following us?" Mandy panted.

"I don't know."

Neither knew where they ran, just that they had to. When it seemed like the sounds of pursuit had faded, they slowed and caught their breath. Aiden pulled out his phone. "No signal," he said.

"Who the hell shot you?" Mandy asked between gasps of air.

"Hunters? Had to be a mistake."

"They almost got me, too."

"It had to be a mistake. It had to be a—"

"Maybe they thought you were the bear or—"

"I can't use my hand. Take my phone," he said, handing it to her. "The password is—"

Another thunderclap pierced the air. Mandy instinctively ducked.

"That sounded far away," she said.

But Aiden didn't reply. She turned to see him leaning up against the tree. He looked slowly at her before he seemed to vomit up blood. He coughed up crimson goo all over his shirt. He'd been hit right in the stomach. His hands fell away from a pumping wound that leaked out over the forest floor.

"Ohmygod," she said.

"Run." He coughed again and more blood fell from his mouth.

"I'm not leaving you, I'm—"

Another gunshot exploded and the side of Aiden's skull burst outward, showering her face with brains and bone shards. She screamed and finally ran. She never even considered looking back, just pumped her legs and moved. She heard hooting and hollering behind her.

"Wowee, you bagged 'em," someone shouted.

"Big feller, too."

"Looks mighty weird."

She had to tell someone. She had to find help. She had to get the others. But mostly, she had to get the hell out of the forest before it was too late.

* * * *

"It doesn't look like anyone's home." Sally peered into the darkened windows of the ranger station. Nearly swallowed by the surrounding forest, the small wooden structure seemed abandoned. "The curtains are drawn. That or the windows are painted black on the inside."

"Why would someone paint the inside of the cabin windows black?" Greg asked.

"I don't know, maybe there's a darkroom in there. Or the glass is just dirty. Whoever's in charge should probably clean them and—"

"Be sure to leave that in the suggestion box," he said sarcastically.

"Just knock again."

"I did. There's no answer."

"What part of again did you not understand?"

He looked like he wanted to say something back to her, but Sally shot him the dirtiest look she knew how and he thought better of it. He turned back to the door and made a big show of knocking loudly. "Hello? Ranger person? We need help."

"Ranger person?"

"Are there gender specific ranger terms? Like, would you say Rang-ette? Or Ranger—"

"It's just ranger," she spat back. "There is no gender specific term. Like baker. You don't say baker-ette."

"Baguette." He raised a finger in the air as if he'd just made the greatest joke in history.

He hadn't.

She knew exactly what he was trying to do: use humour to soften her mood. He always did this when they fought, but she couldn't understand how he could be so flippant about the fact that their two kids were lost in bear-infested woods.

Her heart was racing and an empty pit was growing larger in her stomach each second that she didn't know where Max and Sophia were. And here he was cracking stupid jokes.

"Just shut the fuck up," she said.

"Hey, I just—"

"Not in the mood, Greg," she said, cutting him off. "Every second we waste here is another second the kids are lost and alone out there in the forest."

"I can't make the ranger appear, alright? I'm knocking and there's no one home." He knocked again to show her.

"Did you try the knob?" she asked.

"No, why would—"

"You stupid fuck." She grabbed the handle, turned it and pushed the door open. She shook her head at him. He was proving to be more useless than she'd thought possible.

"There, you see, open. Took all of half a second to figure out. Good thing I have a real man's man like you around."

He blanched. His jaw hung open. He stared inside the cabin in stunned silence while she looked at him in barely repressed fury.

"Nothing to say for yourself? No jokes?"

Perhaps it was stress, or maybe it was just the boiling over of long simmering tensions, but she was calling into question her judgement at having married him in the first place. How could she have ever fallen in love with this sack of rusted nails?

"Mr. Freelance Artist. How does your studio, portfolio, scarf collection, vintage blazers, carefully manicured side-burns and facial hair help us now? Bears don't give a shit that you like to drop flowery words or drink obscure teas. You incredibly selfish, full of shit asshole. Oh wait, you're making vitally important art, right? Art that eventually someone will notice and pay you money for. Then you can stop teaching at the community centre, doing elementary school visits, selling prints at comic cons, drawing posters for your brother's shitty band. Become a real player."

He wasn't even looking at her. He'd become focused on the cabin, letting her vent without anything to say for himself.

"Couldn't even watch the kids for ten minutes. Couldn't do much for them ever really. I changed the diapers, did the two am feedings, sat in the ER with fevers and cuts, found the daycare, met the teachers, drove to pediatrician appointments, bought the new shoes. You needed time to create," she said mockingly. "Horse shit. You just can't be bothered. I'm the bread winner and the homemaker. You draw squiggles that—"

"I-I-I…" he stammered while his face turned green.

"Your spell's worn off. I realize I've been blind. Here I was thinking I had it all, that I was happy. Do you know I defended you to my friends and parents? You're doing all the work while he mooches off you like a sponge Sally. They said that, you know. But I refused to listen. To think all it took was you losing the most important thing in my life while I took a swim to make me understand how stupid I've been these past eleven years."

But still he just looked past her and stammered gibberish.

"How could I have been so brainwashed?"

She imagined grabbing the edges of his styled facial hair and yanking until they tore off his lip in a great bloody gash. Then slamming his head onto the rocks until all his teeth came out in a thick puddle. Kicking him in the balls so hard they came out of his ruined mouth. Then stomping on those balls until they were flattened like pancakes. She almost slapped him right there. But she knew that violence wouldn't get their kids back.

"Can't you even try to defend yourself?"

She was about to chew him out some more when she decided to turn around. And that was when she saw what he was looking at and screamed. The cabin was the stuff of nightmares. Chains dangled from beams in the roof. At the end of each hung an eight-inch curved hook with what looked like the limbs of what had once been a man stuck on. An arm, a leg, an open-mouthed severed head with the hook forced through the back to come out of a ruined eye socket. The torso, hacked beyond recognition, lay on the desk, with bloody slashes revealing the dark crimson insides. The walls were smeared in blood. Strange markings covered the map of the park and the various black and white photos that lined the wooden cabin. She understood now that her thoughts of the windows being painted black were wrong. They were painted in blood.

Someone had been nailed in a crucifixion pose to the wall. Her skin had been peeled back away from her body, dangling from her chest like an unfurled roll of parchment paper. She had no eyes. Tree branches had been lodged into her head. A penis had been nailed next to her left hand. One of her legs was missing.

Directly across from her Sally saw most of a man nailed to the far wall. A huge hole had been cut out of his stomach and the inner organs were piled at his legs. Next to his hands, someone had nailed the intestines, draping them around the room like a strand of lights.

"Kill me," a hoarse voice croaked.

She vomited and collapsed into a heap, unable to process

181

the grim tableau. She stammered unintelligibly. Her mind threatened to snap.

She heard Greg enter the room, then a thud. He came back out after slamming the door shut and helped her up.

"Something is terribly wrong here."

She could only nod, momentarily forgetting the English language. He pulled her away from the slaughter and led her back down the path.

NOW

"Now who in the world would leave a perfectly good car parked out in the woods like this?" Frank examined the old dust and dirt covered Bel Air with a devotee's eye. The vehicle was mostly obscured by the encroaching forest. He'd nearly walked right past it without noticing it.

From the looks of it, it must have been sitting here for years. The remaining windows were filthy, the tires long since flat, the roof sagged inwards. One of the doors wasn't latched. There was enough space where it failed to close that there could be animals or anything living inside the car. The windshield was surprisingly intact, but the Bel Air itself had clearly outlived its usefulness.

Frank pulled on the unlatched door and it fell off its hinges onto the ground.

"Hello?" He leaned inside.

A ratty old blanket covered the rear seat. Empty beer bottles lay strewn all over the floor mats. One was still sealed.

"Hey, jackpot," he said, pulling out the familiar old Labatt logo on a vintage stubby. "Somebody left me a present."

The bottle was filthy, but the brew inside looked as inviting as always.

"No bottle opener?"

He fished around the car, found a yellowed plastic bag of joints in the glove compartment. "Well now, looks like someone forgot his party."

An old concert handbill, some guitar picks, women's underwear, road maps, expired insurance, no bottle opener.

He hooked the edge of the bottle on the corner of the glove compartment and tugged. The cap came off and a mouthful of beer spilled over the old maps. He quickly brought the beer to his lips and sucked back some of the warm brew.

"Not cold, but it'll do."

He wiped his mouth and looked for any signs of someone having passed this way recently. The car certainly seemed to have been stuck here for a long time. He doubted if whoever had left it was coming back any time soon.

"Somebody should fix this beauty up," he said, admiring the old monster of a vehicle. "They don't make 'em like this anymore, that's for sure."

He finished his beer and tossed the empty bottle in the back seat with the others.

"Doesn't look like Derek came this way. Or if he did, he didn't find the car."

He fished once more through the vehicle for any more hidden beers, but came up empty.

"Alright, old man, I know you're out here somewhere, so how about making this easier by you finding me? Especially since I'm not exactly sure where I am either."

* * * *

They'd come from the direction of their camp. Panicked

screams. A woman's cries. It was hard to tell whose they were, but Beth knew that one of her friends was in trouble. She dropped Ashley's book in the sand next to the beach chair and stood up.

"Sorry, Wounded Heart," she said, "I'll have to find out how the man—woman—Sasquatch love triangle turns out later."

She clasped the phone and jogged back towards the path they'd taken from camp. Over a slight rise in the sand, then up a gravel ridge into the woods, where it wound back around to the clearing where they'd left their tents.

The woods were silent as the day wound to a close. She checked the phone. Still no signal. She listened for the voices, but they'd fallen silent. She didn't know if that was a good sign or not.

She crept down the path. She could see the clearing about twenty meters ahead, but something was wrong. It was empty. Their tents were gone.

"What the…?"

When she met the edge, she stopped, saw nothing but flat turf and trees. A brick firepit in the centre was empty and unlit.

"That wasn't there before."

She walked forward and crouched down, touching old soot and charred leaves that crumbled beneath her fingers.

"Did I make a wrong turn?"

The woman's screams echoed again, this time faintly, from behind her instead. Beth spun back the way she'd come.

"That sounded like it came from the beach?"

Footsteps from the other side of the clearing. She tensed up, gripped the phone and swiped it open. Still no signal. She was totally exposed, out in the open. She had to run, but before she could move, two men in fishing hats carrying tackle boxes walked out of the path from the other side of the clearing. One had a moustache, the other thick-framed glasses.

"Oh, hi there, miss," the taller one said.

Her voice was caught in her throat. Neither looked threatening, but who could tell these days? They wore flannel shirts and hip waders, with fishing rods over their shoulders.

"Did you get turned around in the woods?" the bigger man with the glasses said. "They can play tricks on you if you don't know where you're going."

"I—"

"I think you might have the wrong spot," the tall man said. "We booked this site with the park a month ago and—"

He was about to approach her, but the bigger man blocked him with his hand.

"It's alright, miss," he said. "These things happen. No harm done. But you might want to get back where you belong. Sun's about to go down. You might not be able to find the way in the dark."

She didn't feel like she was in any danger, but she understood that he was telling her to go. The clearing was all wrong anyway. She had to have taken a wrong turn somewhere. She rose while the two men watched her curiously and backed away to the path.

The big man nodded slowly. "Make sure you watch where you're going," he said. "There's bears around here."

She turned and ran back down the trail, not bothering to check if they were following, somehow knowing they weren't. The turns were the same, she knew they had to be. The route she followed came right back to the beach.

There, in the middle of the sand, exactly where she'd

left them, were her chair, the fallen book, the towels, and inspecting them all with its snout, a massive grizzly bear.

THEN

"Ron, Ron, can you hear me?" Candace said from her position on the other side of the tree where they'd been hastily tied.

A low moan came from the man that she couldn't see, but could feel near her.

The sun was setting. It had been only a few minutes since the horrible man in army fatigues and his quiet friend had left them. For some reason, he'd tied them up while talking to himself in half sentences.

"Come on, man, don't—" the other had pleaded.

For a moment it seemed like he was going to gut them with his huge knife, but something must have gotten through as he'd instead tied them both to the massive spruce tree, back to back.

"Please," she'd begged. "Don't leave us."

He hadn't responded. He'd stared at the tree, muttering under his breath before finally storming away. For all she knew, this was simply some trick. He'd be back any moment with some other plan for them. He wasn't sane and his friend offered no help either.

"Ron, we have to get out of here. They could be back soon. We need to untie the ropes."

She knew he was there but not if he was conscious. He'd been so badly beaten that his face had swollen up like a red melon. She could still hear his raspy breathing, but even that was growing fainter.

"Please, Ron, baby, wake up."

He didn't seem to be able to hear her. It was going to be up to her if they were to survive. She started squirming under the ropes. Each movement rubbed her bare back against the thick bark of the tree, scraping the skin raw. The assholes hadn't let her get dressed. She wore only her skirt, wrapped around her waist. The rest of her was completely exposed to the cooling air.

She felt her skin shredding under her every motion. The ropes were above and below her exposed breasts, with her arms pinned to her sides. Her legs were splayed out in front of her on the ground. She couldn't force herself up the tree. Ron's body on the other side was too much of a counterweight. Maybe if they both stood up at the same time, they could grind their bodies to an upright position and try to loosen the ropes, but he was no help.

Something small moved on her leg. She stopped squirming and saw an ant crawling along her skin, towards her core.

"Shoo, go away."

More tiny legs met her. A line of ants now, moving in a march along her warm skin, around her thigh, right to her exposed—

"Stop," she said. "Shoo."

She tried blowing, shifting, but they kept climbing up with aimed precision. The tickling of their tiny feet, the alien faces she'd remembered seeing magnified in a National Geographic magazine. They crawled to her exposed flesh and began inspecting the folds of skin, tapping her with their mandibles. She suddenly pictured them all climbing inside her and she began to panic.

"Ron, please."

A branch broke on the other side of the tree. She tried to turn to see, but the trunk was too large. She momentarily forgot the insect assault on her womanhood and froze.

"Is someone there?"

Breathing. Hot and heavy. She could feel another presence nearby.

"Ron?"

Footsteps.

The ants had free rein over her. They began a massed march over her entire body, exploring her for some secret only they knew. How many more were there? The line seemed to stretch forever. The swarm was coating her. She screamed.

The tree vibrated with a massive force. The ropes fell slack. She stood up and frantically swatted at the things that crawled all over her. She ran unthinking from her spot at the tree, turned the corner to see something even worse than the thousands of bugs.

A massive bear, ripping at Ron's stomach. It looked up, muzzle coated in blood, and roared at her. She screamed once, turned to run, but went face first into the tree. She fell backwards directly in front of the massive beast. She tried to rise, but a single massive paw pinned her down.

"Ron," she cried as the thing's maw crushed her face.

* * * *

"Bagged 'em, just like you said," the man in the flannel hat said proudly.

"He was running through the woods," another said. "Real suspicious-like, too."

Frank moved around the body of the young man the hunters had strung up from the tree by his feet. The man looked around twenty, twenty-five tops. His glasses were shattered and the wounds from where the rifle blasts had hit him left him with a destroyed face and torn stomach. Derek stood back, leaning on his rifle silently.

One of the park rangers looked over the deceased killer with interest. He'd radioed Frank with the news that the hunt was over, and they'd rushed right back to find these two hunters showing off their kill like it was a catch of the day.

"He does look suspicious," the ranger said. "I've never seen clothes like that before. What are those pants and that—"

"How do you know this is the killer?" Frank asked.

"Well," the first hunter said. "One, he's dressed weird and—"

"The ranger was convinced we were after a bear."

"I saw him turn from a bear to a man," the other hunter said. "I saw it, I swear."

"You what?"

Derek perked up at this and came to stand beside Frank.

"Uh, yeah. See, me and Zeke here were following a bear. The thing went behind this big rock, then what comes out the other side but this guy. Walking like a, well, not like a bear that's for sure, more like a—"

"So you assumed he transformed from the bear to the man," Frank said, cutting him off.

"We practically saw it."

Frank rubbed his temples with his fingers. "Oh, fucking hell."

"The evidence is pretty compelling," the ranger said.

Frank threw up his hands in disgust. "This man's as hairless as an Egyptian cat. He's wearing shoes, pants, a shirt. Haven't you seen a goddamn werewolf movie before? If he'd been a bear, they'd all be torn to shreds."

"Not a wolf," the second hunter said. "A bear."

"Sure, buddy," Frank said. "That's going to look great in the papers. Hunters swear bear became boy. Blew half his face off. Fuck, this kid's parents are going to sue the shit out of you both."

Derek approached the corpse and leaned in. He sniffed it once.

"This is nothing but a boy, Frank," he said. "He was scared, too. Smells off."

"Uh, thanks, Derek. But I knew that without having to smell him. What we have here are two dipshit hunters who killed an innocent kid in their overzealousness. This is the kind of thing that gives gun-toting posses a bad name, guys. You should be ashamed of yourselves."

The two hunters dropped their eyes. One removed his hat and clasped it at his stomach as they were admonished.

"Fuck. Okay, Ranger… wait, where's the other guy? Smith, was it?"

"Jones. And he's still out in the woods looking."

"Whatever, you all look the same to me."

"But I'm Ranger Ross and—"

"It doesn't matter what your name is, just call this in. We're going to need the RCMP in here to deal with this. In the meantime, Derek and I will go back out looking for the actual killer. And I promise you, neither one of us is going to get confused enough to think we're dealing with a bear that turns into a boy."

"Or a boy that turns into a bear," Derek said.

"Don't you start now."

"But you said—" the first hunter started.

"Dipshits. A bear can't fucking string people up by their insides on meat hooks. It's no goddamn bear, it's a godforsaken man. Now we're going to catch him and you two are going to stay right here and give your statements to the Mounties when they show up."

Frank waved Derek forward.

"Come on, buddy, we'd better get moving before some other idiot out there shoots another hiker thinking he's a motherfucking half-boy half-mountain lion."

NOW

"We're lost, aren't we?" Sandy said as Greg intently studied a fork in the path.

"I just want to make one hundred percent sure we go in the right direction," he told her in the calmest voice he could manage.

"Why didn't you think to mark the fucking trail as we went?"

"I was looking for Max and Sophia, not playing Hansel and Gretel. You could have dropped breadcrumbs, too, you know," he said. "Unless you remember which route we took. Do you?"

"I never even noticed a branching path before. I was more concerned about our missing kids, Greg," she spat back.

"Just let me think for a minute, okay?" he said. "You're not helping."

"Do you just sleepwalk through life?" she asked. "Don't you remember the way or—"

Finally, he'd just had enough. All of her nagging had pushed him too far.

"You know what," he turned and shouted at her. "I wouldn't even have been so tired that I fell asleep on the beach if I had just gotten enough sleep last night. Or any night for the past ten years. Your fucking snoring could warn passing ships in the night, wake the dead, rattle the fine china in the cabinets at Buckingham Palace, test the earthquake readiness of the tallest skyscraper in—"

"I don't snore."

"Yes. You do. Unbearably. I can't sleep, I can't wake up, I can't focus. I'm sick all the time. It's affecting my creative process."

"You're being overdramatic."

"Am I? Really? I'm so fucking tired I can't concentrate on anything long enough. All my unfinished projects, I feel like my brain is a fried egg and you don't even—"

"I had invasive fucking surgery to fix my deviated septum. Remember that? They drilled into my face. It was swollen for four days. Remember the bandages? Do you? Because I sure do."

"Yet here we are four years later and you're still snoring so loud I want to ram cotton swabs into my ears to make himself deaf just to stop hearing you."

"I want to do that to stop hearing you right now," she said.

"Counting sheep, pillows over my head, ocean relaxation tapes, white noise boxes, all wastes of—"

"Maybe if you had a real job we could afford a house with separate bedrooms."

"Or maybe if you kept your legs together in the first place, we wouldn't be supporting two sponges who—"

She just stared at him, expressionless. He hadn't even finished his rant when he knew he'd already gone too far. It had just slipped out. The subject he was never supposed to bring up: the accidental pregnancy.

"Do you want to audit this whole marriage instead of trying to find our FUCKING MISSING KIDS?"

"This will be just like that time Max ran off in the mall. You went nuclear then we found him splashing in the fountain and—"

"Was there a killer stapling people to the walls then, too? Oh right, he was down at the Orange Julius getting a fucking hotdog."

"Look, maybe that was entirely unrelated. Maybe it was a movie set. Maybe it was—"

A primal scream shattered the night sky. They both froze and looked back up the trail they'd taken to get to this fork.

"That's coming from back the way we came," he said.

"Do you think—?" But she never finished her thought as the cries became frantic, desperate, inhuman. The sound travelled closer, bouncing off the trees, echoing, then seemed to be coming from all around them in every direction, jabbing into their skulls as if from invisible knives.

She held her hands over her ears as the piercing wails bombarded them from all angles. Greg stared back down the path they'd come, his eyes locked on something emerging from the darkness beyond. The shadows of the forest were moving. They gave off a palpable warmth even from tens of metres away. A force rippled towards them through the forest floor. There was some kind of entity in the stygian mists. A presence was approaching, leaving washed-out, lifeless trees in its wake. As the voices of the forest spun around him and danced through the leaves, they moved through his ears, pierced his mind, assaulted his thoughts. The thing on the trail strobed towards them, black lines sliding along the path, questing like fingers from an invisible hand. He knew he couldn't wait for whatever it was to reach them.

He looked at Sally. She didn't notice the approaching thing.

Her eyes were shut, teeth clenched as she desperately tried to bury her head in between her legs.

He poked her, tried to get her attention by hitting her shoulder and motioning back down the path, but she refused to look up. So he did what he had to do.

He left her and ran down the left path.

* * * *

"I think he's coming to." Jack watched as the unconscious man's eyelids slowly began to flutter open.

Ashley ran from her spot sitting at the fire to join him next to the canoe, where they'd propped the unknown visitor up. They'd wrapped the naked man in one of the blankets from the tent after having dressed his wounds the best either of them could.

"Where…?" the man croaked.

"You drifted downstream in the canoe," Ashley said.

"You look like you've been in a fight with a combine."

The man leaned up on his elbows, grimaced in pain and looked around him. Then he peered under the blanket to see the state of his badly ravaged body.

"Who…?"

"We both did," Ashley said. "There was a first aid kit in the tent."

He examined his surroundings as if he was trying to get a bearing on where he was, then looked over his shoulder back at the river.

"I floated all the way back here?"

"Do you remember where you were originally?" Ashley asked.

He sat fully upright, braced by the canoe. "I'd made camp upriver. We were... well, you can imagine what we were doing."

"Something where you're both naked?" Jack asked.

Ashley elbowed him in the ribs.

"What? It doesn't have to mean anything—"

"Making love under the stars, if you must know," the man said. "It was magical. Like it always is. Although it was my first time with her and—"

"Making love?" Jack said with a raised eyebrow.

"He means fucking, you jerk," Ashley said again.

"I know, it's just such a... lame way of saying it. Why not just—"

The man coughed. "Is there any water?"

"I'll get it." Jack ran over to the tent.

"Don't mind him," Ashley said. "He's a bit of a tool."

"A tool? He's a carpenter?"

"Not that I know of. I meant he's a moron."

Jack was back in a flash with a canteen. He passed it to the man who drank eagerly. When he was done, he wiped his mouth and stared at the green metal container. "I'm glad I made her leave this here. She didn't want to, but I had my own. There was no sense in overloading the canoe and—"

"So what happened?" Jack asked, cutting him off.

"Alice and I went canoeing. She said she'd never gone. I found that hard to believe, so I took her out on the river. We went a little further than I intended and decided to make camp for the night and then come back in the—"

"Alice who?" Ashley asked brusquely.

"I never actually got her last name," he said. "I feel like a bit of a cad now, but it honestly never came up and—"

198

Ashley pulled out the driver's license from the wallet in her pocket. "This her?"

He took the card in his hand and nodded. "Yeah, it is. McCormick, eh? Nice name."

"Who the fuck are you?" Ashley said.

"David Horten," he said. "I'm—"

"How long have you been with my aunt?" Ashley said. "How the fuck did you keep her away from us for so long?"

"I don't understand," he said. "Aunt? You look older than she is."

"That's impossible. This is my aunt." She took the card back and waved it in front of his face. "She's been missing for forty fucking years. Now where is she?"

He shook his head. "I don't know. Like I said, we were making love. Then this huge bear came into camp. I grabbed some fire to chase it off, but it knocked me away with one paw. I remember landing hard, then it hitting me again and I ended up in the canoe. I have no idea how I came back here, I swear."

"A bear?" Jack said. "You were attacked by a bear? See, I told you his wounds were—"

"I don't give a shit what he says he was attacked by," Ashley said. "You have to take us to where you were with my aunt. You have to show us where—"

"The bear could have got her," Jack said.

"We don't know that," she said. "If he knows her, he can take us back there. She might be in trouble and needing help. You have to take us."

"You're right. She was alone with that thing. She might have climbed a tree or run off somewhere and gotten lost or—"

"Eaten or been—" Jack said.

Ashley elbowed him again in the ribs.

"What? It's entirely possible that—"

"Can you manage?" Ashley said, ignoring him.

"I think I can. But there's one thing you can do for me first."

"What's that?"

"Can you get me some pants?"

* * * *

The bear was just sitting there, sniffing at the beach chair, digging its nose in the fallen book, turning pages curiously. Beth crouched low behind a bush and watched, hoping the thing didn't have a dog's ability to follow scents. She really had no idea how bears' senses worked, what their traits or habits were, even where they were supposed to live. But judging by the presence of this massive grizzly, she had to assume that the Whiteshell was one of those places they called home, or at least was a stop on their route to it.

"Come on, go away," she whispered. "Go find a deer or something."

The great paw finally swatted at the book on the sand, knocking it away.

"Yeah, it was pretty lame, I know."

Then, it slowly collapsed back onto the chair, crushing it under its massive weight.

"Oh shit, Ash is gonna be pissed. She just bought that."

She didn't understand why the bear was choosing to use that particular spot as its rest area, but as long as it was, she wasn't going to be able to wait there. She dug out the phone, found that it still had no signal, then shoved it back into her pocket silently.

In that brief relaxation of focus away from the bear, she looked back to see it had left the chair and was moving towards her. It had closed almost half the distance between them already.

"Oh fuck."

She crouched back but it was clear that the thing's eyes were locked on her location. Somehow, it knew where she was.

She rose to run back down the trail, but in turning back, she saw the impossible. The exact same bear moving towards her from down the other direction of the path. Swivelling her head, it was as if she was seeing double. Two massive grizzlies, each stalking her from opposite places, draining colour behind them.

Her mind formed the idea after her legs. She ran at an angle towards the lake. Maybe the other bear would get into a fight with the one who'd wrecked their beach chair, and she could get away in the chaos.

The sand resisted her feet, slowing her. She stumbled, nearly fell and heard an angry roar behind her. She refused to see which bear had made it and bolted to the water. Splashing in, she leapt over the gentle waves with a hurdler's grace. She pressed further out, first waist high, then shoulder. She sprinted until she was forced to crawl as fast as she could out to the middle of the water.

Only when she was sure she was past any point the thing would chase her did she feel safe enough to turn around.

The scene was all wrong. Only one bear stood on the edge of the waterline. Where was the second one? Why hadn't it followed her, too?

Scanning the beach, there was no sign of it. Treading water, she waited to see what the thing was going to do. The way it looked at her was unnerving, as if it was making calculations far beyond what a creature like that should be making.

Then, it splashed into the water towards her.

"No, go away," she shouted. "Find something easier, find—"

But it wasn't going to listen. It slid in deeper, then began paddling. It slowly started inching towards her, the huge head staying just above the water line as it zeroed in on her path. She kicked back and started paddling to the other side of the lake.

* * * *

Branches tore at her face as she pushed through the trees in mad desperation. She had to put as much space between her and whoever it was that had attacked them as she could. Mandy hadn't looked back once; she didn't dare. There was no inner voice scolding her cowardice, she knew unequivocally that Aiden was dead.

Everything had happened too fast. She never saw who had shot at them. But the sight of his head exploding outwards would haunt her for the rest of her life. Aiden was gone. She wasn't. She had to survive.

He's dead. He's dead. He's dead, but you're not.

It could just as easily have been her. They were standing so close together, the sniper could have aimed at her head instead. Then her brains would have splattered all over Aiden's shirt. Would he have acted like a hero and stayed with her corpse? Would it have mattered? She kept running, pushing herself past the point of exhaustion. She had no idea where she was going. It was so dark, she could barely see her hands in front of her face. The moonlight briefly popped through gaps in the thick tree canopy above. She didn't dare use his phone as a flashlight for fear of giving herself away. They could still be after her.

Heart pounding in her ears, she finally risked stopping for a moment to catch her breath. Bracing herself on a tree, she listened to the still night sounds. It didn't seem like anyone was in pursuit, but then there hadn't been any warning the first time either. Her lungs throbbed, while her legs began to stiffen up.

"Fuck, fuck, fuck, fuck."

Everything had gone to hell.

"You could have just stayed in town and watched Netflix, played video games, washed your hair, done a seaweed facial, waxed your legs, anything. But no, you had to listen to your friends and come to Rock Peak Lake. Meet some single guys, it'll be fun, they said. A nice break."

She looked back in the direction she'd come, waiting and watching, listening as she muttered under her breath.

"Rock Peak Lake. Roughing it. No phones. Definitely no massive animals in the woods or hunters that shoot the first cute guy you've met in a long time. Now I'm alone and talking to myself hoping I don't die, too. What a great fucking weekend."

Something stirred in the woods to her left and she froze. She crouched lower and tried to see through the thick brush. She could feel her heartbeat slowing back down. She caught her breath. A mosquito landed on her arm and she swatted it. The slap sounded like a gunshot in the quiet night. More of them began to swarm her. She waved them away with her hands.

"You can't stay here in the dirt, you'll just be a bug buffet. You have to find your way back to the others. Then you can get the hell out of here and get the authorities. The rangers, the police, the fucking army can come down here and deal with this."

But she didn't want to move. She felt safe crouched low in the darkness, less of a target. But as she stared back the way she had come, she heard another sound in the distance. Footsteps? Branches snapping at the pace of someone's gait? Her heart started racing anew and she gasped. Someone was coming.

"Fuck this." She rose up and ran in the opposite direction.

A forest path crossed in front of her. Had it been there a moment ago? Who cared? She leapt out of the brush and looked both ways, trying to figure out which direction would lead her where she needed to go. The route was winding, twisting around through the dark mass of trees that seemed to be closing in on her. But something about this part of the trail had a feeling of familiarity.

"That fallen log," she muttered, "I'm sure I've seen it before. Unless it's another fallen log that looks exactly like it. There could be more than one fallen log in a forest of this size. Oh, fuck it, it's not like you have any better ideas."

She ran in the direction that felt right. After about two hundred meters, there it was, salvation. The trail's end. She could see the huge moon again, shining down on water as smooth as a black mirror. The calm lake reflected the massive sphere and twinkling stars in its undulating calm. She was back at the beach, and at the lake they'd started from. At least, she thought so. The sand, the shape of the water, it looked exactly like where they'd been swimming when the guys had come and this whole nightmare had begun. But something was wrong—there was no one here.

"Beth?" she called out softly. Nobody answered.

The chair, their stuff, it was all gone. She must have left. Maybe the others, too.

Oh fuck, they fucking left me.

"Which way was it to the campground?" She tried to remember how they'd approached the beach. From the north? The west?

She hadn't been paying enough attention on the way here. She'd been too busy enjoying the sun, laughing with her friends, hoping she'd get a tan, anxious to show off her new bathing suit. It seemed like so long ago. Were they all okay? Had they run into anything in the woods like she had? Maybe they were all dead and she was the last one left.

"Beth?" she called again and walked towards where they'd been sitting earlier in the day.

She looked for anything familiar, a note, trash, a lost towel, but the beach had been swept clean. There weren't even any footprints from bare feet or sandals.

Then it hit her. While this seemed like the same beach, it couldn't be. The woods, the lake, the night sky—nothing but nature surrounded her. She knew there were cabins on the other side of the lake, she'd seen them before. At this time of night, they should be lit up, but she couldn't see any sign of lights from their windows in the distance.

"Maybe they're all asleep. Maybe it's later than I thought. Or maybe this is the wrong fucking beach."

Could she swim across and find out? If there were cabins there, she could get help. Unless this was the wrong beach, then it would be a waste of time. How far was it? How many kilometres could she swim after running through the forest for the past hour? And what if she hit the other side and there were no cabins? What if she got halfway out and drowned in the lake from exhaustion?

I need a better idea.

She had to find her friends and the car. She scanned along the beach, the tree line, the edges, desperate to find something familiar enough to jog her memory.

She spotted another trail diverging on the left. That must have been where they came down to the beach. She'd simply emerged from some alternate route. She was pretty sure she knew where she was now. It made sense. It should just be a quick jog up that path to the campsite.

"It's the best option you've got," she muttered and ran.

NOW

"Can't you hear them?" Matt said. "They're telling me she's close."

"Who?" Josh asked, looking at the forest that surrounded them and not knowing what Matt was hearing. "You keep saying—"

"The voices in the forest. The trees. Parts of it all. The intelligence that forms in the places we're not supposed to walk."

"The same voices that said that girl was—"

"I did what I was told."

"You're really scaring me, man," Josh said.

Matt crouched down and wiped his knife on the forest floor. The clean blade reflected the moonlight. He touched the turf and his eyes rolled back in his head.

"You have to open your mind to the things that have always been here, before we came. Before anyone came."

"I think all those energy drinks fried your brain," Josh said.

"You don't get it. They want me to find her. They understand my pain. They want to help."

Matt's reflection in the blade danced from edge to edge as he played with the knife. His eyes rolled back, and he slid the blade into the holster at his leg.

"The same way they told you to leave that poor couple tied to the tree?"

"Are you going soft on me?"

"It's not that, it's just… you abandoned them to what exactly?"

"We abandoned them," Matt said matter-of-factly.

"You could have let them go. You didn't have to—"

"Untrue," Matt said, cutting him off. "It needed a sacrifice. The girl had seen my face. You blurted out my name like a dipshit. You want to go to jail over a case of mistaken identity?"

"What do you mean, sacrifice? We left them alive and—"

"What happens next isn't for us to know. We simply appease."

Something in Matt had broken beyond repair. His mind had left and it was scary. His actions at the old car were a side of him Josh had never seen, nor could he have imagined was there in the first place. A visible change had overtaken him since they'd come here. He'd become inhuman. It was all there in the eyes. Hollow. Washed out. A lack of awareness of what he was doing and yet, a total control of his brutality. He was there, but he wasn't at the same time, as if something else had taken root inside of him.

"I'm going back," Josh said. "I shouldn't have let you leave them and—"

"You can't go back," Matt said, suddenly lunging the knife to Josh's throat before he could even react. "If you've learned anything on this trip, it has to be that."

"You haven't been making sense for hours," Josh said, freezing in place. "This has all been one big fucking mistake."

"No," Matt said with finality, pressing the knife in tightly.

"Everything is happening according to the old ways. How they've always happened. The cycle. We're just a part of it. One of many. Now there's still a lot of forest out here, but it's not as dense as it appears. I know where to go. So decide right now. Are you coming or does the forest get another sacrifice tonight?"

He felt the cool metal separating the skin of his neck in millimetre cuts. Josh looked into Matt's eyes and knew instantly that if he said the wrong thing, he'd slit his throat.

"Be cool, man, I'm with you. I'm coming. I—"

The knife was gone and back in the holster as if it had never been at his neck in the first place. But touching the spot, Josh's hands came back with a faint line of blood on his fingers.

"Better."

Josh knew now that the man was truly dangerous. Maybe it was the lack of sleep, maybe it was the pills or energy drinks, or maybe it was just some dark part of him finally coming to the surface. The best he could hope for was going with him and trying to stop him from killing whoever he found.

"So where do we go?" Josh asked.

Matt looked off into the night, as if he'd heard a sound. He took two steps forward, before stopping again, then sniffed the air and slid the knife into his holster. "Yes, yes, I understand," he said and started walking into the bush.

"Uhhh," Josh said, following him into the darkness. "Wait for me?"

* * * *

The trailer was just where he'd left it, not that he had any reason to think it wouldn't be. But there was no sign of Derek.

He hadn't gone to the public restrooms and he hadn't come back here. Unless he was inside taking a nap.

The trailer wasn't much to look at; a partially rusted hitch at the back of a vaguely square-shaped cream-coloured box with windows on either side, a propane tank at the rear, and a series of faded and peeling stickers from a continent of travel; Mount Rushmore to Disney Land to Las Vegas to Fort Lauderdale to Yellowknife to Moose Jaw. It had almost as many miles on it as Frank did.

"You taking a siesta, old buddy?"

Frank pulled open the sticky side door and stepped inside. The place had all the accoutrements of a home away from home, small sleeping area, tiny kitchen, storage, cooler, folding table raised up against the wall. The only thing it didn't have was indoor plumbing. One smell was instantaneously obvious.

"Shit…"

Someone had taken a dump inside. The two cots at the back were unfolded and messy. It was completely quiet and weirdly lonely. But the smell…

"Either something crawled in and died, or Derek got confused and thought this was the public washroom."

Stepping gingerly, he approached the bedding. He pulled back the sheets of the cots and found nothing. He checked in the small toaster oven mounted near the cupboards, in the fridge, still found nothing. He looked under the cots, opened the drawers, nothing. But then he saw it on the small chair at the edge of the hitch wall. A dark blobby shape, resting in the centre of the fabric like a sleeping animal. He stepped closer and took a big sniff.

"Yup. That's a deuce."

But was it animal or human? He reached for the internal lighting hooked up to the small gas-powered generator. He hoped the thing still had some juice. This was the moment of truth. He held his breath, hoping that Derek wasn't so far gone that he'd taken a crap in the trailer. But as the lights flickered on, he saw the horrible reality.

"Definitely shit."

He switched off the lights and stepped outside. There was no way he was picking that up. It was just going to have to stay there for now. It would sure give old man Ulster one hell of a shock when he found it. Frank would blame it on vagrants.

"Unless I run into someone else out here, Derek's suspect prime. Poor guy. Hope my brains aren't scrambled eggs when I'm his age."

Derek was only six months older than Frank, a fact that seemed irrelevant as he walked back to the opposite trail leading deeper into the woods. In a way he pitied his once virile and cognizant friend for facing all the horrors of aging before him.

"If I'd just taken a shit, where would I go next?"

Food. He would go looking for food.

Frank took a deep breath of the night air, trying to discern the different smells that bombarded his senses.

"Pine. Wood. Smoke? Fire?"

Another few sniffs and he had his answer.

"Hotdogs."

He followed the gravel path in front of him, hoping that his nose really did know where it was leading him.

THEN

"—and that's why they say if you listen closely to the call of the loon, you can hear the echoes of the things that have been and will be. The ghosts of the forest speak through the voices of the creatures that move in the darkness. You just have to listen."

Trooper Stan leaned back proudly from the fire. Twelve scouts sat hypnotized, their faces shadowed by the flickering light of the burning centrepiece of their campsite. Rotund Georgie had dripping marshmallow smeared all over his face and sucked more melted goo from a stick in his hand. Bespectacled Darryl clutched his wrist to keep it from shaking; the others had all gone quiet.

"That's not scary at all," Jonah finally blurted out.

Trooper Stan turned to the chubby kid with the curly red hair, who stared at him with a smirk of superiority. "Oh, really?"

"Really," the kid said defiantly. "My cat's coughed up scarier stuff than that."

"Okay, Mr. Smart Ass," Trooper Stan said. "You don't think that's a scary story, then how about you tell one to the group. I'm sure everyone's all ears, right, gang?"

A few of the kids looked at each other unsure, others

murmured encouragement, but nobody took the initiative to seize control. They all knew that was Trooper Stan's job. At least, all of them except Jonah.

"No objections? Then by all means, Jonah, tell us a story that's scarier than one about the ancient, unfeeling, inhuman consciousness of the life that existed before humanity, that sees us as nothing more than blips in time, sand that will be washed away as if we never existed at all."

"Uh," Jonah said. "I thought your story was about a tree?"

The others chuckled and Trooper Stan felt a modicum of their respect for him slipping through his fingers. This kid was always pushing at the edges of what he could get away with, looking to challenge his authority as scout leader.

"There are trees that have existed for thousands of years, Jonah," Trooper Stan said. "On that kind of geologic timescale, our lives would seem like those of insects. Isn't the ultimate unimportance of our pitiful existence truly the scariest thing to think about? How whatever we do or know is nothing more than a tiny figment in a larger tableau of which we are but a microscopic speck? The forest is bigger than us, sure, but space and the infinite is beyond our very comprehension. Why, it's enough to bring someone to madness if they tried to make sense of the reasons why any of us were here in the first place."

"Uh, Trooper Stan," skinny Randy said, raising his hand. "We're here because our parents signed us up for the weekend and—"

"I know that, Randy," Stan said harshly. "I was talking philosophically, okay? Asking the big questions. But since none of you think that's scary, then how about we all just sit and listen to what Jonah has to tell us, okay? Then we can douse the fire and go to bed. We've got a long day of canoeing tomorrow."

Jonah stood up and stared at the collected crowd of his fellow scouts. He theatrically cleared his throat. "Imagine a bear," he said. "A really, really big bear. And that bear likes to eat children!"

The kids all screamed in terror and Trooper Stan rolled his eyes.

"Oh, come on, that makes you scream?"

"And that bear is—"

"Run," a woman's voice shouted. "Run! There's a bear chasing me."

Trooper Dan turned to see a woman in shorts and a billowing shirt, opened to reveal a tiny bathing suit that barely covered her bouncing breasts, run through the camp. He was all set to tell her that what she was wearing was inappropriate for the children to see when she leapt over the fire like a hurdler and ran right past them all. He watched her go then turned back at the sound of a massive roar. The biggest goddamn bear he'd ever seen bounded into camp and started to turn his troop into its dinner.

"Holy shit," was all he could say as the thing swatted and clawed the poor screaming kids.

He wanted to do something to stop it, but the bear darted forward and lashed out before he could even react. It struck him on the chin with its huge clawed paw. He tried to speak, but no sound escaped him. His face didn't seem to be responding at all. His tongue felt like it was dangling out of his mouth. He reached up and touched it, felt the loose dangling muscle against his neck.

That's not right.

Then he understood what had happened. He had no lower jaw. The paw swipe had taken most of it clean off and his tongue was flopping loosely below. He began to choke on his own blood. The bear roared and swatted his head. He was knocked to the ground off the path, landing hard on the dirt. He could only see out of one eye. It was enough to catch flashes of more kids being butchered, but there wasn't much time to make sense of any of it as the great thing lumbered towards him and stepped down on his skull. His entire cranium popped like a zit. He had a fleeting conception of his eyeball popping out before the world went dark.

* * * *

"I'm starting to think we're dealing with more than just your run-of-the-mill madman, Derek," Frank said as he examined the newest crime scene they'd stumbled across.

"There's certainly a motif here."

A small clearing in the woods had been turned into a scene from Satan's Christmas Eve. An upside down corpse hung from a tree with his stomach torn open and his guts pulled out. The coils were draped around the clearing from tree to tree like twisted, rubbery, intestinal garlands. Tiny droplets of blood fell to the forest floor intermittently. A crow watched them from a branch where it perched. It pecked away at the entrails as they stood inspecting the carnage.

Another victim was nailed to a tree. Her legs had been pulled around behind the trunk in some kind of disturbed reverse hug. Slashed beyond recognition, both of their eyes had been gouged out leaving bloody sockets that exposed mangled darkness deep inside. Their tongues had been pulled out to dangle at their feet in the wind like dead eels.

"Demented interior decorator?"

"Or one hell of an ingenious bear," Derek replied.

"You're actually thinking bear?" Frank said, surprised.

"They can be damn clever."

"This goes beyond clever—it's demonic."

"You think it's a devil-worshipping bear?" Derek asked as if he hadn't considered that option.

"It would explain a few things, but I'm still leaning towards one of those not so ordinary, padded room psychos here."

"You keep your theory, I'm putting a fiver on Satanist bear."

Frank looked over the chaos for some sign as to which one of them was right, but the bodies offered no clues. Nor were they talking.

"My detective nose tells me what's left of the guy's face looks like he's been through twenty-eight rounds with Kid Howard and the propping up of the bodies was done by someone with opposable thumbs," Frank said. "That just about eliminates the bear hypothesis."

"Have you considered that it's entirely possible the bodies have simply been arranged in order to make us think that it was done by someone with opposable thumbs? To throw us off the scent?"

"Hmmmm," Frank said, rubbing his chin in consideration. "No, not really. So I'm going to take your bet and put five down on regular human deranged lunatic. Maybe a hairy one, but no bear."

"Suit yourself," Derek said, shrugging. "I'm going to buy scratch tickets with my winnings."

It wasn't just that someone had done these horrible things to the poor people in the clearing, or that they'd taken the time to display them in this awful manner like the ones in the cabin, it was that whoever was doing it was doing it all while Frank was looking for them. That took some nerve. The bastard felt so secure in his or her or its crimes that they were taunting him by committing more of them with each passing hour.

"I'd say we're closing in on him," Frank said as he examined the corpses more closely.

"How can you tell?"

"This stuff is still fresh."

"They teach you how to read intestines at the academy?" Derek asked, unconvinced.

"You don't need a degree in depravity to tell that the bodies are still warm. The carrion eaters haven't gotten to them all yet. Shit, this one still has his eyes. That's the first thing a crow goes for. They like the juicy taste."

The crow in the branches eating the entrails cawed in agreement.

"I'm suddenly rethinking bratwurst for supper," Derek said, frowning at the bird watching them.

"Really? If anything, this makes me want 'em more," Frank said. "Now be careful around the crime scene. Somebody's going to have to lock it down and look for evidence."

"I'm not sure anyone can find any truth in this," Derek said.

"You're an accountant. This is my world."

"But this is ritualistic. This is a sacrifice. This is—"

"Any sign of sodomized bodies?" Frank asked.

"You seen that kind of stuff before?"

Frank crouched down to see if the killer had, in fact, sodomized the victims. "You haven't the foggiest idea of what goes on out there in the big city."

"The same way you don't know what goes on out here in the forest. It's a whole different world. It has its own rules and—"

"You crunch numbers, I crunch crime. But I'm the only one who can do it regardless of the location." Frank stood up and took one more look around the macabre scene. "Time's a wasting. Each second we spend here gawking at the man or woman's handiwork—"

"Or bear's," Derek interrupted.

"Right," Frank said, rolling his eyes. "Each second we spend here gawking at the man, woman or bear's handiwork, is another second he, she or it gets to find more victims. So double check that rifle and let's get on the march."

Derek slung the rifle over his shoulder and together they walked off into the night.

NOW

"I don't understand it," David said. "I know this was where we made camp."

They stood in a small clearing a few meters away from the river's edge. The canoe had been dragged to shore and David, wearing a too-small sweater and a pair of ill-fitting shorts, stood incredulously examining every tree and blade of grass.

"Are you sure?" Ashley said, watching him disbelievingly.

"Of course," he said. "I've paddled this river plenty of times. I know this place like the back of my hand. This is my usual spot."

"Your usual spot to bring women to prey on?"

"What? No. I brought her here because it was a great spot," he said. "I mean, look at the view." He waved his hands outward, showing off the beauty of the secluded area.

"It is a pretty nice view," Jack said.

The moon was huge. The lake reflected it back, giving the illusion of a split surface. The calm waters drifted slowly by. The silence of the forest surrounded them. It was as if they were in the middle of nowhere and everywhere all at once.

"Yeah. The kind of place you bring some unsuspecting girl and say, oh no, look at the time, it's too late to go back. Let's make camp here and then I can pressure you into having sex. And if you say no, who's to save you? Big strong man, weaker innocent woman. It's not rape when you're surrounded by the beauty of nature, right? God, it's all so rehearsed."

"You've got it all wrong," David said. "It was a completely natural thing. It just happened and—"

"Yeah, your dick just happened to fall into her vagina over and over again. Didn't matter if she wanted it or not."

"I'll have you know she did, but that's not the point. I didn't rape Alice. We made love and—"

"This bullshit has gone on long enough," Ashley said. "How about you tell us the real story? How do you know my missing aunt and what did you do to her?"

"I didn't know she was missing. And I still don't see how she could be your aunt. You look older than she does."

"Is that some kind of crack about my age?"

"No, I—" He turned to Jack. "Do you have any idea what she's talking about?"

"Sorry, man, I'm just—"

"Don't ignore me." Ashley stepped in front of Jack and jabbed a finger into David's chest. "Don't patronize me. Don't talk around me. Don't treat me like I'm not important. Just tell me how you know my aunt Alice who has been missing for forty fucking years. The aunt I never met. The aunt whose fucking driver's license I just found in a tent downriver. The aunt you claim to have made love to a few hours ago."

"Wait, forty years? We can't be talking about the same person then."

"So your story is that there's another Alice McCormick who looks exactly like my long-missing aunt? Wow, some—"

"What do you mean, long-missing. Did she run away from

home or something?"

"No, she came out to the Whiteshell alone. She made camp at Rock Peak Lake forty years ago and never came home. There was a search, missing person posters, the whole thing. She was never found or heard from. I've grown up with her as my vanished aunt. Presumed dead. Someone I never got to know. I—"

David braced himself against a tree. "This is impossible. I must have hit my head. Forty years? That's completely insane. I only met her this morning and—"

"Could Alice have had a daughter?" Jack asked.

"That she named Alice as well?"

"It makes about as much sense. Unless you're trying to say that this guy somehow travelled forward in time forty years."

David and Ashley both looked at him like he was mental.

"Maybe we just came to the wrong spot," Ashley said. "You said you'd left your tent set up and I don't see any signs of that. Could it be further downriver?"

"I don't think so."

"Then where's your stuff?" Jack asked.

"Maybe Alice came back and packed it up?"

Ashley shook her head in frustration. "This is getting us nowhere. Your story has more holes in it than Swiss cheese. Maybe you took more of a shot to the head than you thought from that bear. But we can't stand around here all night waiting for you to remember more. We need to get back to our friends. Let's just paddle back to the tent we did find and look for some more clues. Then we can try again in the morning if we have to."

"Uh, yeah," David said, taking another look around in confusion. "Yeah, that's a good idea."

* * * *

The piercing screams dug at her ears, stabbed into her mind, became shrill bleats of white noise. Her skull seemed to vibrate. She could feel blood seeping between her fingers, pouring from her ears.

Her balance gave way and she fell to her knees. She tipped forward and tried to bury her head into the dirt. Anything to stop the sounds that pulsated inside of her.

Some kind of force swept over her, like a warm breeze flying past, taking the horrible sounds with it. The screams faded away as if being dragged deeper into the forest.

When the noise had dissipated, she opened her eyes and saw only the empty path that they'd followed. She spun in the dirt and saw the two directions of the fork going the other way. Greg was gone.

"He fucking left me…"

A moaning wail pierced the night air from the left-hand side trail. A loon's call answered. But the forest was otherwise silent. Whatever had made that shrill cacophony was gone.

"Which way did he go?" She stood up and regarded both routes of the fork. Twisting into darkness, neither seemed like the way they'd come.

A faint light blinked on further down the right-hand side path. Like a flashlight briefly switched on, then off. Could it have come from Greg's phone?

"Greg?"

She took the right-hand path. But at the point where it seemed like she should have come to the source of the light, she found nothing.

"Greg? Max? Sophia?"

None of this brush looked familiar. Not that there was all that much that would stand out in a forest, but the further down this route she went, the more she was almost sure they couldn't have come this way. She was all set to turn back when she saw that blinking light again, farther ahead of her. Too large for a firefly, too bright for anything but a phone or flashlight. Someone was out there. Were they signalling her?

The moon and stars above offered little help down at the level of the forest floor. She hesitated for a moment. What if it wasn't Greg? What if it was the person who'd created that disgusting morgue back in the cabin? The light flashed again. She heard the sound of children's laughter.

"Max? Sophia?" she called out.

No answer.

Listening intently, she thought she heard the faint echo of Greg calling out to the kids much deeper into the woods. Then, more laughter nearby. She dug into her pocket and took out her phone. She flicked on the flashlight and pointed it towards the source of the sounds. There was nothing there, nor behind her either. She slid the phone back into her pocket. She considered stepping into the woods when the light in the distance flicked on again.

Torn between the two options, she went towards the light. The path seemed to circle around a huge rock. The more she followed it, the less it made sense. It felt like it was turning around inward on itself. The route went all the way around the rock and seemed to come right back to the other side, yet never met its source. Had she just made a complete circle?

"Max? Sophia?" a woman's voice called out.

She heard the sound of footsteps approaching. Something made the hair on her arms stand up. She stepped off the trail

223

into the woods and crouched down. With a moss-covered trunk obscuring her from the gravel path, she waited.

The footsteps grew closer and closer until she saw a shape emerge from the darkness. It was a woman. She paused and looked back the way she'd come. That was when Sally's mouth dropped. It was her standing there. She was wearing the same shorts, the same yellow shirt over her bathing suit. She held her phone in her hand and swiped it on, shining the light around her. Sally ducked down as it passed over the tree she was hiding behind. The light scanned more of the forest then shut off again.

Almost too scared to look, Sally eventually forced herself to slowly rise. She saw the other version of her walking down the path around the rock formation.

"Impossible."

Then, an echo from back down the path.

"Max? Sophia?"

She turned towards the source, shaking in place as she heard more footsteps, then, exactly as before, another Sally came up the path. She stopped in the exact same spot and took out her phone, repeated the same action of scanning the area before shutting the light off.

Sally stayed low and waited for this second version of her to leave before she felt she could step out of the woods.

Behind her, the trees rustled noisily. She spun around, half expecting something to emerge, but the low-hanging branches stayed still. Heart racing, she reached into her pocket, as if compelled to by some unseen force. She swiped open her phone and turned on the flashlight. She shone it towards the spot, saw nothing but shadows, then scanned the other sides of the path. When she was back to her starting point, she turned it off and replaced it in her pocket.

She looked down the route the two other Sally's had gone. The same one she had. What was happening? How could there be other versions of her?

She took tentative steps before finally following them back around the rock. Each step made her expect to bump into one of them, but instead, she was alone.

She seemed to hug the circumference of the huge stone in an endless loop. The sense of disorientation was profound. It felt as if the path had gone alongside the entire rock surface multiple times, but the more she followed it around, the more it seemed to stretch around endlessly.

Finally, the trail branched and pivoted into the rock to a worn path leading to the peak. She looked up to the top of the huge stone formation. It was about ten meters up to the summit. She couldn't see what was up there. She began to climb awkwardly up the smooth surface of the boulder. The summit was near the top of the tree line. Looking out over the vast expanse of the dark forest, she couldn't tell if she facing east, west, north, or south, nor where they'd started from. It was all an endless sea of dark green. Like an ocean.

"Max? Sophia?" a voice called out.

She spun to see another her looking out over the forest at the other side of the rock. She hadn't been there a moment ago.

Sally couldn't speak. She stepped towards the other her, who had no idea she was there either. She reached out to grab her shoulder, inching closer.

"Max? Sophia?" the woman said again.

"Who are you?" Sally said softly as her hand landed on the woman's shoulder.

"Mommy?" The woman turned around but it wasn't Sally's face staring back at her, but Sophia's. The child's innocent face was gouged with bloody trace marks from scalp to chin. Her eyes were empty sockets. Her mouth hung open in a cavernous darkness.

Sally staggered back. She slid on the rock and landed hard on her backside. She pushed herself away from the other her who slowly walked towards her.

"Mommy?"

"Max? Sophia?"

Now there was another voice behind her. Sally looked over her shoulder to see the second version of her standing at the edge of the rock. It, too, turned, but instead of Sophia's face, it was Max's. Pale, sickly, with white eyes and exposed facial ligaments in the torn cheeks.

She pushed herself away from it, too. Her hand slipped on the edge of the rock and she went sliding down the sheer face all the way to the base, landing hard at the bottom. But she was on the path again.

She scrambled to her feet and started running. Ahead of her came another light. Someone stood in the path scanning in all directions. She didn't wait to see if it was her again, she instead turned into the bush and ran. The branches swiped at her face and tore at her clothes as she pushed deeper. Running through the stygian darkness, hopping over a collapsed tree, stepping around a large moss-covered rock, her leg caught on a root and she tripped, crashing to the forest floor in a painful heap. She knocked the wind out of herself. Her hands were cut and bloody. She'd ripped her shirt. She pushed herself up but felt an excruciating pain in her leg the second she put any weight on it. She fell to her side in the dirt. Not able to see more than a few feet in front of her, she moved her hand down her leg to find something lodged in the skin. Sticky to the touch, a jolt of electricity pulsed up her side when she pressed against it.

She dug into her pocket for her phone. She took it out and switched on the flashlight function. As she shone down on her leg, she gasped in shock. She'd broken the limb, badly. A chunk of bone was jutting out of her calf and blood leaked down into her shoe.

"Oh God," she said.

This was bad. Really bad. She could go into shock if she wasn't careful. It might already be too late. There was no cell signal out here. She needed to know where she was. She looked away from her leg and shone the light around her, but surrounding her in the darkness wasn't trees. It was a circle of her, all watching with empty eyes.

Sally took a deep breath and shouted, "Greg," at the top of her lungs.

* * * *

Greg stopped and listened for the sounds of pursuit. It was deathly silent in the woods. He didn't know if that was a good sign or not. A moment ago he was sure that he'd heard the faint voice of Sally calling out to him from further in the woods. But she'd since grown quiet, too. Had the thing found her?

He'd been running for almost fifteen minutes. There was no sign of whatever it was that he'd thought was coming for him. He must have gotten away. The only problem was that he was sure by now he'd be back at the beach, which meant that he'd been going the wrong way the whole time.

"Fuck," he muttered.

He needed to go back. Going this way was only going to get him even more lost. Unless somehow he was able to find the kids out here. That would be almost too coincidental. He'd be a hero, she'd be shut up, but it would all be a fluke. Then again, even if he did save the day, she'd still never let him live this down. Assuming they could even patch things up after all of this. Assuming there was even anyone left to patch things up with.

No negative thoughts. This is all going to work out.

He peered into the woods for any sign of Max or Sophia, not expecting to find any, but looking for any excuse not to go back the way he'd come.

"Where the hell could they be? How could two little kids manage to elude us for so long? They wouldn't have wandered so far away, they'd be too scared and get hungry. At some point they'd stop to call for help, or turn back, find one of the dozens of trails and work their way back, anything. So why no signs?"

He didn't want to think about what might have happened if they'd stumbled on the ranger cabin, the perpetrator, or the bear that seemed to be roaming around.

"No, if they can hide from us, they'd hide from that, too. Stay positive."

He refused to imagine that outcome. He would find them, and they'd all be back to having a weekend of fun family togetherness in no time.

"Greg," a voice called out faintly. Distant, more like a whisper on the wind. It sounded like Sally. Had she found the kids?

"Sally?" he shouted.

"I'm hurt."

He tried to isolate where in the woods it was coming from. "Where are you?"

"Here," she said. "Help."

The voice was so far away, muted, more like a recording played on low volume, but it had to be her. She sounded like she was in serious trouble.

"Help."

"I'm coming."

Based on the direction of the call, she was deeper in the woods to what he guessed was the north, but he had no idea just how deep. So instead of going back down the trail, he plunged into the brush. The paths had to link eventually; the park was full of interconnecting routes. They'd charted them all at the big park sign when they'd arrived in the afternoon.

"Sally," he called out as he moved branches away from his face.

"Greg," she answered faintly.

He ran further, following the general direction of the call until he came to a huge rock formation that met the top of the trees. A path hugged its circumference. He was about to leave the confines of the tree cover when he saw something casually saunter around the rock from the blind side. A massive bear.

"Oh, shit," he whispered.

The fur seemed to absorb the darkness around it, sucking away the vibrancy of the trees as it moved. The nebulous shape of the thing on the path obscured the moonlight above. The thick muscles covered in shaggy fur gave it the look of a mangy stuffed animal. But the sheer size of it was daunting. Even from where he was standing, he could feel it giving off tremendous heat.

He backed away slowly, keeping it in sight at all times. The thing hadn't noticed him. It simply walked around the path with its oblivious lumbering gait, then went off into the darkness. When he was sure it was gone, he released a held breath.

"Greg, help," Sally called out again.

The voice was close. Much closer than it had been the last time she'd called out. But it was also behind him. That wasn't the direction it had been before. He turned and pushed through the hanging branches towards the new source.

"Sally?"

"Here. Help. Here. Help. Here, help. Help."

She was repeating her words oddly, like they were playing back on a skipping record. Was she delirious?

"I'm coming, hang on."

He knew he should never have left her in the first place. That thing coming for them had set off something primal deep within him and he'd bolted. He was a coward and now she was paying the price. But he could still fix this. He would fix this. He ran faster, feeling the branches gouge at his face.

"Help."

Then he saw a light. Through the trees, some kind of signal. Blinking like a beacon or a lighthouse. He pushed through the final few metres and came to a small clearing. The light flashed in his eyes. He covered them from the burning that brought tears.

"Sally," he said. "I'm here. Where are you—"

He realized then, it wasn't a blinking light, it was a beam being cut off by people standing in front of it, moving back and forth in some kind of strange swaying march.

"Who...?"

The light hit him in the eyes again and he had to cover them. A hand grabbed his shoulder. A warm breath hit his ear. He felt the light blink out and opened his eyes. He stared into two dark pools set in Sally's face, which had become a ruination of death. Another hand landed on his other shoulder. It was another Sally. Then hands found his legs. Sally lay on the forest floor with a twisted leg, hands outstretched, pleading with him as her back was ripped out by the bear he'd seen earlier.

The other Sally's grabbed his head and pushed him towards the thing's massive open jaws.

* * * *

Beth was near exhaustion when she reached the other side of the lake. When her feet hit the sand and rock-covered ground, she stumbled forward and fell flat on her hands, scraping them raw. Frantically crawling towards the shore, her palms burned and her nails broke. She shot a look back to see how close the bear was to following her onto land.

The smooth lake surface was unbroken. The massive reflection of the moon gave no sign of the creature that had pursued her anywhere. Scanning the whole of the lake brought no further clues. Had it drowned in the swim over?

"Where did you go?"

The stars above were as bright as she'd ever seen them. The view itself, of total calm, was the kind of thing you could put on a postcard, yet there was something not right with this place. She'd started from the other side of the lake, on the beach where she'd waited for the others. She'd swum towards the lights of the opposite bank's cabins. She'd seen them on her way over. But now, dripping wet, hands bleeding and cut, staring back at the expanse of the lake, they were all on the opposing bank.

"That's impossible," she said.

Looking behind her, she saw the beach chair, her dropped book, the towels, even Ashley's hat. She walked over to see if they were figments of her exhausted imagination.

She touched the chair. It was solid. She picked up the towel. It was dry and full of sand. The hat was as real as the rest. Even the book was exactly as it should be. It still had the bookmark she'd left inside.

"But…"

She couldn't reason any of this out. Somehow, she'd swum across an entire lake only to end up where she'd thought she'd been all along. And yet, where she'd started from hadn't been where it was supposed to be either.

"There is something very wrong here."

She suddenly felt very exposed. Why had she agreed to stay here alone? She should go back to camp. At least there, she could start a fire. But if the others came here, they'd never knew where she'd gone. She had to leave them a message. She didn't have a pen, lipstick, paper, anything useful. But the beach was a mixture of sand and small, smooth rocks. So she spent nearly ten minutes gathering up and writing "BACK AT CAMP" with the small stones near the chair.

When it was all done, she gathered up the blanket, book, and chair and headed towards the trees, finally knowing where she was.

Reaching the trail, she turned back towards the rocks, as if looking at them would somehow ensure the note did the trick for the others. But she froze when she saw that the message she'd left had been changed to:

"ALL ARE DEAD"

She spun around, half expecting to find someone behind her with a giant knife about to stab her. She was alone. As alone as anyone could be.

She looked again at the rocks, thinking maybe she'd imagined the change. The stones seemed to glow with a pulsing rhythm, like a set of Christmas lights plugged into nothing.

"Who's there?" she meekly croaked.

The words must have been left for her, but who did it and how? She'd only had her back turned for a moment. They couldn't have moved them all so fast and found a hiding place in such a short time.

Whoever did it, must have been hidden nearby, watching her. Waiting. That meant they could still be here.

"If you're trying to scare me, it's not going to work," she said defiantly.

But it was working.

She turned to the trail. It was empty. She could just run.

But when she turned back to the beach, the rocks had moved again, this time spelling out:

"HE IS COMING"

"Who?" she shouted. "Who's coming?"

But the night didn't reply.

Was this a hallucination? Did she dare inspect the rocks to see if something was making them move? Or should she just get the hell out of here?

She made her choice.

She turned and ran.

NOW

"There's no one here." Matt kicked a can of beer across the deserted campground and into the bush. Four tents had been set up with an equal number of lawn chairs circling a long since extinguished fire. The ground was littered with empties. A cooler full of melted ice and packages of hotdogs had been tipped over near the firepit. Some animal seemed to have gotten through the plastic and chewed most of the wieners. "They told me we'd find her in camp."

Josh peered inside one of the tents. "I'm not so sure this was their camp." He saw scattered men's clothes in a pile next to an open backpack.

"Of course it's their camp," Matt replied. Looking in a second cooler for a beer, he found a fresh one and popped the top. "Tents. Beers. Hotdogs. What more proof do you need?"

"Maybe some buns?"

"You didn't think she was going to—"

"There's only men's clothes here."

"So what?"

"If Beth was here, she'd have brought her own—"

"Out skinny dipping with her new boyfriend. Maybe fucking him in the lake in front of everyone. They're despoiling the sacred grounds of—"

"Face it. This is a different campground. All guys. Separate from Beth and her friends. Just bros here for a good time. Entirely coincidental and not at all a part of your fantasy."

"No. No. No, you're wrong. The forest wouldn't lie. The trees told me she was close."

Josh dug around inside the tent and came out carrying a large hoodie with a faded Blue Bombers logo on the chest and two empty bottles of whiskey.

"Well?" he asked. "What about this evidence?"

"Looks like one hell of a party," Matt said, impressed.

"There's nothing to connect Beth here. This is a huge fucking park and you have to accept reality. With a million people in Manitoba, it's entirely probable that another group is—"

"Shut up." He threw the beer bottle against a tree and shattered it into a million pieces.

"What?"

Matt's eyes darted to the west. He raised his finger for quiet.

"Would you just tell me what you—"

He began muttering under his breath. "They haven't been here for a while. The fire's a day old."

"Okay, but how—"

"They've moved to the girls' camp."

"So you finally admit this isn't theirs?"

"They told me it isn't. The two groups each had their own site. Fuck, it's so obvious now. A decoy camp. To throw me off the scent."

"Dude, listen to yourself, there's no—"

Matt stormed off. The trees seemed to part for him, revealing another of the endless trails in the woods. Josh blinked. Had he seen what he'd just thought?

"Was that path—"

"We were closer than either of us realized. Distracted. Yeah, I see that, too. Fucking hell. We didn't see the goddamn forest for the trees. But she's close. So very close. Yeah. Yeah. I understand."

His hands fingered his knife as he moved down the new path and left Josh in the empty camp.

The trees began growing, reaching out to seal the route behind the man. "Oh no, I'm not letting you out of my sight." Josh ran after him. He leapt through the closing edges of the elongating branches, just as they locked together and cut off all sight of the other camp. He wondered if he was making the right decision, but as Matt jerkily ran ahead of him, he understood that he had no other choice.

* * * *

Guided through the woods in a seemingly random way, each turn as natural as any other, he pushed his way through the brush until he came to a clearing that told a familiar story.

Echoes from the past repeated. A woman hung upside down from a tree with her stomach torn open and her guts pulled out, stretched around the clearing, draped from tree to tree. The entrails wrapped around her neck attached her to the second victim—a man nailed to another tree. His legs had been pulled around behind the trunk. Cut to ribbons, covered in bloody gashes, their eyes had been gouged out. The ground was soaked in blood.

It was a message and a sacrifice all in one. The depravity was purposeful. The warning clear. He rubbed his hands on the bark of a tree and they were quickly covered with blood.

Voices spoke through the remnants of the victims. He saw what had taken place here. It had happened more than anyone knew. Done by a multitude of hands throughout the life of the forest, dating back to the first meeting of those who came with those who had always been.

He sniffed the air and examined the pinned limbs. The entrails were almost devoid of blood. A crow pecked at some of the offal dangling on a branch above. The fog in his mind struggled to remember why this all looked so familiar.

The crow cawed, staring right at him. The words made no sense. Should they have? Had they once?

He stuck his finger inside the gaping eye socket of the dead man. He closed his eyes and let his thoughts wander, trying to discern what had been seen before this one met his unfortunate end. Who'd begun the cycle?

The images came quickly. So fast that he struggled to make sense of them all. Eventually, the truth broke through. He removed his finger from the bloody socket and sucked off the remnants of blood and brain. He knew what was coming next. Now he only needed to find out where.

* * * *

"Fucking hell, Derek. Where in the goddamn world have you gone?" Frank said, stopping on the trail and leaning up against the rough bark of a nearby tree.

He was getting tired. He'd been walking all day. He shouldn't feel this rundown; he'd been walking most of his life. But the streets of River City were a far cry from the overgrown gravel paths of the Whiteshell. The lack of noise was off-putting. No cars honking, no screaming, no swearing, no jackhammers, not even a gunshot. Who could stand it?

"I'm starting to understand why people moved to cities in the first place."

A loon called off in the distance. The moon shone down overhead. The temperature was dropping enough that he felt goose pimples rising on his arms. The trees were losing their colour.

"What I wouldn't give for a mustard, onion, and sauerkraut dog about now. Maybe from old—"

He snorted derisively at the mere thought. "You're letting yourself get as distracted as old Derek. Stick to the path. Find your pal and go home. Forget all about this fucking place."

He stared down the seemingly endless trail ahead of him and knew he had a lot more walking to go before he found either his friend, or his car.

"Almost enough to make me wish I'd forgotten it all in the first place. Maybe Derek had the right idea after all."

THEN

"You catch anything?" Derek asked from his spot knee deep in the river a few metres downstream.

"Sure did." Frank held up their dinner, a fresh catch of walleye pulled from the water.

"You give them names yet?"

"Uh, yeah, first, seconds, and thirds."

Derek waded next to him and inspected the catch with an appraising eye. "That one is thirds," he said, pointing to one of the fish.

"If you say so."

"Then how about we go and clean the things? I've got some butter in the cooler that's gonna go nicely with seconds."

"Which one is he?" Frank asked.

"We'll decide on the grill."

* * * *

The crickets were singing him a tune in bug language. He didn't speak it, but from the sounds of it, the song was either meant to lull him to sleep or hypnotize him. Whatever purpose the little things had for crooning at the night sky wasn't for Frank to worry about. He was more concerned with the fact that he had no recollection of finishing the bottle of Jack that lay at his feet. The last time he'd noticed, it had been about half full.

"I couldn't have drunk it all," he muttered, trying to reconstruct the time that had seemingly vanished as he'd sat in his chair in the woods under the bright moon and stars. That was the problem with time. It never added up right when you'd been drinking. One sip led to another and the next thing you knew you were laying on the grass vacantly staring at the fire in a puddle of your own piss.

"You're supposed to be my pal, Jack," he said to the empty bottle. "You've always been there for me. It ain't easy being a cop, top secret missions, undercover, women, wives, dead partners, the memories of old friends and…" He trailed off, staring at the last swill in the bottom of the bottle. "Tag. You're it."

He took the final drop and let it glide down.

"You never talk back, demand alimony or threaten to cut off my testicles in the middle of the night."

He took a sniff of the remaining fumes in the bottle. It wasn't enough.

"Now go join your ancestors in the great circle of life. Return to the earth from whence you came."

He lobbed the bottle far away into the brush.

"Come on, Frank," Derek said from his spot near the raging fire. "You shouldn't litter. This is a pristine wilderness. Or at least it was before they carved it up with roads and campsites."

"That's progress," Frank said.

"Not to some."

"How come I'm the only one who's drunk?" Frank asked. "You should be blasted, too."

"Not tonight," Derek said. "I have to listen for the voices of the forest."

"You sure you ain't drunk? Cos that sounds like bullshit."

Frank knew if he stood up, he'd find out he was far drunker than he felt. Right now, he had no reason to stand so he'd just sit by the fire and do his best to stop the ground from spinning.

"Most people forget the calls of the land," Derek said. "Especially when they've lived all their lives in the city. But they're still there for us, if we just open our minds."

"You really sure you're not drunk?"

The big man laughed as he picked at the remnants of the walleye on his plate. "No, I'm not, I'm sorry to say."

"I wish you were."

"You may not remember this tomorrow, Frank, but what matters in life are the moments we share. They're not just embers of a fire that fade away in a puff of smoke."

"I must be drunk. You're going Shakespeare on me."

"In places like this, where time has no meaning, all things are possible. The rules of nature don't follow our perceptions. They exist beyond our notions of now and then, how and why. The forest has its own trajectory. We tread on it where and when, but not the same where and when. And what was then can be now and what might never be could have already happened."

"Okay, I'm going to pass out now," Frank said. He stood up and fell face first into the dirt.

Derek heard the rhythmic snoring of a contented man and put his plate down on the ground next to his chair. He stared at the fire and waited. Then he looked up as a much older man strolled into camp, his clothes dirty and disheveled, his hair wild and white. The posture had stooped, but the eyes were as alive as they'd ever been.

"Where the hell were you?" the old man said. "I've been wandering all over looking for you."

"I'm afraid you haven't found me right now either."

The old man came to the fire and warmed his hands. His breath fogged, betraying the chill in the night air. "I forgot how cold it could get out here at night."

The man saw the passed-out form of Frank snoring on the ground.

"What's the matter with him?"

"Drunk."

"He's got the right idea. That's what I came up here to do, by the way. You and I, getting drunk and fishing one last time before you wasted away."

"I'll expect your coming," Derek said.

The old man plopped down in the empty chair and put his feet up on the snoring form of Frank. He reached into a cooler and pulled out a beer.

"Mind if I?"

"Go ahead."

"I hadn't seen a stubby in years and now I get two in one day. Where'd you find one?"

Derek just smiled as the man took a sip.

"Now this takes me back."

"The forest has a way of condensing—"

"I don't need the lectures, Big D, I just need a drink."

"I'm afraid that's all I can do for you. You don't belong here."

Frank shifted in his sleep and the old man caught a glimpse of his face. He took a look at his beer as if it had been poisoned.

"I must be hungry, I'm hallucinating."

"You're just visiting. Memories are like that."

He finished off the beer and looked at his reflection in Derek's great thick glasses, then back to the younger version of himself that lay before him.

"I should have brought a sweater," he said. He noticed a plate of half-eaten fish on the ground. He scooped up a handful and popped it in his mouth.

"Not bad. Ain't no loaded dog, but it'll do." He finished off the plate and took another sip of beer. "Well, as much as I appreciate the siesta, I should get back out there. I was looking—"

"You'll find what you're looking for," Derek said. "But you might have to make a decision you never expected."

"You never were this weird when we came up here before," the old man said.

"This is a special time. A convergence. The spirits of the forest have awoken again. As they do in each cycle. As they will continue to do long past mine and your time. I can only hear them for a short period. Just like how you can only be here for a brief moment."

The old man stood up and dropped the empty beer into the cooler. He brushed off his pants and looked back to the trail he'd come in on.

"So I just keep walking?"

Derek nodded. "Trust me, he's out there and he's still inside. He just needs the right prompting."

"And?"

"And you'll know what to do when the time comes."

"That's your big advice?"

"Just remember it all, Frank. For the both of us."

The old man nodded and walked away.

NOW

"Someone is messing with us." Ashley leapt from the canoe and ran to the now-empty clearing where they'd found Alice's potential campsite originally.

David beached the canoe and Jack stepped off to follow her onto land.

"This is the spot," Jack said. "I remember that tree at the edge... wait, it looks bigger, doesn't it?"

Ashley followed his gaze to a large spruce tree that loomed over the riverbank. Some of the branches were bare, like withered and burnt arms stretching out, desperate to touch the water.

"I can't remember," she said. "But I think if it had been so dead, it would have stayed in my mind."

"I swear it wasn't like that," Jack said. "I—"

"He's right," David said, joining them. "When I met Alice here, the tree was full of life. This looks like it's half-dead or years have passed and—" He trailed off, checking the bark for clues.

"This *is* the spot," Ashley said. "I know it is. I was paying attention when you took us in the canoe. I remember the route. Now we come back and it's been swept clean. There's not even a crumb left."

"You think someone buried it all?" Jack asked.

"There'd be fresh dirt piles, wouldn't there?"

"Unless they did it in the bush."

"Then we'd never find any of it."

"Maybe they just carted it all off?"

"Sure, but who and why and—"

"Guys," David said, standing up from his inspection. "I can't explain it, but this is both the same spot and not the same spot."

"You're right," Jack said. "You can't explain it."

Ashley turned to see David pacing the clearing, checking the other trees, peering back out to the lake, looking at the position of the moon and stars, doing math in his head.

"We were here," he said. "I was here with Alice before that. But where we were wasn't where we are now. It was, but it isn't anymore. It's changed subtly. As if it's been aged."

"You're still not doing a very good job," Jack said.

"And I really can't do any better. What was here isn't. But what is here, used to be here."

Ashley sighed. "Look, everyone's exhausted. You were attacked by a bear, Jack and I have been wandering in the woods and canoeing all day. I'm starving and my brain feels like mush. And not just from trying to understand what the hell you're talking about. As much as it might hurt to hear this, Jack, I don't think we're finding your friend tonight. I think we should head back to the camp. Our camp. We can cook some hotdogs, get some sleep, and figure out a plan in the morning. With any luck, the others will all be there waiting with a big fire going and—"

"And maybe they found John."

"Maybe."

David continued to pace the clearing, muttering to himself.

"You should come with us," Ashley said.

"I should keep looking for Alice," he said. "I—"

"In the morning."

"There was lots of beer in our camp," Jack said.

He turned to both of them and considered the idea, then took one more glance back at the river. "Yeah, maybe that would be a good idea."

* * * *

Frank could see his breath fogging in front of his eyes. He knew he should probably grab a sweater if he didn't want to catch a chill, but heading back to the trailer would be admitting that he'd lost his oldest friend.

Derek was alone somewhere out there, maybe lost to his vascular dementia, maybe pooping in the trailer again. Or maybe he was just wandering around confused, seeing every trail as a place he'd never been, finding himself deeper and deeper in the forest with no way to ever find his way back.

"It's my fucking fault," Frank murmured.

What was worse was he was beginning to doubt his own sanity. Maybe it was the all-encompassing, oppressive scenery that was messing with his mind, but he was seeing things, hearing things. The forest itself seemed washed out, drained of its vibrancy. He needed a rest, but he didn't want to give in to his declining stamina.

He knew Derek wasn't long for the world. If what the family had told him when he'd been put in the care home held true, soon enough the final shreds of who he was would eventually fade and he'd be nothing but a shell, barely able to control his bodily functions. Then he'd stop eating and quickly waste away. Was that a fate better than starving to death alone in the wilderness?

Frank sighed with resignation. While it pained him to see his friend like that, he didn't blame the man. He was the victim of fate. The least Frank could do was find him and get him back somewhere comfortable. He was the one who'd brought him here after all. The man was almost his responsibility until he returned him to the care home.

"Come on, buddy," he muttered. "Give me some kind of sign of where the hell you went."

Then he saw it. Just off the path. It looked like blood, but how could you tell if something was actually blood when there was so little light? The moon barely reached through the trees down here. It gave just enough illumination for him to see dark blotches all over the leaves and bark of a tree. The potent stench of rotting meat was enough to confirm it.

He crouched down. It took him a while to understand what he was looking at. It had been badly mauled, but when he finally realized the truth, he began to piece together what was going on.

It was a chunk of what appeared to be a human leg.

"Here we go," he said.

The bloody flesh, deeply gouged, with visible bone and gristle, had been chewed on. Flies buzzed and crawled around it. A thin white worm burrowed into the meat.

He raised himself back up to his feet and looked for some clue as to where to go next.

"That's my sign, I guess," he said. "So assuming that's not your leg, old buddy, it looks like I'm on the right path."

* * * *

The campsite was empty. The lawn chairs and tents were positioned exactly as they'd been left. Donna's tent's open flap blew gently in the breeze. The extinguished firepit of ashes offered no warmth and the chill in the air told her that she needed to get it started soon.

"How can I be the only one here?" Beth said as she went into her tent to find a sweater. Sliding it on, she felt a little better, but it wasn't going to be enough.

The phone wouldn't turn on anymore. The swim across the lake had bricked it. She didn't have Ashley's car keys. All she could do was sit and wait for the others.

She wondered if she should have just waited on the beach. Sure, it was more exposed, but at least she'd know if someone was coming. She could have used one of those rocks as a weapon. Now, in the small clearing they'd chosen for their campsite, she felt hemmed in, surrounded by the thick forest that could hide an army ten feet from her and she'd never know.

"Guys, where are you?"

Visions of the bear coming back flashed through her mind. Her sitting down in the lawn chair as it, vicious and hungry, snuck up on her. Then growling, it charging in and attacking her before she could do anything about it. She'd scream but it would simply swat her and eat her.

Or maybe a mountain lion would find her. They lived here, too, didn't they?

Her breathing quickened. Sweat dripped down her brow. She was starting to feel a full-fledged panic attack setting in. Strange sounds in the forest. The calls of birds. Insects.

Rustling in the trees. Every noise was closer than the last. No matter which direction she looked, they came from behind her. The darkness taunted her. There was no time to run. There was nowhere to go. Footsteps. Branches moving. Louder. Louder. This had to be it. The bear was coming for her. All she could do was wait for the inevitable.

No. I don't have to be a victim.

She grabbed one of the burnt logs from the fire and held it up as a weapon, ready to strike at whatever was approaching. Even if it didn't save her, she'd at least go down swinging.

Then Ashley emerged from the trees.

"I sure hope you were about to start a fire with that," she said. "I'm freezing."

Beth breathed a huge sigh of relief. She dropped the log and ran to hug Ashley when two men following behind her emerged from the trees and she stopped. One was Jack, the other she didn't recognize. He was hairy, wrapped in bandages, dressed in too-small women's clothes. She backpedalled and picked the log back up. She held it ready until she had some explanation.

Ashley noticed her tension and waved her hands. "This is David. We ran across him near the river. He was attacked by a bear."

"A bear? I was chased by one, too," Beth said.

"And you got away?" David said. "Bears are fast runners."

"I swam across the lake. But when I got to the other side, it wasn't the other side. Does that make any sense?"

"No. But a lot about today doesn't," Ashley said.

David stayed at the outskirts of the camp, waiting for Beth to let him in. Finally, she lowered the log and tossed it back into the firepit.

Jack collapsed into one of the lawn chairs. "Oh God, my feet are killing me."

"Did you guys find John?" Beth asked.

"No. We're hoping the others did. Have any of them come back?" Jack asked.

"No."

"Shit, and it's getting late, too," Ashley said. "I hope they're not lost."

"I hope the bear didn't find them."

David gingerly crouched down at the firepit and started rearranging the logs. "Anyone have matches? Mine were in my pants back… well, wherever the hell I left them."

Beth opened her mouth to ask a question, but Ashley waved her hand to stop her. "Don't. It's too complicated. I'm not even sure I understand what the hell is going on."

"I've got matches back at our camp," Jack said. "I could go get them."

"No," Ashley said. "No more splitting up."

"Then how—"

"I can get it going with sticks, it's just a pain in the ass," David said. "Give me a minute."

He went to work rubbing sticks over some dried leaves, gently blowing and cradling the tiny sparks, fanning them into something more.

He's a real outdoorsman, Beth mouthed to Ashley. *Kind of hot, too.*

Ashley just shook her head as if to tell Beth to keep her hands off. She must have called dibs.

"Almost got it," David said.

"Damn, I didn't know you could actually do that. I've only seen it in movies," Jack said.

"Trust me, matches are preferred. But you never know what you might have to do when you're out in the bush for six weeks."

Ashley tossed her bear spray into her tent and dragged the cooler over. She placed it near the fire. "More hotdogs. The ice packs won't be cold, but at this point, anything will do."

"Won't the smell attract the bear?" Beth asked nervously.

"He was all the way downriver when I last saw him," David said. "I doubt he would have wandered this far in."

"But I—" She stopped herself from saying anything as if doing so would keep it from being true. If she never told them the bear was just at the beach, then it would never have been there in the first place.

"Ta-da," David said, stepping back proudly as a small fire began slowly picking up size in the pit. "Man brings fire. Lights up night sky."

"Is that supposed to be a racist stereotype?" Ashley said, shocked.

"No, I meant it as a caveman."

"I doubt they spoke English," Beth said.

"If I grunted, would you have understood?"

"Doubtful they grunted either," Beth said. "They most likely had their own language and—"

"You could've just thrown in a grunt here or there instead of saying the whole thing in grunts. That would have made more sense," Jack offered.

"Like Ugga Bugga?"

"Yeah. That would've worked."

"Oh God," Ashley interrupted. "This may be the most pointless conversation I've ever heard. Let's just get these dogs cooking."

* * * *

"Well now," Frank said as he stood on a rock formation that overlooked the lake. "Look who we have here."

Down below, at the edge of the forest, he saw the thing silhouetted by the moonlight. A massive grizzly, sitting on its haunches, chewing on something he couldn't make out. The creature seemed to glow with an ethereal haze that drew the colour away from everything around it.

Oblivious to his presence, it finished its meal then looked up to the sky. If he didn't know any better, Frank would have thought it was looking right at him. But of course, bears didn't have eyesight that strong. Or did they? Maybe the biggest ones, like this monster, were more powerful in ways beyond strength. He really should have paid more attention to David Suzuki, then maybe he'd know if he'd just been marked by Yogi's big brother.

The thing finally raised itself up and turned around, marching into the woods away from sight. Frank relaxed. He hadn't been spotted.

"You're not getting away that easily," he said.

He clambered down the rock face, doing his best to stay oriented in the twisted, thick woods. He pushed his way through the trees until he saw the lake in the distance.

Emerging onto the beach, he found he'd managed to stay almost exactly on the straight path. Or he'd been allowed to stay on it.

The bear was long gone. The beach was deserted. It was almost peaceful again, except for an odd rock formation. As he stepped closer, he saw that someone, or perhaps the bear, had arranged a series of small stones into a message. Maybe someone was leaving a note for anyone else who came this way, or maybe some teenagers were playing a prank on him. He didn't know or care. Each rock was smooth and rounded, coloured in greys, blacks, and whites. Together they spelled out:

"TIME TO DIE"

"I don't think so, buddy," Frank said and followed after the bear.

* * * *

"There's no one else coming," Beth said. "Where's Donna and Mandy or Percy and Aiden?"

"They must still be out there," Ashley said, looking out into the forest.

"I could go check our campground," Jack said as he sat at the fire and roasted a wiener. "They could have just decided to crash there."

"It's better if we stay together," Ashley said. "If there is a bear roaming the woods, it probably won't bother a group and if it did, we can use the fire to scare it off."

"The one I met wasn't scared of fire," David said.

"You're not helping," Beth said.

Ashley and Jack roasted hotdogs over the fire. David was busy holding his bandaged hands over the flame while Beth held tightly to a can of hard lemonade. They'd started cooking, assuming the others, when they finally showed up, would be as hungry as they were and thankful for the prepared food. But so far, it was still only the four of them and Ashley was beginning to worry.

"I had no idea it could get so freaking cold out here at night,"

Beth said.

"You here last night," Jack said.

"Sure. But I was bottle-of-wine warm. I had no idea what was going on."

"We were all pretty hammered."

"You think we should put on some music?" Jack asked. "It might signal anyone out there we're here."

"The forest has a way of obscuring the noise from carrying," David said. "Fifty feet or fifty meters plays tricks on you."

"One of us could go and try to find the ranger," Beth said.

"That would be splitting up. Which I've already said we are not doing. Besides, we've got fire and hotdogs. We've all been hiking non-stop. I can't go another step. I'm sure the others'll start filtering in soon. They're not going to want to be in the woods all night." She found herself saying things out loud to convince herself they were true.

"But we have to find the ranger in the morning. He needs to know what's going on."

"Do those guys live in woods twenty-four seven?" Jack asked.

"Your guess is as good as mine."

They cooked in silence for a moment, letting the night air and sounds of the forest surround them. Finally, Jack slid his wiener into a bun and leaned back, chewing eagerly. "I have a question relating to the whole not splitting up thing you mentioned."

"Which is?" Ashley asked.

"Does that mean you're okay with guys sleeping here?"

"The jury's still out," Ashley said curtly.

"Oh, come on, haven't we proved we're harmless?"

"You're close," she said, "but he may have raped and murdered my aunt, or at least kidnapped her for forty years and left her to die in the woods."

Beth sat up and shot a panicked glance at David.

"Now wait—"

"He did build the fire," Jack said, cutting him off.

"Yeah," Ashley interjected, "and I built ours last night, what's your point?"

"Wait a minute, David did what?"

"I didn't do anything," David said. "I've told you this. Alice and I were making love when the bear attacked. I was almost killed and—"

"And you're the one alive and she's not here to contradict you."

"Ashley, come on," Jack said. "You're being—"

"Don't tell me what I'm being. This has been one fucked-up day and I'm not about to let my guard down for anyone. Especially not some strange handsome hippy we find in the woods and—"

"Handsome?"

"Then how does this work?" Jack asked. "We can't stay here and we can't go. We're like Schrodinger's campers."

"The others will come," Beth said, refusing to stop staring at David. "Then none of this will matter. Everyone can go back to their own camps and Ashley can stop being Mother Superior."

"Sorry for being the only one with any sense around here," Ashley said.

"I can go back to the canoe," David said. "I was sleeping alone for weeks before I, uh, met the woman you think is your aunt."

"Why does everyone keep trying to find reasons to split

up?" Ashley said. "Are you all so desperate to be horror movie victims?"

Beth blanched. "You think everyone's dead?"

"I didn't say that. I just don't want to separate the group now that some of us are finally back together. So just sit and eat and don't get caught up in—"

She trailed off as they heard a rustling in the trees. Everyone fell dead silent. Ashley looked to Jack. He reached for a large stick and held it over the fire to get it ablaze. David did the same. They all watched the woods, looking for the source of the noises. Could the smell of cooked meat have attracted the bear? Or was it someone from their group finally coming back?

"Well, well, well. Look who we have here."

Two men entered the campground. One was dressed in full camouflage and carried a massive knife, the other was in jeans bringing up the rear. Ashley could see Beth's heart sink when she realized that under all the smeared makeup, was Matt.

NOW

"You thought you could sneak around on me?" Matt brandished a huge serrated knife. He stood a few feet away, at the edge of the campground. "You thought I wouldn't find out?"

"What are you doing here, Matt?" Beth asked.

"Didn't think I'd find you, did you? You thought you were so smart."

"It's not what you think," Beth said.

"You don't get to tell me what I think." He pointed the knife at her.

They all froze. There was something very wrong with his face. It was contorting and stretching out, looking like some kind of melting halloween mask. The paint was swirling around and changing shape. His eyes glowed with red fire, and he seemed to be absorbing the light that filtered down through the trees into some kind of negative space that haloed him.

"My girlfriend goes away for the weekend without telling me. She meets some guys with her friends. They all start having a big laugh at my expense. Ha ha ha. Matt never has to know. What happens at the lake stays at the lake. That right? We can suck as many dicks as we want. We're on a hall pass."

"Look, uh, Matt, is it?" Jack said. "You've got the wrong idea—"

"You don't get to talk." Matt, impossibly fast, was on Jack before anyone could stop him. He batted the flaming log away and shoved the knife under his nose. "You do not count. She's the one I want. As far as I'm concerned, you're just a cock with legs."

"Hey."

"Wrong idea," Matt said. "Wrong idea? Do you think I'm a fucking moron?"

Jack seemed to want to say something but a glance from Josh stopped him.

"Beer." Matt pushed Jack down into a lawn chair and grabbed one of the cans from the ground. He crushed it in his palm, but the beer can wasn't quite empty and splashed him with warm alcohol that evaporated as soon as it hit him.

"Check the fucking tents, Josh," Matt said.

Josh hesitated a moment, then ducked into Donna's tent. He emerged with a pair of obviously men's jockey shorts.

"Oh ho, more proof. A man's gitch. Which one of these two are you fucking, Beth?"

"Matt, I swear, I'm not—"

"That was Donna's tent, dipshit," Ashley said. "Those must be Percy's. They must have snuck a quick one in when no one was looking."

Matt swung the blade to David. He ran up to him and jammed the knife down into his leg. David screamed out in pain and dropped his log in the fire. He fell back into his chair. The girls cried out as Matt dug the knife around back and forth, sending dark red blood leaking out over David's extremities.

"Please," Ashley screamed. "That's not Percy, that's David. He's—"

"Not Percy?" Matt stopped gouging the man's leg, leaving the knife embedded as David grimaced in pain.

"No."

Josh ripped the knife out, letting the blood fly over David's face. He kicked the chair over to land hard on the dirt. He leapt over and threw a punch, then another one, raining down heavy blows. David could only meekly hold his hands held up in front of his face in vain as he took shot after shot to the face and body. Eight, twelve, thirty punches. Finally, Matt pushed away from the battered man. Ashley moved to go to him, but he waved her back with the blade.

"Stay."

"What else is in the fuck tent?" Matt asked.

Josh crawled back inside the tent and in a few moments emerged with a condom wrapper and a small vial of white powder.

"Someone was sure having a good time," he said.

"Cocaine?"

"Well, it could be sugar or salt or—"

"Who the fuck keeps sugar and salt in a small vial in their tent?"

"Maybe someone who planned on using it to cook."

"Oh, for fuck's sake, those are Donna's, too," Ashley said. "She and Percy were getting high and having sex. It's hardly a—"

"One way to find out." Matt snatched the vial from Josh and unscrewed the cap. He dabbed some on his hand and snorted it up his nose.

"Should you really be doing that? You don't know what that

is and—"

"Fuck off, Josh. I could use a pick me up." He shuddered once as the stuff hit him. The fire in his eyes seemed to be expanding outward now, even as the darkness deepened.

"Anyone else?" he said, holding it out.

"Go fuck yourself," Ashley said.

"Suit yourself." Matt took another snort then threw away the vial.

"What are you going to do here, Matt?" Ashley defiantly moved over to the fallen David, who was bleeding all over the forest floor.

"Get back," he said.

"He's badly hurt, bleeding out. I need to get that thing bandaged or you're going to have to add murder to your list of crimes."

"You don't get it. They're asking for another sacrifice. He's as worthy as any of you."

Beth looked confused. "What are you saying? What did you do?"

"You don't want to know," Josh interjected. "It wasn't pretty—"

"Shut the fuck up, Josh. It's not about what any of us want anymore. It's what it wants."

"What is it?" Jack asked.

"Here," Matt said. "Let me show you."

Before anyone knew what was happening, Matt lunged at Jack. He plunged the knife through his neck. The man gargled in shock as the blade pierced his windpipe. Blood shot all over the hilt and down Matt's arm, coating him in red. He grabbed Jack's hair and held him up as the man began to lose the ability to stand.

Beth screamed. Ashley watched in shock as she cradled David's head on the forest floor. Josh just backed away, shaking his head.

"It's coming," Matt said. "You can be the first to meet it."

He began twisting and grinding the knife, slowly ripping the flesh of the man's neck until he reached the edge. Then, part of the body slid down and he went to gouging the remaining flesh. He started speaking in some otherworldly tongue as he severed the head of poor Jack. Blood saturated his arm, poured over his body and down his leg, soaking his boots. The headless corpse collapsed to the ground. Beth screamed anew. Ashley retched. David simply stared in horror, holding his own wound, trying to staunch the bleeding.

Matt turned away from the fire and looked to the heavens, holding the head high. The lifeless eyes of Jack absorbed the moonlight as the dripping of the remaining blood rhythmically splattered on the dirt.

"It's coming. It's coming."

Matt turned to Beth, approaching her with the head held out like a lantern. She cowered away from him. He reached out with his free hand and gently caressed her chin, coating her in blood. She shivered in fear. She didn't dare speak or move, just remained pinned to her chair in primal terror as he wrote some kind of arcane symbol on her face.

"Don't touch her," Ashley said meekly.

"Josh, tie that bitch up. She's starting to annoy me."

"I-I-I—"

Josh kept backing away to the edge of the campsite. His head moved back and forth rapidly, his eyes wide with terror, his breathing rapid and shallow.

Matt turned to look at him.

"You can't escape what's coming," he said. "In fact, it's already here."

* * * *

"What was it, forty years ago?" Frank said as he moved through the trail in the woods. The route kept shifting and turning, the trees opening new paths, closing off others, as if they were herding him. He'd lost his sense of direction now, everything was all so confusing in the dark.

"Maybe longer," he said. "Haven't thought about it since. Hard to remember one case over the others. Forty fucking years." He spoke aloud to try to put what had been going on in some kind of order. Now that it had started to make more sense, he was coming to the realization that this was a repeat performance.

"I don't know how you picked up on it before I did, Derek, old buddy," he said. "Some part of your brain must still be working right. Must be why you wandered off. You wanted to make sure the ending was different this time."

He kept pressing into the woods, letting them lead him where they would. He felt the cold comfort of his gun under his flannel jacket.

"After it was all over, I just put it out of my mind and moved on. Shit, that was before I lost Daphne to that disco, the Camponelli crime wave, that blasted robot who wanted my job, the worms, the patchwork men, the pool party, that kid who thought I was his dad. How many chiefs and partners in that time? Then there was Morty, Jessica and the gang. Those kids who played video games for money, Southside Annie. Goddammit, I guess I was so busy with life that I never remembered. To think after all this time, we'd be back where we started and I'd forget to remember not to forget what we did in the first place. The mind's a strange thing when the guy with vascular dementia recalls more than the one with a steel closet full of stories. Maybe I'm the one going senile after all."

"You're not making any sense, Frankie," Derek said. "Like less sense than you usually make, I should say."

Beside him now walked Derek, as he used to be so many years ago. Young, virile, with fiery red hair and all of his football player physique. But he was just a ghost of the past. Frank understood that he was only a phantom memory temporarily made flesh, a trick of the light.

"You get into your pappy's homebrew again?"

"I wish this was all just a case of some bad liquor. But the Van Lundgren stuff is long gone and Pappy's been dead sixty-five years at least. Any buzz I might have had today has worn off and I'm thinking clearly. In fact, I think I finally know exactly what's going on here. Maybe for the first time this whole trip. I don't believe in fate, but whatever brought us back to the same place after all this time sure has a sense of humour."

The younger Derek walking beside him smiled. "Glad to hear it, Frankie."

"How'd you know? Or I guess I should ask, how will you know?"

"The call of the wild places never really leaves you. Even if you leave them. Sometimes it just takes a little prompting to get through all that other noise."

"Any advice?"

"You've got this covered. You always do. But remember

to tell yourself to change the channel. Even if you won't remember doing it, you'll remember to do it when the time is right. Oh hell, maybe I'll have to remember to do it. I sure hope I can remember not to forget to do that when the time comes."

"Now who sounds drunk?"

"You know, that's a good idea," Derek said. "Still plenty of beer back at camp."

"Drink a few for me. With me, too."

"Just what the doctor ordered."

Derek seemed to step down an invisible trail into the woods. Frank barely saw him go, but knew that he was again alone with his thoughts.

The woods kept opening ahead of him and closing behind him. He marched, knowing that he would get where he needed to. He was wanted there.

"Hey, Grampa," a voice said beside him. "You know the way back to the public washrooms? Something sure didn't agree with me and I've got a real three flusher brewing here."

Frank saw another ghost walking beside him. A ghost of his own past this time. The same features, the same wild eyes, but without the wisdom and burden of age wearing him down. This was a guy who hadn't seen shit yet.

"Let me guess," Frank said. "You used some old butter you found at the back of the fridge on the walleye you caught."

"Hey, good guess, old man. Sounds like you've done it, too."

"Sure, once or twice. Let me give you some advice. If it stinks going into the pan, it's sure going to stink going into the can."

"I'll try to remember that," young Frank said.

"You won't. But that's okay. You'll deserve it."

"So, uh, do you know the way or not because I'm feeling thunder down under and the levee's about ready to break?"

"Sure, sure. It's just down the path near the highway past the big wooden sign."

"Great, thanks," young Frank said and started to leave.

"One thing though," Frank said. "Trips like these are for memories. As in making them. There'll come a point in your life that they might be all you have. So don't forget what you did and who you did it with."

"Sounds like you've brought some dames up here."

"A few. But also some good friends."

"I'm here with my oldest friend, too," young Frank said. "Just finished his accountant's certification and we're getting blasted drunk to celebrate."

"That's as good a reason as any. What are your plans?"

"Me? I was thinking of joining the army."

"Go for it. It'll do you good. But when you get out, a man with your skills would be invaluable on the police force."

"You think?"

"I know."

"Hey, thanks again, old man. I'll consider it. But right now, I've really got to unleash this time bomb in my pants before—"

He started to run off and Frank shouted after him.

"Remember to change the channel."

"What?" Young Frank stopped and looked over his shoulder.

"You won't remember why, but when you're my age and you're visiting an old friend who's not all there, he's going to be watching something terrible on TV and you should change it for him. Can you do that?"

"Look, I'm not sure what you're getting at here, but yeah, okay, if it'll stop you from giving me any more advice, I'll remember."

He started to fade away down his own path. Frank stopped to watch him go.

"Remember all of this. The hunting and fishing and—"

But the man had disappeared, leaving Frank alone again.

"Well, this whole place sure has brought back the past in a big way. Must be something in the air."

Frank took a deep breath and tapped his gun. "What we have here is an example of history repeating itself. Only this time, I'm ready for it."

The trail ahead turned. He followed its lead.

"Take me to the show. I'm ready."

THEN

"Okay, look, pal, you've had your fun. You had us running around in circles for a while, but it's over now. I'm putting a stop to your little weekend misadventure."

Frank had his gun trained, ready to pull the trigger at the slightest movement towards him. The man was cornered now, with nowhere to run, but in Frank's experience, that meant little. The sick and deranged ones didn't play by the same rules as the rest of us. They sometimes did things you didn't expect. But he expected the unexpected and was more than ready for it.

"I don't want to have to shoot, but I will. I'm a crack shot, too. That means I won't miss what I'm aiming at. In case you're confused, I'm aiming at something vital. I don't think you want to know what it feels like to bleed out. To slowly die as your body fills with stomach acid or bile or shit. Believe me, it's not pretty. Hurts like a bitch, too. Now if you try anything and I'm forced to shoot, it'll be hours before an ambulance can get here. That means even if I shoot something a little less vital, say a kidney or spleen, you're still going to croak. So why don't you just relax, put down that man's intestines and put your hands up?"

Face to face with the killer on the ridge overlooking the lake, against a massive black rock formation that pointed to the sky. It wasn't a cave, wasn't a cliff, but it was the closest thing you were going to get around these parts they called the Canadian shield. Here and now though, it was the public's shield. Like the one he had in his pants back home.

"You're cornered, you know. Oh, sure, not in an actual corner, but you get the idea. Sheer drop on one side, man with a gun on the other. Call it a rounded corner."

Frank was the only thing standing between this sick monster escaping and murdering more people. He'd already killed too many campers and forest rangers. It would take a while to connect all the missing pieces to figure out just how many.

"That's right. The rock. Frank. The gun. The drop. Who's going to blink first?"

The killer took deep breaths, his blackened eyes darting back and forth for any escape. The hunk of guts in his hand dripped blood to the forest floor. It had taken all of his smarts to get to this point, the endgame, and he wasn't about to let the man slip through his fingers, even if there seemed to be something very wrong with him. He was absorbing the light around him, giving off some kind of ethereal glow from his skin. Skin that was stretching and bubbling on its own. He must have some kind of serious rash.

"This time, I'm bringing you in. There's some bleeding hearts out there who want the courts to have their chance. They want the brain doctors to get a look inside of your head, figure out what secrets they can learn about psychopaths. They think it will prevent more like you from coming back."

Silence. An eagle soared overhead.

"What do you think about that? How do you feel about

the full force of justice getting to work its magic instead of a bullet ending it all here? I shoot you, where would we be? One more corpse but no answers. Nobody'd ever know the why of a crime like this, or how to prevent it in the future. Unless you want to tell me and spare a bunch of people the work."

No answer.

"Didn't think so."

Frank didn't want to shoot the guy either. A bullet was too final. It stopped the cycle only for the briefest of moments. It would just start anew with someone else. More victims. More killers. More bullets, more broken lives.

He'd seen a lot in his life so far. He'd killed a lot of people. Most deserved it even if a few might not feel that way. This one was different. He'd gone to new lengths of depravity. This was major news headline material. Frank didn't want to kill this killer. He wanted to see them cuffed and dragged in front of a judge and jury. Not because they kept telling him it was the better way, but because this guy wasn't written about in any books. There were no case studies for what he'd done. He broke the mold. And maybe he had some serious skin condition, too. Who knew what secrets he could reveal alive?

Bringing a man in alive. There was always a first time. A case like this was Frank's ticket to make detective. If he wanted to work his way up in the ranks of the force, they told him that he couldn't just shoot everyone who broke the law. He had to show that he could arrest them, too.

Rules.

Face contorting, skin emitting some kind of phosphorescence, lack of noticeable verbal skills, the bit of intestines he was chewing on; this guy was a career maker.

"Still don't want to talk, eh?"

The killer lowered the handful of human tripe and looked at Frank with eyes that didn't see the world in the same way as the good and just. They were so black, they might not see at all actually.

The man appeared to relax. Maybe he'd talked the monster down. Maybe there was something to this whole not shooting people thing. Or maybe the guy was about to make a move.

"That's it. Drop the squishy bits and put your hands in the air."

Their eyes met. Cop vs killer. Law vs disorder. Good vs Evil. Who would blink first?

* * * *

The more she ran, the more the trails seemed to disappear. She was sure she'd started back to the camp, but after passing the lake four times, Mandy now had no idea where in the hell she was going. Her legs were tiring. She'd sweated through her loose shirt. There were scratches all over her bare legs below her shorts. Her hair was frazzled, she looked and smelled awful. She needed a shower and more deodorant. But no matter where she went, she seemed to end up nowhere.

Finally, she slowed to a jog, then stopped, put her hands on the nearest branch and caught her breath.

"Hello?" she called out. "Is there anyone out there?"

Only a loon answered.

"Fucking hell. Where am I?"

No phone, all because of Ashley's stupid rules. Alone because her escort had been shot. No signs of humanity, no clues that she was anywhere closer to where the others were. And yet, she'd seen the same lake so many times that she knew she had to be only a few kilometres from the highway, or at least some of the hiking trails. So why wasn't she seeing them?

"Oh God, I don't want to fucking die in a provincial park. I just want to go home."

That's when she heard the faint noises of music. She held her breath and stared off into the thick woods, trying to zero in on the source. Some kind of violin? A vibrating? What was it?

"Folk music?"

She pushed herself deeper through the clinging trees, despite her exhaustion. The music grew louder as she approached. There came a glow from what seemed like a bonfire. She heard voices. Singing and raucous laughter. The music grew in intensity, a kind of dancing tune unlike anything she'd ever heard.

The light drew her. She finally came close enough to see a group of men sitting around a roaring fire, surrounded by supplies and two huge canoes. Some were dancing, others drinking, a few chewing on what looked like cooked rabbit. They were dressed in furs, striped wool, with thick beards and long hair. Tanned skin, ruddy faces, crooked teeth.

"Is this some kind of reenactment society?" she muttered.

The sight of the food, the warmth of the fire, the smells, they all drew her out of the bush.

One of the men spotted her and pointed.

"Regardez les garçons, c'est une femme!"

The music stopped and all eyes turned to her.

"Uh, hello. Is this some kind of history channel thing?" she asked. "I saw the canoes and—"

"Anglais? C'est une fille anglaise."

"No, c'est impossible. Elle doit être autochtone."

A man with a heavy fur hat rose up. "Alors, comment nous avez-vous trouvé mademoiselle?"

"I'm sorry," Mandy said. "I only took two years of French. I don't understand what you're saying. My name is Mandy and I'm lost. I'm looking for my friends. They were camping by the lake, and I got separated after one of them…"

She trailed off when she spotted the hungry looks in their eyes. These were men who clearly hadn't seen a woman in a long time. They were all so heavily dressed and she realized how little she was actually wearing. Their lecherous gazes made her intensely uncomfortable. She suddenly felt that she had to get out of here fast.

"Uh, right. So I'm going to get going now and…" She backed away slowly, hoping to hit the tree line so she could turn and bolt, but she hit something firm enough to know that it was one of the men behind her. Huge warm hands closed on her shoulders.

"Où vas-tu, madame?"

"I'd just like to get back to looking for my—"

"Rejoignez notre fête," he said. "Moi, j'aimerais vous présenter quelque chose dans ma poche."

The way he was looking at her made her understand what he meant better than knowing what he was saying could. She saw him grab his crotch, then spun to see the others all licking their lips. All she could do was swallow once and hope that they'd be quick about it.

"He—"

She tried to raise up her almost forgotten can of bear spray, but the hands closed over her mouth and she was hoisted up. The can fell from her grasp to the forest floor as she was carried over to the fire and too many men to count.

NOW

"I'm going, man," Josh said, backing away. "I can't be a part of this any more and—"

He didn't see the massive bear emerge from the woods. The thing was easily nine hundred pounds, standing over a foot taller than the man when it reared up. It seemed to emit a rippling shadowy haze from its fur, glowing in a kind of negative image of reality; a much stronger halo than the one around Matt. The bear's teeth were as large as a human thumb, yellowed and gleaming. A line of drool fell from the jaw as it roared.

"It has arrived," Matt said. "As promised."

"What?" Josh said but before anyone could shout a warning, the massive bear's jaws clamped down over his head, seemingly swallowing the entire skull whole. The bite sliced through the weaker flesh of the neck with wild abandon and tore the cranium clear.

In a flash it was over, and a second headless corpse fell forward as the bear gnashed the flesh in its jaws with sickening crunches. They all saw poor Josh's head being ground up like it was nothing. The man's shocked expression cried out silently as his eyes saw the inside of the bear's jaws as their final vision.

It was too much for Beth—she collapsed backwards and crashed down to the ground in a faint.

"Good God," David said.

Ashley screamed.

"It is a god," Matt said proudly.

The bear finished the grisly meal of poor Josh's head and swallowed. It regarded the corpse at its feet, then turned to Matt, who stood holding the severed head of Jack.

"Seconds?" He lobbed the thing to the bear. It hit the ground in front of it and rolled, looking up at the creature.

The bear sniffed it once, then clamped its teeth over the top and crushed the skull, leaking brains and blood over its jaws. A couple more stomach churning bites and Jack's head was gone, too. The monster licked up the spilled gore on the forest floor and seemed to become sharper, the haze more potent. It even appeared to grow larger before their eyes.

"You see?" Matt said. "Offer a sacrifice and it comes."

"What is it?" Ashley croaked.

"It's a bear, stupid," Matt said.

"That's no bear," David said.

Matt grinned, his mouth seemingly stretching beyond the confines of his face. "You're right."

"What do you mean, he's right?" Ashley said. "It's obviously a fucking bear."

Matt dropped the bloody knife and stepped towards the creature. The thing began chewing through the torn neck of Josh, digging out strips of flesh and gnashing them happily.

"It's so much more than that," he said. He stood awestruck in front of the thing as the light he absorbed from the stars above began flowing into the bear and back from the bear to him. "This is the embodiment of the natural world. This is life. The life of the forest. The anger and the revenge of the forest. This is what was promised to me."

His face began stretching, his body convulsing. The light transferring from the bodies increased, like a growing elastic energy. The bear grew larger, and Matt began swelling outward.

"Yes, I'm ready. I want it all."

The bear stared silently at him as he screamed in some kind of orgasmic ecstasy.

"You can all be next if open yourselves up. I think you—"

But he never finished what he was trying to say. Beth rose from the ground with Matt's dropped knife. Screaming in primal fury she swung down as hard as she could at Matt. He turned to look at her but had no time to react as the blade embedded itself in his skull almost down to his nose. His eyes rolled back in his head. His face stopped its transformation and returned to normal. He went limp and fell to the ground like a collapsed mannequin. His remaining energy haze seeped out of his body and flowed into the bear, draining the colour out of what was left of him.

Beth screamed in horror at what she'd done.

"Beth, get away from that thing," Ashley shouted.

"I killed him. I killed him."

She dropped to her knees and cradled Matt's head in her lap. She gently touched the knife, trying to see if there was any way to get it out. Blood leaked from the wound down his temple, dripping to the forest floor.

"Matt? I didn't mean it. I don't know what came over me," she said, stroking his cheek. "It's going to be okay. I'll get you some help. I'll call an ambulance."

"Beth," Ashley said. "He's dead."

"No," Beth screamed. "He might not be, he—"

Whatever had been happening to his skin had done more damage than it appeared. The two pieces of his head, cleaved by the knife, split apart like an avocado skin. His brain slid out onto Beth's lap.

She stared down at the greyish mass and screamed again.

"Put it back, put it back."

"Get away from—"

The bear's great head leaned into Beth. It snorted in her ear, sending a spray of warm breath over her face. It seemed to snap her out of her panic. She slowly turned to come face to face with the massive primordial monster.

"I- killed- him."

"Let the body go, back away slowly and—"

The bear leaned down and sniffed the corpse of Matt as the last of his colour was sucked out. Then, it turned back to Beth. She remained locked in place, unable to move, simply shaking in abject terror of the creature. Weeping, she refused to let go of Matt's head, gently caressing his hair, trying to avoid touching the leaking brains. She stroked his cheeks as bits of grey ooze slid down her lap.

"Beth, I'm serious, you have to move," Ashley said but it was clear the girl wasn't hearing her. She refused to even look at her. She'd snapped.

"He's still alive, I can feel it."

Head split in two like a coconut, skin turned a sickly blueish white, no sane person would think the man had a chance.

"I have to get her," Ashley said to David.

"No, don't," he croaked meekly. His face was swollen and misshapen, battered and bruised into a kind of inhuman mask. Blood poured from his nose. His eyes were shut. He looked more like the elephant man than the handsome outdoorsman he had before. His breath came in short gasps from puffy lips and a broken nose. "You don't understand. That thing isn't what you think it is."

"It isn't a bear?"

She turned back to the scene of her friend, refusing to leave the side of her dead ex despite being mere inches from a massive grizzly that stared at her with a kind of intelligent curiosity. Each breath of the thing sent Beth's hair flying. The drool falling from its jaws soaked the ground next to her. The smell of its musk was overpowering. The rippling fur, the strange dark glow, the impossible size of it all.

"No, it's—"

That was when the bear finally made its move. It happened so fast that David never had a chance to finish his thought. Ashley's scream cut him off as she realized that the creature was mauling Beth. It tore off her face with one bite, ripping out most of her neck along with it in a great splash of red, then brought its massive claw down and rended the skin from her head to her lap, slicing through to the bone, nearly cleaving her in three sections.

It lifted its maw, saturated with flesh, and roared. Ashley backpedalled away, letting David fall to the ground. Something inside of her broke then, unable to comprehend what she was looking at. The animal, far bigger than a man, covered in thick fur, with its gargantuan square head, six-inch talons, huge, pointed fangs dripping flesh, dark intelligent eyes, dropped back to all fours and stared at her across the campsite.

The giant grizzly bear, wild, feral, consumed with bloodlust, took a few lumbering steps over the twin corpses of Beth and Matt. A piece of flesh fell from its jaws.

"Go," David said, "run."

Ashley couldn't budge. She was pinned in fear looking at the beast as if she didn't even think it was real.

"Ashley," he said again but she was blind in her panic.

He awkwardly rose to his feet and stumbled to the fire, grabbing a log and brandishing it like a torch.

"You didn't like this much once," he coughed. "Let's see if you can handle seconds."

The beast reared back onto his hind legs, towering over David. It was even bigger than before, almost a meter taller than he was. He gulped in fear but refused to back down.

He moved to lunge the fire into the thing's torso, but the fire somehow extinguished itself the closer it came to the beast. David recoiled, a charred log now in hand.

"Oh, fuck," he said meekly.

THEN

He didn't normally bring handcuffs out to the lake, especially when going fishing. He found fish were just too slippery to latch on to, but Frank always had a spare set in his glove compartment. Luckily, before the search party had begun, he'd remembered to take them along. He approached the killer, who finally looked docile enough to lock up, ready to snap the cuffs on a fresh pair of wrists, and knew that the old adage of always being prepared was one lesson he'd retained from his boy scout days.

"That's it," he said calmly. "Easy does it. Just let me slap on these shiny bracelets and it'll all be okay. We'll get down from here and go back into town. We'll get you some help and this will all just be a bad nightmare."

He was a meter away, watching for any subtle cues of impending movement. He had to be ready for anything.

Half a meter. Reaching out non-threateningly, acting like a friend.

He clicked the cuff on the first wrist.

"Almost done. Just relax."

The clasp was closing over the second wrist, nearly locked in. He breathed a momentary sigh of relief and that almost cost him his life. The killer lunged forward and wrapped the cuff chain around Frank's neck. They both fell backwards onto the rocky ground. The force of the landing knocked the wind out of him. He lost his grip, then his ability to breathe.

Choking.

The killer was choking him with the cold metal chain. He tried to reach up and hit the attacker but he had no leverage to get in a solid blow. Pinned down, struggling under the weight, his brain cried out that he had to get loose. He consciousness was fading...

NOW

B acking away from the frothing creature, David fell
to his butt and slid in reverse towards the fire. His
hand brushed the edge of the pit. He felt the heat at
his back and reached for another log. He pulled one out and
threw it ineffectively at the approaching bear. The flame was
doused inches from the beast and the blackened log bounced
harmlessly off the monstrous form.

The behemoth took slow, lumbering steps towards him,
each footfall vibrating the ground like a tiny earthquake. The
fur rippled from the motion of the powerful muscles as the
thing stalked forward. He could smell the sick stench of its
hot breath, the musk of its fur overwhelming him. There was
nowhere to go, nowhere to hide, nothing he could do but
await the inevitable.

"Stay back," Ashley shouted. "Leave him alone."

She'd pulled the knife from Matt's split cranium and
stabbed forward at the thing's face. The knife pierced its
eye, embedding deep in the skull almost to the hilt. Ashley
let go and backed away, thinking she'd done serious damage.
David took the opportunity to crawl around the fire to his
feet, putting the flames between him and the monster.

"You did it," he said. "You—"

But the bear showed no sign of pain. It just turned to look at her, one glowing eye focused, the other split down the middle by the huge knife.

"Is it dead?" she asked. "Is—"

It reared up again, silently this time, towering over her. David knew what was coming. Ashley simply stared dumbfounded as the paw came up.

"Out of the way," he cried and ran to her. He leapt, grabbed her around the waist, felt the edges of the claws scrape his already damaged back, slicing through his sweater, the bandages and skin. He landed hard on top of her right against the edge of one of the tents.

"Hey, Yogi, leave those kids alone."

The bear turned to the source of a new voice shouting from the edge of the clearing.

As if some primal instinct deep inside of her took over, Ashley crawled inside the tent, dragging David along. She zipped up the flap and buried her head under a pillow, leaving him moaning and bleeding on the tent floor.

"Never thought I'd see you again," the voice shouted from outside.

"Someone's here," David groaned. "We can't let him—" But he never finished his thought as he finally collapsed unconscious, the strain of his rescue having drained the last of his adrenaline.

"David," she said, coming up from under the pillow. She crawled over and touched his neck for a pulse. Then she carefully opened the zipper of the tent and peered outside. An old man dressed in a flannel shirt and hip waders stood at the edge of the campground. He held a huge handgun pointed at the bear. His stark white hair was sweaty and wildly out of control. His wrinkled visage said he had to be a senior citizen, but his fiery eyes seemed much younger than the rest of him. He was tall but stood with a slight stoop. He pointed the gun with a confidence that told her he knew how to use it. The bear just looked at him.

"Don't remember me? I'm crushed."

The bear didn't move.

"The man who tracked you down all those years ago. The one who, in a moment of weakness, didn't fill you full of lead."

The bear said nothing.

The old man seemed puzzled. "Come on. I had you dead to rights and you were shitting your bear pants."

Still the bear made no reply. Ashley was confused—was the old man expecting the bear to talk back?

"Seriously," he said in frustration. "You go senile, too? It's me, Detective Inspector Sergeant Frank Malone of the River City Police Department, err, retired."

Now the bear seemed to understand. It roared and stood on its hind legs to issue a challenge. The thing towered over the old man and could kill him with a swipe, but the guy showed no fear.

"Yeah, yeah, yeah. I hear you," Frank said. "You're still a blowhard, you know that?"

"Mister, watch out," Ashley said. "That thing killed my friends."

Frank noticed her head poking out of the tent. "It's killed a lot of people, girlie," he said to her. "And it's all my fault. I should have put him down forty years ago. I didn't pull the trigger when every instinct told me to. I was soft then, but I'm rock hard now."

Ashley scrunched up her face at the unfortunate choice of

words the old man used. She knew what he meant, but—

"Eww... mental picture."

The bear roared again, as if it wanted Frank to pay attention to it. It was suddenly acting very strange for a bear, not that Ashley knew exactly how a bear was supposed to act in this kind of situation.

"Where do you want it, Boo-Boo?" Frank said cockily. "Between the eyes, in the chest? Maybe two in the balls first?"

While that was a huge handgun in his hands, Ashley wasn't sure it was going to be enough to take out something this big. A knife in the eye hadn't fazed it and didn't bears usually take high-powered hunting rifles to bring them down? She'd never seen a movie where Dirty Harry had to shoot a grizzly, so maybe it could do the trick. But if it didn't, then he wasn't going to last long against those massive claws.

Frank had a confident grin on his face, but he still wasn't shooting. He was just staring the animal in the eyes, like he was waiting for it to do something. Why was he insisting on talking to it like it could comprehend him?

"If you think I'm going to take it easy on you after all you've done, you've got another thing coming. Ain't no coming along quietly today. No hospitals, no courts, no jails. No more reintegration. This ends tonight, buddy. So what'll it be? Two in the head?"

The bear growled again. It quickly dropped to all fours and charged the old man. This was it. He was done for. Ashley couldn't look. She shut her eyes until she heard the shots. She heard a man cry out. She knew it was over for all of them now.

THEN

F rank couldn't fight off this guy; he was surprisingly good at staying on top of him and keeping him pinned flat to the ground. He cursed himself for going down to such a punk. His lungs struggled for air. Just when he thought his number was up, something crashed into the killer, knocking him off Frank's body and releasing the grip he'd had fastened on his neck.

"Hands off," Derek said.

Frank leaned up. His vision cleared. Stars twinkled at the edges of his eyes. He saw his buddy standing over him like a great protector with a rifle at the ready.

"'Bout time you got here," Frank said, coughing.

"Sorry, had to take a leak."

"That piss was almost the death of me."

"Me, too. Those beers went right through me."

"Alright, alright, you're here now, just keep your gun trained on this asshole so I can get the cuffs on him."

Frank stood up. He brushed the dirt off his pants, cracked his knuckles and neck. He gave the killer a cocky grin. "Ready to play nice now?"

"The demand for a sacrifice," the man said. "The thing in the darkness. The voice's call."

Then something happened that left Frank dumbfounded. The man cried out, dropped to his hands and knees, and started convulsing. His skin stretched, his clothes ripped off, hair sprouted from his back and arms. The now nude body became covered in fur that kept growing into a shaggy mop. With a sick crunch, his face elongated into a snout. His eyes turned dark, his teeth grew, his ears stretched to a point, his nails became claws. Right before their very eyes, he transformed from a man into a bear. A massive grizzly bear, four times the size of what he had been before.

What the hell was going on?

"Jesus, Mary and Joseph," Frank said. "Would you look at that? He's a fucking bear! He's a fucking bear? How the hell is he a fucking bear?"

"Werebear," Derek said calmly. "You know, like werewolf."

"But he's a fucking bear."

"It's not that complicated," Derek said. "It's like that old movie. Only instead of turning into a wolf, this guy turned into a bear."

Frank took the information in stride. The logic seemed to check out, even if it was completely out of this world. He looked at the tiny handcuffs in his hand and at the bear's huge legs. "I don't think the cuffs are going to fit on him anymore," he said.

The bear roared once in defiance and bared its teeth at the both of them.

"And look at the size of those chompers. He could bite a watermelon in half."

"He could do more than that, Frankie," Derek said, still remaining oddly calm about all of this. "He's got a bite force of about twelve hundred pounds per square inch. He could chomp through a skillet, a tree, even your bones."

"What about two watermelons stacked on top of each other?"

"You just stay away from that mouth, okay?"

"Don't worry," Frank said. "I don't plan on playing lion tamer with that thing."

"Good. Now hold on to this." Derek handed Frank his rifle.

"What the hell are you doing? Just shoot the thing."

"Sorry. It doesn't work that way," Derek said.

NOW

"What's wrong?" the girl screamed.

"What's wrong is that damn bear has taken three shots right in the chest and keeps on coming."

Frank hadn't expected that. He was used to Big Bertha stopping things in their tracks with one shot. She always did when he pulled her trigger. "You sure blew it this time," he said into the barrel.

The bear roared again and took a step towards him.

"Oh hell." He resigned himself to a quick death. "Don't watch this," he said to the girl. "It's not going to be pretty."

The monster's breath was hot and wet. It smelled of rotten meat. When one of those paws lunged out for him, he was finished. He wondered what the headlines might read, assuming they found anything left of him. "Frank Malone, famed River City cop, found partially digested in the woods" or maybe "Frank Malone, hero of River City, missing and presumed to have wandered off. Possibly suffering from dementia." He hoped it would be the former.

Moist breath hit him. He watched the thing rise up and its paw recoil, wondering if he should try to shoot the thing in the testicles. Would *that* kill it or would it just piss it off? It was one of those questions that would never have an answer. He wouldn't live long enough to find out. But he was surprised when death didn't come. Instead, something stopped the beast in its tracks with a heavy thud. He opened his eyes again to see another bear rolling around in the dirt, wrestling with the massive monster like a couple of Vachons. It was an old and grey grizzly, just as big as the other one, but lacking some of the muscle tone. Glowing faintly with a bluish phosphorescence, it looked like it had been wandering in the forest for generations. It looked as ancient as the trees and as tough as their bark. Not unlike Frank.

The two monsters bit and clawed at each other, neither one giving an inch. Bloody gashes formed all over each of their bodies. It wasn't clear who was going to come out on top. They batted and swatted and roared and butted heads. Panting and trampling the forest floor, they took it to each other with a ferocity no human being had ever witnessed before. Well, almost no human being. To Frank, this was another echo of the past playing on repeat.

Frank watched the fight as he calmly reloaded his gun, getting ready to use it once more on the bad one. Would the testicles be the magic spot that stopped the thing? Maybe he would find out the answer to his question.

THEN

Derek grabbed his shirt, ripped it off his body and cried out in a rage. Then he, too, dropped to his hands and knees and started shaking spastically.

"What in the holy hell is going on?" Frank could only watch incredulously as Derek's skin stretched and sprouted hair, his face contorted, his teeth and nails elongated, his unassuming face and football player physique transformed into a giant fucking bear. His fur was shiny and thick, his claws pointed, his teeth as long as Frank's fingers. In a flash, his best friend had become a beast.

"Two of you?"

Derek the bear roared at the other grizzly with a ferocious challenge. The other bear stepped backwards a moment in confusion. It clearly hadn't expected to meet this. But it quickly recovered, then roared back as it stood up on its hind legs and tried to tower over Derek with some kind of intimidation technique.

Derek the bear rose up to meet it eye to eye. For the briefest moment, the two towering giants blocked out the sun. Then, as Frank could only watch with gaping mouth, the two animals crashed together and started fighting.

NOW

"Come on, old buddy, show that asshole a thing or two about how to fight dirty. Just like the last time."

The struggle was titanic, the immovable object meeting the irresistible force. The old bear managed to latch on to the other's neck and held strong, clamping down with all of its remaining strength. But the other beast was much bigger and stronger. It swatted at him repeatedly, battering his old and broken down form with each clawing strike. Despite his vice-like grip, the grey-haired bear weakened. He finally just couldn't hold on anymore and fell to the side, exhausted and bloody. Laying prone in the dirt, his breathing was raspy and weak.

The other beast roared to the heavens in triumph. It dropped to all fours and made ready to finish off its rival. That was all Frank had to see. He took aim at the darkened animal.

THEN

Frank had once seen Stu Hart wrestle a bear in front of twelve hundred people. That bear was tiny and brown, but it had played with the great grappler like a toy, hugging him with its long arms, and rolling around on the dirty old Stampede Wrestling mat until, muzzled of course, it managed to get on top and get a quick three count. The prize had been a bottle of Coke and the spectacle amazed the entire Calgary crowd who hooted and hollered as Stu gentlemanly shook the thing's paw in a truly honourable display of sportsmanship.

But that was a match between a man and a baby. This was two full grown grizzlies fighting like the vicious wild animals they were. Derek, who was now somehow a bear, smashed the other beast up against the rock. He was bigger than it and he clawed at its face, bit its neck, twisted and rolled until he got on top and pressed down as hard as he could on the thing's flattened body. The other beast squirmed and snapped at him, but couldn't escape the pin.

"One-two-three," Frank counted out in awe.

Then, in another sight Frank would never forget, the great grizzly on the bottom began leaking some kind of black fog. The wispy substance seemed to evaporate out of its fur, into the air, into the soil, into the trees. As more and more of the strange dark mist left the animal, the thing shrank back into a man. The fur recoiled into the skin, the nails shrank back to human ones, the face retreated from muzzle to nose. Now he was dwarfed by the massive grizzly on top of him. Naked and completely at the mercy of the victor, he held his hands up in submission.

Derek the bear roared once in its face and for a moment, Frank thought he was going to bite the man's head off, but instead, he simply held him down. The strange white phosphorescence that encompassed him began flowing out, just like the dark energy of the other. The glow seeped into the trees, the ground, the air, the stars, enriched the colours around them, somehow made the forest seem more alive and healthy. The stars shone just a little brighter and the forest floor pulsed with new life.

The Derek bear leaned forward with his snout and took hold of the man. As he shrank back into his original form, his human teeth held onto the other man's neck. When the transformations were complete, two nude men stood before Frank, locked in the remnants of a bear wrestling match.

Both of their naked bodies were covered in scratches, bleeding out in deep gashes that looked like they were going to need a hell of a lot of stitches to close. The great swaths of hair that had once completely covered them had turned back into normal manly hairy backs. Their manhoods dangled between their legs and their flabby, white skin glistened with sweat in the light.

Derek released his teeth clamped on the man's neck and pushed himself off his vanquished opponent. He wiped his hands proudly. "That's how we do it," he said enthusiastically.

"One man-bear champion wins, the other loses. Survival of the fittest."

Frank slapped the cuffs on the loser. He pulled him up to his feet and shook his head in disgust when he saw the total submission in the man's defeated, bloody face. The strange black glow in his eyes was gone; they'd returned to their original cool grey. The dark haze that had enveloped him had been replaced with some pretty nasty BO.

"Nice try, Ranger Smith, but it looks like you weren't the only one who could turn into Yogi."

NOW

T he old bear lay unmoving on the ground, unable to defend itself. It tried to lift a paw to take another swat at the larger creature, but the poor thing was so weak, the battered limb collapsed under its own weight.

The blueish phosphorescence that surrounded it began to seep into the larger bear, evaporating into its own darkened halo. The life seeping away, the poor creature looked like it was deflating.

The other grizzly swung its great maw to Frank and roared in triumph. But Frank had taken the opportunity to calmly put his gun right up to its head and fired point blank from only millimetres away. There would be no mistakes this time. Three quick BLAMS pierced the eye socket and skull and two more between its legs and it was all over. The beast toppled to the ground, its head now a bowling bowl. It lay unmoving. The energies that encompassed it began slinking away, back into the trees and ground, stars and air, letting those that it had been absorbing from the poor weak old elder go free in the same way, restoring life and colour to the clearing.

THEN

"I told you already, my name isn't Ranger Smith! It's Ranger—"

"I don't care what your name is," Frank said, cutting the man off. "I'm calling you under arrest."

The man struggled in the bonds, but Frank had put them behind his back this time. He wouldn't break through or be able to use them against him.

"Those are one hundred percent solid Canadian steel, Smith, you're locked up tighter than my ex-wife's who-ha."

"You can't possibly contain the forces of the natural order," the ranger said. "You or your friend. They are coming back. I will be here waiting for them. They've chosen me, you know. They—"

"Oh, shut the fuck up," Derek said. "You have no idea what you're talking about. You weren't chosen for shit."

"No, no, I was. I heard the call, and I was given the greatest gift of—"

Derek slapped him across the face. "You really are a moron. You were no one special. The forest seeks out a host to embody and you were here. Your weak mind was open and that was all it took."

"Bet you didn't expect me to come with backup, eh, ranger?

Shit, even I didn't realize it, which makes it even more of a shocker."

Frank proudly waved his hand to Derek who was putting on his flannel shirt gingerly. His wounds hampered his ability to button up. It barely covered his great girth and did nothing to hide his dangling cock and balls. His pants lay shredded on the forest floor and he picked them up, eyeing them with a frown.

"Well now, these aren't going to be much good, are they?"

"You should have taken them off before you changed. Am I going to have to look at your Johnson the whole way back?"

"Sorry I didn't have time to drop trou' before saving your ass. I'm just thankful I could get the shirt off, I paid ten bucks for it at Merv's."

"I guess I shouldn't complain. You could be as buck naked as him."

"You got a problem with the naked male form?" the ranger asked.

"Of course not. But I don't know how the hell I would explain to the RCMP boys showing up with *two* buck ass naked men covered in bloody scratches out of the woods."

"Just tell them it was one hell of a bush party."

"I guess it was, in a way."

The ranger turned to look at Derek as he adjusted his shirt. "What are you? Why do you have the powers that I was promised were mine alone?"

"Shut up." Derek slapped him across the face again, this time with more force than Frank had expected. "You're nothing but an instrument of something you don't understand."

Frank himself didn't quite understand what in the hell was going on here either. He kicked Ranger Smith in the ass. The man lurched forward. "Yeah, what he said. Say, uh, Derek. If it just so happened that there were other people here who while maybe not instruments, still didn't understand just what in the fuck was going on, you'd, you know, fill them in. Right?"

The ranger was about to speak but Derek shot him a glance, and he mutely dropped his head in defeat. Frank waited a moment while Derek finished buttoning up his shirt. He touched one of the trees and closed his eyes, as if he was listening to something being said through the bark. But he stayed quiet. There didn't seem to be any further explanation coming. Then, he let go and took a deep breath.

"Things are back in balance again," he said. "We can get moving."

"Uh, okay," Frank said.

"No, I won't go. They will come back to me. They spoke to me of revenge and—"

"And you failed," Derek said. "It's all a part of the cycle. The forces of nature build and build and finally lash out. Then a counter force comes and puts things right. You played your part, I played mine. It's the way it has always been and always will be. You did not earn what you were given nor can you ever receive the gifts again. Sorry, I didn't make the rules."

The ranger looked to speak but somehow Derek's words hit him deep enough to break his thoughts. Frank pushed him forward and he began walking. They followed closely behind the nude man. Derek held the gun over his shoulder and glowed with a kind of post-coital glee. It was nice to see his teeth back to human size. He pulled a huge wiry hair out of his mouth and tossed it to the ground. They walked for a few moments in silence before Frank finally couldn't stay quiet.

"So," Frank said.

"So," Derek said.

"That was a thing."

"Sure was."

"We good?" Frank asked, wondering how long his best friend had been like this.

"Yup," Derek said.

"And him?"

"He's not turning back any time soon."

"Good to hear."

They walked back down the ridge, towards the campground. Frank used the gun to prod the ranger in the back. He stumbled forward, but kept moving.

Frank stayed silent for a while, letting the noises of the renewed forest surround them, hoping Derek would enlighten him more. He tried to go over what he had just seen to understand it all. Two men turning into bears then fighting. One bear wins, they both turn back. This was a little beyond anything they'd ever gone over in training. He needed answers.

"Okay, old buddy," Frank said. "I've got a couple of questions here."

"I'll bet you do." Derek laughed. "Fire away. We've got a few clicks to walk before we get to the truck."

"Right. Let me think about the best place to start. Hmm, I guess the first thing is, since when the hell did you turn into a fucking bear? I've known you since we were six and I ain't ever seen that shit before."

Derek laughed again, a deep-throated belly laugh. He patted Frank on the shoulder. "Frankie, there are more things in heaven and earth than dreamt of in your philosophy."

NOW

Ashley knew she had to leave the tent to see what had gone on. She'd been scrunched up in a ball hoping and praying that the monster would leave her alone after it killed the old man. She'd heard sounds of a struggle and lots of animal cries, then gunshots.

"Hello?" she meekly said.

After that last couple of shots, there'd been no other noises. She had no idea what happened to the old man, or where he'd even come from. If the bear was eating him, surely she'd hear crunching or chewing or something, right? But it was deathly silent out there. Maybe he'd killed the animal instead? He hadn't called her to tell her it was safe. But what were those other sounds of a struggle? She mulled over what she should do before finally, taking a deep breath, she turned to her injured companion.

"David, I'm going to go check," she whispered. He seemed to have fallen unconscious. He was still breathing, though. She picked up her tossed can of bear spray, turned from him, slowly unzipped the tent and crawled outside.

"Hel—"

She couldn't even finish the word. What she saw was beyond belief.

The old man was alive. He crouched over a naked man on the ground. He laid a flannel shirt over his slashed body. The man was breathing, but barely. His body looked like a jigsaw puzzle. He was covered in scars and gaping wounds. His weathered flesh was torn into sections, bleeding badly. She could see the crimson of muscles and the white of bone inside the cuts.

But there was another man laying on the ground nearby. He was also naked. He wasn't moving and with good cause. A huge chunk of his head had been blown off. Brains, bone and blood leaked from the shattered skull and soaked into the forest floor. His crotch was a mangled mess, too. A disgusting gap between his legs poured even more blood, with long strands of innards slowly sliding out.

The sight of so much gore made her retch. She dropped the bear spray as the hotdogs came back up and she decorated the side of her tent in avant garde food art.

"Don't worry about it," the old man said, seeing her now. "That's how everyone reacts the first time they see insides on the outside."

Ashley wiped her mouth on the back of her hand. She watched in confusion as the man checked on the wounded senior. He was looking for a pulse. He found it, but his face looked grim.

"What happened here?" she asked. "Where's the bear?"

"There," the old man said, pointing to the naked dead man. "Here, too." He motioned to the other wounded man.

"I don't understand. Those aren't bears, they're people?"

"Lady, there are more things in heaven and earth than are dreamt of in your philosophy."

THEN

"Let me get this straight," Frank said as they marched down the trail. "You can turn into a bear whenever you want."

"Not whenever I want," Derek said. "There are conditions."

"Like a driver's license?"

"Not exactly."

"Full moon? Is it controllable? Could you, say, turn into a bear to surprise your baby girl's first suitor? Put the fear of Yogi into him good?"

"It doesn't really work like that," Derek said.

"What about for Halloween? That'd be one hell of a costume. Save you all kinds of time and money."

"I think they'd call animal control if I did that."

"What about as a prank? You bring a woman back to your place, tell her you're going to make yourself more comfortable. She thinks that means silk pyjamas and then BAM, you come out full Smokey, scare the pants right off her."

"Frank, Frank, Frank. It's not like that," Derek said. "It's not some party trick. It's not a game. It's not even something you're supposed to let others see."

"But I saw it."

"And I should kill you for that."

"But of course you're not going to do that."

"Of course."

"Why not?"

"Because you were just as much a part of this as I was. I was gifted the change in order to save your life."

"And thanks for that, but when in the hell did all this start? Was this a puberty thing?"

"No," Derek said. "I've been me since I was born. But I'm not like you."

"Yeah, no shit. You're half-bear."

"Werebear. I told you that it's called werebear. And it's not something you're born with. It's not like I'm descended from a long line of them who used to prowl the forests all over Canada until the white man came. This mystical line of warriors who now, unfortunately, have only a few of left and—"

"Is your dad one, too?" Frank interrupted. "What about your mom? Christ. I wonder what that bedroom is like. That's one case of if it's rocking, I'm sure as hell not knocking."

"They weren't bears when they had sex, Frank."

"But they could have been, right? How would you really know?"

Derek paused and rubbed his chin in thought. "You know, I never thought about that."

"There might be money in that blue movie. The Werebear in Miss Jones."

"Look, Frank. You don't get it. This change only happened because I heard the call. It could have been anyone really, as long as they have an open mind and are close to nature."

"Shit, I'm those things, why didn't I get to turn into a big fucking bear?"

NOW

"Is he going to be okay?" Ashley asked Frank as he tended to the injured old man. "He looks in rough shape."

"What's your name, kid?"

"Ashley."

"Ashley, I'm Frank. I'm a- I used to be a cop."

"A cop?"

"Retired, unfortunately."

"But you—"

"This is my friend, Derek. He's dying. He's not built for this stuff anymore. He's old and beaten down like me. But he heard the call and he did it again anyway. He saved my life and yours. He's a real hero."

"Did he chase the bear away?"

"You could say that he chased away the animal inside."

"I—"

"But it cost him, see. He's just too badly hurt and too old to heal. There's nothing I can do. Nothing anyone can do."

She turned back to the other naked man. "Then who was he? He looks like the ranger at the gate when we came in—why is he dead and naked?"

"That right there is the echo of the infamous Ranger Smith," Frank said. "I don't know if he's his son or cousin or neighbour from down the street or—"

"Wait, so the ranger from the gate got shot in the head? By who? And why? And—"

"This all started before your time, Ashley. Before mine, too, to be honest. See, this story started forty, fifty million years ago. This is just another rerun."

THEN

"So, Ranger Smith here is, what, a rogue werebear? Has he gone rabid? Is he from some kind of evil clan that you're sworn to fight? That sort of thing?"

"Nope," Derek said. "It's nothing that organized. The forest is a living thing, just like you and me really. And a part of that life is defending itself against invaders. Invaders like us."

"Invaders? We just came to hunt and fish."

"Exactly. See, it's a cycle. When the balance gets too out of whack, the forest takes action. In this case it reached out to Ranger Smith here and corrupted him. He let the spirit of vengeance take over. He was given the gift of transformation and drew life from those he killed."

"Like a vampire. Shit, a vampire werebear. Is that even possible?"

"Because he was alone out here, the spirit found him and took him over. He's not a vampire or anything. It was all in the quest for revenge for—"

"Camping."

"Sure. And building roads and cabins and docks and—"

"So you just hate progress, eh, Smith?" Frank said.

"I'm merely a servant to the great—"

"Shut the fuck up."

"So how did you transform?"

"I wouldn't have had any idea if the forest hadn't reached out to me, too."

"Why the fuck did it choose you?"

"I told you, you lose something surrounded by concrete and skyscrapers all day. I was here with an open mind and heard the voices."

"So you can't do it again? Shit, if I could, I'd be doing it every weekend and—"

"It's not that simple, Frank. It's a part of the circle of life. I was allowed to transform because he had tasted the flesh of man. He'd let the darkness overtake him and was moving beyond his mission. It's a part of the ritual. The battle between two to determine the path of life. Does the forest remain peaceful and tranquil or does it become a cursed place of evil and—"

"This is all getting fucking convoluted. Who made those rules?" Frank asked, disappointed. "Sounds like a real killjoy if you ask me."

"The who is lost to time, old friend. The why as well. All I know is, in this day and age, no one remembers how long this has been happening or how often it's going to happen in the future. Maybe it's every hundred years, maybe every five or twenty or thousand or—"

"Wait, did you say eat the flesh of man? This guy's a cannibal?"

"He wasn't truly human at the time," Derek said. "I told you he was the acting embodiment of the anger of the natural world and—"

"Humans are delicious," Ranger Smith said.

"Shut up." Frank butted him with the rifle.

"He's not wrong," Derek said. "People are delicious. I heard the same voices he did, but I'm not a cannibal or an asshole. I fought for the other side."

"How did you turn? What did it feel like?"

"I have a feeling it might have hurt a lot more if I hadn't been drinking Jack all weekend. In fact, it hurts right now, so I think I could use a refill."

"That's the first smart thing you've said all afternoon."

NOW

Ashley patted down Matt's corpse, doing her best not to look at his split-open head. Flies were already gorging on the leaking fluids. In his leg pocket, she found his phone. Miraculously it had survived and still showed a signal. She grabbed his limp arm and used his thumb to unlock the device.

"I'm calling the paramedics," she said when it flashed open. "Maybe they'll be able to get here in time to help."

"It's too late for me," Derek coughed. Blood splattered over his chin.

"Don't say that, old buddy," Frank said. "You don't look that bad really. Just a few paper cuts. Some polysporin and a few bandaids and you'll be good as new."

It was obvious that Frank was lying to his friend. Ashley could see bone sticking out inside a few of the larger gashes on his side. He was growing paler by the moment as his breathing slowed. She was no doctor, but even she could tell that it wouldn't be much longer now.

"No, it's true," Derek said. "You can't bullshit me, Frankie."

"You've known me too long, I guess."

"Heh." Derek coughed, and blood bubbled up from a hole in his chest. "We sure had some crazy adventures, didn't we?"

"Sure did. This one is right up there with the best of 'em."

"I wanted to thank you, Frankie. For springing me. For getting me out here. I didn't want to die in that place."

"I didn't want you to die in this place either."

"You did your best."

"No, this is all my fault," Frank said. "If I'd just kept a better eye on you, you wouldn't be bleeding out in the middle of nowhere right now."

"I was called here, Frank. This was what I was supposed to do. Unfinished business. I have a feeling once you ID that guy, you'll find he was blood with Smith. You were right all those years ago. The corruption he absorbed, it tainted his line. All it took was for someone, his son maybe, to come out here and for the cycle to start all over again."

"See, what'd I tell you? If I'd just blasted him, none of this would have happened."

Derek coughed. "Maybe, maybe not. It's a part of it all, Frank. The cycle. But things are speeding up. The whole world's getting out of balance. The forest was just fighting back."

"Tell that to all the corpses out there."

"The blood will appease the spirits. For a while."

"So what about the other guy?"

"It's good the girl killed him. He was about to become another one. There's no way we could have stopped two forces of nature like that."

"One stopped you bad enough."

Ashley called 9-1-1 as Frank and Derek talked. Their words were private, and she let them have their moment.

The dispatcher answered and Ashley told them where she was and that there were injured and dead that needed attention. When she was off the line, Frank was giving Derek a sip of water from one of the bottles strewn about the campsite. He gently cradled the man's head, giving him a drink like to a baby. There was obviously a lot of love and history between the two, but Frank was betraying no emotion on his face. He laughed at something Derek said and took a drink of the water himself.

"Help is on the way," Ashley interjected, snapping them out of their private moment.

"Hear that, buddy?" Frank said. "You might just pull through after all."

"Fat chance I'm going back to that nursing home. I go in there, I can't even remember my name anymore."

"At least you'll be alive."

"That's a fate worse than death. No," he said glumly. "While I can still think clearly, while the spirits are still talking to me, you gotta make sure I don't go back. You gotta let me join them. It's all a part of the cycle. I become another voice for the next forest warrior. Please, let me go. End it for me, Frankie."

"I can't do that."

"What do you think is better? I bleed out slowly while the girl watches? Or I go back and my brain turns to mush? Then I can't hear anything."

"Aren't there any dames in the place you could—"

"I look like I'm in any condition to do anything with 'em if there were?"

"There's got to be something you—"

"I thought we were pals," Derek said, cutting him off. "I want to join the choir."

Frank sighed deeply as he realized he wouldn't change the

man's mind. "So what are you asking?"

THEN

"What do we tell the cops about all this?" Frank asked Derek. "I doubt the, uh, forest wants all this getting out. The papers get wind of there being werebears and nature forces and all that, you'd have all the eggheads in Ottawa down here messing with the place."

"He's not going to convince anyone." Derek poked Ranger Smith. "He knows they'll lock him up in the nuthouse."

"So we just say the maulings were caused by a bear and no one is the wiser? We can't let this guy go. What if he transforms in custody?"

"He can't. And no one's going to buy that he could do to the victims what was obviously done by a bear. He lost the fight. He's banished from the forest forever. The forces of nature would never grant a loser the powers again. He's cut off from that world now."

"I could just shoot him," Frank said. "That would solve the problem."

"Hey—" Ranger Smith said.

"I couldn't let you do that. This is a part of the cycle. One winner. One loser. The loser never hears the call of nature again and lives their lives in an empty pit of despair knowing they're a failure."

314

"Not good enough. We hand the man over to the authorities with what charge? Being a loser?"

"He did eat people. Can't he be convicted for cannibalism?"

"That's the angle then. Let the Mounties pump his stomach and find out who he chowed down on."

"I also ate a deer and—"

"Imagine the press," Derek said. "Weirdo loner posing as a park ranger snaps and eats dead campers. What's the sentence for cannibalism?"

"I'll have to check the manual on that, but we can definitely pin the Satanic Christmas stuff on him. Defiling corpses has got to be more than a simple misdemeanour. What do you think, Ranger Smith? Rotting in jail sound like a good deal?"

"I'll find a way to break the curse," he said. "They'll listen to me. I'll have my reven—"

"Shut up." Frank butted the man in the head with his rifle.

Derek laughed a great big bear laugh.

"I'll tell you something," Frank said. "When this is all over, I aim to sit and get so blasted drunk I don't remember the image of your dangling cock and balls or the fact that you turned into a bear."

"That can be arranged."

"And I don't want to even look at another tree for years."

Derek looked down at his exposed dick and then the vibrant forest surroundings. He raised an eyebrow. "If you can keep a secret, then I promise to never mention this as long as I live."

NOW

I n the basement of the downtown River City Police
Department precinct, Jacob the coroner finished the
last bite of his hoagie and wiped the Italian dressing
off his chin. He rolled up the paper wrapper and threw it
into a nearby garbage can, already overflowing with trash.
On his computer screen, a Matrix-themed screensaver cast
green light over a stack of paperwork messily crammed into
a corner.

He shook the mouse and pulled up his email inbox. There
was a new message from the forensics lab in Toronto.

Opening it up, he found a response to a sample he'd sent in
over a month ago.

He lit up as he read the results.

"Hey, Becky." He waved his assistant over. The brunette
with the thick glasses looked up from her desk.

"What's the matter, Jacob?"

"Remember that cold case I sent out east?"

"The unidentified person found in the Whiteshell in the
seventies?"

"Yeah, the guy nobody claimed, and no one reported
missing."

"What about him?"

"Turns out we've got an ID now."

"Really? How?"

She rose from her chair and came over to his desk.

Jacob clicked the link in the email and came to a police record. "This guy," he said and pointed to the image of a man taken from an arrest.

"That doesn't make any sense," she said. "That says he's currently twenty-two. That puts him born almost twenty years after the body was discovered."

"Right. So unless he somehow went back in time to avoid appearing in court for this dangerous driving ticket, I'd say those clowns out east are trying to mess with us."

"I guess you really don't have an ID, do you?" she said snarkily.

"No, I guess we do not."

"This is almost as big a nothing-burger as those archeologists who found that can of bear spray mixed in with voyageur artifacts and thought they'd discovered some heretofore unknown element of French fur trapping. You know the one. Turned out to be a completely common brand sold everyday at Canadian Tire and—"

"Okay, okay, you don't have to rub it in."

He reached for his can of orange crush and sucked the last drops out through the bent and chewed plastic straw.

NOW

Ashley sat in her lawn chair, sipping a warm beer, trying not to look at the headless corpses of Josh and Jack, the mauled body of Beth, the split cranium of Matt, or the unmoving battered form of David. She knew this scene would be burned in her mind forever and the less she focused on the gore, the better it would be. The nightmares would come in time. For now, there was calm and quiet as the sun began to rise and the forest came back to life.

She heard a faint cough from the tent. It was David coming to. In all the insanity, she'd forgotten that he wasn't dead. At least, she hoped he wasn't.

She leapt from her lawn chair and ran over to him, laying in the open tent. His face was red, purple and swollen, but his eyes were partway cracked, and he showed a flash of recognition at seeing her.

"David. You're still alive."

"Thanks for remembering," he wheezed.

"Don't worry, help is on the way. Just hang on."

"Is it over?"

She nodded grimly. "It's just you and me left."

"Everyone is—"

"Everyone," she said, understanding what he meant.

"So it was a bear?"

"One hell of a bear."

"Did you get it?"

Ashley looked to the dead ranger and then off in the direction Frank and Derek had gone. In the distance came the loud crack of a rifle blast. So he had done it. He'd helped put the old man out of his misery and let him go the way he wanted to.

"Sure did," she said and sat down next to him.

* * * *

Frank returned later, alone, feeling tired, like the events of the past day and a half had finally caught up to him. His best friend had gone out the way he asked. He was at rest and one with the forest. Now Frank needed to lay down and sleep for a week. He wasn't young anymore and spending so much time roaming the woods, shooting at bears, not drinking and fishing enough and then finally burying his best friend had taken more out of him than it would have a decade or two ago.

As soon as help arrived, he'd climb in the back seat of his car and just pass out. But first, there was something he had to do. Derek's one last request.

"You kids going to be okay if I go take care of something?"

Ashley looked up from her spot in the tent next to the injured hippie. "Someone else you have to, uh, help?"

"You could say that."

He left them at the campsite and returned to his car, exactly where he'd parked it yesterday. He went to the trunk, popped it and looked inside. There, just as Derek had promised, were

319

two children, a boy and a girl, both sound asleep. They stirred from the noise of the trunk opening and looked up at him, confused. The little forest people were real after all.

"Grampa?" the boy asked.

"Sorry, kiddo. I'm just a retired cop."

"Where's the nice man who told us to hide in here?" the little girl asked.

"Oh, he's still around somewhere. He just had to go away for a while."

"Did he find our mom and dad?"

Frank gently helped the kids out of the trunk and on to the ground. "There's something you should know about your mom and dad."

"I bet they'll be super proud of how good of hiders we were," the little girl said.

"Yup. This was the safest place you could have stayed. There was a bear out here, you know."

The little boy nodded. "Yes, other grampa told us to be very quiet and keep out of sight. He was really nice. He gave us Daddy juice."

"He was, at that," Frank said as he spotted a few open beers in the trunk.

"Mister, I'm real sorry, but there was no place to pee in there and I really had to go."

That was when Frank caught a whiff of the strong urine smell emanating from his trunk.

"That stuff goes right through you, eh?" he said as he heard the sounds of sirens approaching up the winding forest road. He took the kids by the hands and turned to watch the emergency vehicles pull into the campground parking lot.

THEN

Y ou don't understand, they were all dressed like fur traders, and they spoke French. They were doing some kind of historical reenactment or movie or I don't know. Things got out of hand. I don't know how long I was with them, but, as soon as I could, I ran."

"And you came right here?" the ranger asked.

"I don't know where anything is. All the trails are wrong, the signs, the cars. Nothing seems like it should and—"

"Easy, easy, ma'am. You're safe now. I've got a radio here and we can contact the RCMP post down in Kenora. They'll send someone out to help."

"Radio?" Mandy said, confused. "Don't you have a cell-phone? Or a—"

The face the man made showed he didn't know what she was talking about. "Hey, be glad they sprung for the radio. Up until last year we were still using telegraphs out here."

She began to look around the ranger cabin. The map, the photos, the calendar, everything was out of date.

"Is this some kind of museum?" she asked. "Where's the—"

The man shut the door, and she spun to see him silhouetted by the rising sun through the windows.

"Just relax, I'll take good care of you. You know, it gets so lonely out here in the woods all by yourself. You go so long without seeing anyone, almost feels like you're hibernating."

There was something very wrong with his eyes.

"I don't understand," she said. "These dates say nineteen—"

When she turned back to him, he'd somehow appeared right next to her. "They told me what I have to do. I have to give you my essence."

"You have to what?"

"It's a part of the cycle. You're going to have my son."

She tried to back away, but he had her hands held in a vice-like grip. She tried to scream but something flew from his mouth, some kind of dark fog, and filled hers. The heat choked out the air and she found her strength leaving her.

She fell backwards onto the small bed and could only watch helplessly as he did what he wanted.

NOW

I t had taken some doing to find the old man's office. It wasn't listed on Google, nor did it have any website or social media accounts. Ashley had to search through an honest-to-God Yellow Pages to find it and even then, it was above a barber shop.

'The Frank Malone Detective Agency' the sign on the door read. As she and David approached, the door opened and Frank led an elderly man out. His arm was draped over the shorter man's shoulder.

"It's right where I told you. Parked and waiting at Rock Peak Lake. Took me longer than I expected, but I found it just like I promised. If I had a hitch, I'd have brought it in myself, but I don't, so just go and get her."

"Thanks again, Mr. Malone. You really do fine work. I'm going to tell all my friends about you for sure."

"Great, I could use some more clients. Now you go and have fun with that trailer, okay?"

The old man beamed as he walked past Ashley towards the stairs.

The building had to be as old as Frank was, maybe older. It wasn't much to look at, one of those historic old warehouses that populated the exchange district downtown. The place was cleaned up enough to have kept most of the old charm. It smelled of dust and mildew and barber shop chemicals. Faint particles danced in the sunlight that shone in from the large windows.

Frank saw Ashley and David and smiled.

"You kids looking for the barber? He's downstairs."

"It's me, Mr. Malone," Ashley said.

"You're Malone? Then who am I?"

"No, I'm not you, I'm Ashley."

"Should I know you?"

"Come on, Ashley?"

"You need a detective, Ashley, or you just sight-seeing?"

"No, Ashley. From Rock Peak Lake."

"Rock Peak Lake? What year?"

"Rock Peak Lake a week ago?"

"Oh, I didn't recognize you all cleaned up. Nice to see you're alright after that whole situation. What brings you in?"

"This is David," she said, introducing the man at her side. "He wanted to come and thank you for all that you did."

"David," Frank said. "Which one were you? Not the one with the knife in his head, were you?"

"Nope," David said, sharing a confused glance at Ashley. "I was the guy who survived two bear attacks and was beaten unconscious on the ground the whole time. If you hadn't rescued us, I'd be bear food and not even know it."

"Better not to know, kid. Trust me."

"Right. Anyway, I just wanted to say that I appreciate what you did and I'm glad I'm not dead."

"You sure?"

"Yup."

"You came all the way up here just to say that?"

"I would have called, but you don't seem to have a working phone number."

"Really? Give me a second." Frank walked back through the door into his office. They watched him step over to his phone, pick it up and hold the receiver to his ear. Finding it dead, he tapped the buttons a few times. Ashley was surprised to see him still using an old rotary phone. It must have come with the office or something. Frank checked the cord, then disappeared behind the desk and came back up, hitting his head on the edge.

"Fuck," he spat, then came back over to them. "Another mystery solved. The case of not getting any calls for a week. Seems like I forgot that I left it unplugged."

"Why'd you do that?" David asked.

"I can't afford a secretary, and I don't think Gino downstairs would appreciate the thing ringing off the hook all weekend."

"You're that busy?" Ashley asked.

"Not right now. But I could be."

"Right," she said. "Well, I, uh, also wanted to thank you. I also appreciate not being dead."

She and David were holding hands and Frank finally noticed. He raised an eyebrow. "You two kids an item or what?"

"We both bonded over our mutual appreciation for not being dead."

"There are worse things to build a relationship on, that much I can say from experience."

"Can you answer me a question, Mr. Malone?" David asked.

"No, I won't be the best man at your wedding."

"I wanted to know what year it is."

"What year? That's an easy one." Frank walked over to his

desk and picked up his 1993 Angie Everhart calendar. "Why, it… oh hell, I forgot I kept this for the articles. Ashley, what year is it?"

"I keep telling David, but he thinks it should be nineteen seventy-seven. The doctors think it's a symptom of his concussion. You know he doesn't even remember Star Wars?"

"You're lucky, kid, some of us wish we could forget it."

"We're not even sure David's his real name. The only record of David Horton in the provincial records has him born in nineteen fifty-two."

"I can't explain it," David said. "I was so sure, but everything here says otherwise. I guess it's just going to take some time for my brain to recover from the injuries."

"But I'll be right here to help you. Even with the traumatic head injury, he's the kindest and most thoughtful man I've ever met. Almost old-fashioned."

"Hey, old-fashioned never goes out of style. But I wish you kids all the luck in the world. Although surviving the bear attack shows you both already have it."

They looked at each other and smiled. Nothing was certain just yet. They'd bonded during the time David had been in hospital. Ashley had gone to see him every day. There was something about being the only survivors of a brutal massacre that brought them together. But it was still early. They were navigating the fallout and the loss of so many of her friends, but the future did look brighter than it had been for a while.

"I know that look," Frank said, grinning. "Why don't you kids step into my office and we can have a toast? Let's say to new beginnings."

THEN

"And you're sure he's going to be secure here?" Frank asked as he watched the orderlies take away Ranger Jones. He was tied up in a straitjacket and moved with the lethargic gait of a man heavily sedated, but appearances could be deceptive. The man was a killer and belonged in a real jail.

"Of course, officer," the doctor said. The man held a clipboard and marked in something with a freshly sharpened number two pencil. Frank would have to make sure he knew not to let one of those get too close to the sicko. "We pride ourselves on security both for our patients and for the community. Mr. Jones will get the best of care away from those he might hurt."

"It's not care I think he needs, doc," Frank said. "It's a life sentence."

"Yes, of course. But you must understand that we have diagnosed him as mentally ill. He is totally divorced from reality. He lacks the part of the personality able to differentiate between right and wrong that the rest of us take for granted."

"He ate people and strung their guts up like popcorn strands."

"I can send you a copy of my report if you'd like."

"I can send you the Polaroids of the corpses if you'd like," Frank said curtly.

"Poor Mr. Jones thought he was the bear doing all those things. It's a most strange case."

"I was there," Frank said. "I brought him in."

"Rest assured that he'll be well looked after until the day comes when he has been judged safe to return to the community. He'll start with day passes at first, then a gradual intro—"

"Just make sure every T on the form is crossed before you go and do something like that. This guy's an animal and doesn't belong out there."

"You have your diagnosis, and I have mine."

As the man disappeared behind the doors of the institution, led away into the care of the province, Frank sighed. He didn't trust a place like this or a doctor like that, but he had no choice. This was the decision of the judge and he had to live with it. But he'd be watching to make sure the man didn't get out.

"Alright, doc. You do what you have to, to try and cure the man, but take it from me. He's not human."

Frank turned and left, knowing that he'd have to make sure Jones stayed locked away for the rest of his life. It was a promise he'd never forget.

* * * *

Frank forgot all about his promise to make sure Ranger Jones stayed locked up for the rest of his life. Things just kept coming up.

NOW

"**N**ow, Dad, this TV will be perfect for you here. Look," Billy said as he placed the small flatscreen television on the nightstand facing the bed. "It fits here and there's a remote and everything."

Billy flicked the set on and stepped back as it booted to life.

"—and the bear killed multiple campers before it was brought down by hunters and natural resources staff. Authorities tell us it was a nearly one-thousand-pound grizzly."

"Shit," the old man said as he lay on the bed.

"Now, Dad, there's nothing wrong with the set. Look, the picture is crystal clear. Better than that old Zenith you had at home. That thing was a real antique. You must have had it forty years or—"

"I don't want to be here," the old man said.

"We've gone over that. You can't look after yourself anymore. Pine Hollow had a sudden opening and we had to jump on it before someone else took it. They'll take very good care of you and—"

"Bullshit. You're leaving me here."

"Kids, leave me alone with Grandpa for a moment." Billy waved his kids out of the white room and when he was sure they were gone, he turned back to his dad. The man was almost eighty, stooped, suffering from a myriad of ailments, and completely impossible. It had been a huge fight to get him out of the house, but here they were, and he was going to have to face up to it.

"—the park has been the sight of numerous bear attacks over the years with the last such occasion in nineteen sev—"

"That's me. That's me it's happening to," an elderly woman screamed from outside the room.

Billy turned to see a withered woman in a dark shawl sitting in a wheelchair in the hallway. She was pointing at the television with wide eyes.

"Now, Amanda," an orderly said. "You can't go around harassing the other guests. Let's get you back to your room and—"

"I'm not supposed to be here. I was from now. I should be with my friends. I'm young and—"

"I'm really sorry, folks," the orderly said. "I'll take care of this." He pushed the chair away while the old woman shrieked unintelligibly.

"See?" Billy's dad said. "You're abandoning me with crazy people. You're—"

Billy lowered the volume. "We're not going to abandon you here, Dad. We'll visit as often as we can. This is for your own good and—"

"Bullshit. Bullshit."

"Don't be like this. You'll have a wonderful time here and they'll make sure you're comfortable."

"Fuck off."

"Okay. We're going. We'll come back when you've had more time to adjust."

"At least put something good on the TV," his dad said.

330

Billy changed the channel, found an old rerun of—
"The Gong Show, that's fucking better."

NOW

M r. Edward Ulster was happier than he'd been in ages. He'd found his missing trailer at last. He'd thought it was gone forever, but it was back and he could hardly contain himself. It was amazing to him how so much happiness could be contained within a simple object.

He didn't stop to think about how strange it was that the trailer had been parked in his spot at Rock Peak Lake, it was just a fortuitous coincidence. To think that the thief would take it there.

"Strange world."

One thing was for sure, it made picking it up much more convenient.

He pulled up to the parking spot and saw his trailer exactly where Mr. Malone had promised it would be. It was a little dirty and covered in fallen leaves, but it was there in one piece and that was all that mattered. Whoever had taken it, hadn't vandalized it beyond just simple neglect. He had to be thankful for that at least.

Edward parked and got out. He took a deep breath of the clean forest air and approached the trailer. All the stickers pasted on the back told of a lifetime of fun. Just memories now, but so much a part of who he and his wife had been.

The places they'd seen and gone told of lives well lived. He opened the door and walked inside.

It was almost exactly as it was when he'd last seen it. Although, it looked like someone had used it recently. The beds were turned over and there were clothes everywhere. Some were men's, others women's.

"Some hitchhiker or hippie kid probably," he said to himself.

No matter. He could clean it all up and it would be as good as new. But there was one thing that bothered him and that was the horrible smell. He couldn't put a finger on it. Either an animal had died in here or—

He nearly fainted when he saw the massive log of—

* * * *

"Shit," Frank said, suddenly sitting upright in his chair. "I left my fishing rod in the river."

THE END OF ANOTHER FRANK MALONE
ADVENTURE

About the Author

Author, filmmaker, martial artist, collector, gamer, dad; Winnipeg based I.D. Russell has been crafting a shared universe of books and films for the past decade and a half. Beginning with the feature films *The Killing Death* and *Cybernetic Showdown* and continuing with the *High School Hell* and *Revengist* book series, his crazy comedy/horror/action stories have found an international audience. *Beyond the Dark Forest* is another book in the continuing adventures of River City Police Officer Frank Malone and is set during his retirement post *High School Hell Book 3: Heart of Flesh*. Many more books have been written detailing Frank's wild life, so stay tuned!

Check out *The Killing Death* and *Cybernetic Showdown* now streaming on Amazon Prime, Tubi, Vimeo, and Gumroad. Visit the YouTube pages *Ringo Jones Productions* and *Jeremy Sockman Movie Reviews* for additional content or click to www.ringojones.com to stay up to date on all upcoming work!

Follow on Facebook, Twitter, Instagram, and YouTube!

You can connect with me on:

🌐 http://ringojones.com

📘 https://www.facebook.com/IDRUSSELLAUTHOR

🔗 https://www.instagram.com/idrussellauthor

🔗 https://www.patreon.com/ringojones

Subscribe to my newsletter:

✉ http://ringojones.com

Also by I.D. Russell

The further adventures of Frank Malone:

Political Suicide: River City Hell Book 3
When you fight the Authority, The Authority always wins…

It doesn't seem to matter what Samantha Abraham does, the shadowy organization known as The Authority just keeps coming back. With their corruption now spreading beyond just the music industry and professional hockey, she begins to see enemies everywhere she looks; in the campus of the university, the police, and maybe even all the way to Ottawa itself. Can Sam and her friends finally put a stop to the conspiracy before it's too late?

Giving in would be

POLITICAL SUICIDE

Sudden Death: River City Hell Book 2

Killing the song wasn't enough.

Samantha Abraham thought she'd stopped the madness when she ended the pop careers of Radiant Cyanide and Factor 5ive. But little did she know that there was much more to this sinister plot than just a few hit songs. The River City Jets hockey team is the next target for the shadowy figures of The Authority and it's going to take all she has to save rookie sensation Rick Hansen from one monstrous transformation.

Waking up from a Rock 'N' Roll Nightmare, she finds herself facing...

SUDDEN DEATH!

Rock 'N' Roll Nightmare: River City Hell Book 1

High School Hell was just the beginning...

Samantha Abraham graduated, her best friend and golem boyfriend didn't. Hoping to put their deaths behind her, she's off to River City University for a fresh start. Great friends, fun parties; life in the big city was everything she'd hoped. Until she meets Scott, the mysterious, tortured lead singer of the rock band Radiant Cyanide. Their music doesn't just make the crowd go wild, it might be making them go insane...

Suddenly her dream life is turning into a ROCK 'N' ROLL NIGHTMARE

Demon in the Sack
Game Over?

The streaming life isn't for everyone. Spending your time hanging out, eating pizza, and playing as many video games as your eyes can handle takes hard work and dedication. But when one third of the popular *Three Gamers* show decides to start looking for love outside of blinking screens and six button controllers, he finds out that while there might be someone for everyone, he's just become the target of a creature not-quite-human.

This one's not after his fame or money, but his SOUL!

Cursed Words

Some stories should be left unwritten...

Fifty years ago the Van Lundgren estate was the sight of unspeakable acts of evil. The truth has been long buried and forgotten. Now, the house is re-opening as a bed and breakfast and twelve souls show up for the weekend. But some crimes transcend time and when a raging thunderstorm traps them inside, the guests start dropping one by one. Soon the survivors are going to learn that some horrors can never truly be locked away.

Trapped in a nightmare, there's only one truth...

Sticks and Stones may break your bones but Cursed Words can KILL YOU!

Under Blood Lake

Somewhere in the darkness below the surface of Lake Winnipeg, the Deep Ones are waiting.

He thought it was just a simple weekend trip to put his brother's affairs in order and lay him to rest, but when River City's toughest cop shows up in the sleepy harbour town of Lakeshore, he unwittingly steps right into a community suffering under an ancient curse. Someone is pulling the strings and suddenly he's got bigger fish to fry. Off duty, without a weapon and under orders to stay on vacation, can Frank survive when he faces up to creatures more inhuman than real?

The Killing Death

He was ready to retire but then a madman started leaving victims in pieces. Can this aging cop solve one last crime before a killer finishes his deranged pizza?

When an unhinged pizzeria owner stumbles on an ancient Egyptian ritual, he begins a spree of brutal killings that leave a city in shock. It's up to veteran detective Frank Malone and his rookie partner to piece together the clues and catch the murderer. One problem, this isn't just a simple case of catch the bad guy, it could resurrect long dead spirits of evil.

With Egyptian magic, action, gore, and an insane ending you won't believe, this comedy/horror book is a wild good time!

Heart of Stone (High School Hell Book 1)

It's bad enough being the most unpopular girl in school, but when a strange new exchange student shows up, Samantha Abraham discovers she may be in love with a golem.

It was love at first sight for Sam when Joshua, the dark and mysterious foreign student from Eastern Europe, walked in to class. He's dreamy, great at hockey, and she's landed the chance to be his tutor. But the more time she spends with him, the more he seems to harbour a sinister secret. It's starting to look like he's a criminal, but he might also be a monster . . .

With the help of her over-zealous, secretly- crushing BFF Duckie, and with the popular girl bullies nipping at her heels, Sam must go up against a bunch of weird science, and a hellish high school social life, before she has a remote chance of a first kiss . . . or of surviving the Halloween dance.

Heart of Clay (High School Hell Book 2)

Samantha Abraham has the power to magically control her boyfriend's every action, but now someone wants that power—and wants him dead.

After the fallout from Heart of Stone, Sam has learned the truth: that her boyfriend, Joshua, was created in a lab by a mysterious scientist known only as The Professor. A magical ruby gives her the power to control him by thought. It seems like the perfect relationship, until a gauntlet of assassins show up in River City with murder on their minds.

On a quest for the truth that takes her to Toronto and into the den of her enemies, can Sam, Duckie, and hockey-hunk Rick save Joshua's life before it all goes to hell?

Heart of Flesh (High School Hell Book 3)

Samantha Abraham lost everything when she lost Joshua—but the fight for the ruby, and what it means, isn't over yet.

Sam is back in River City and the events of Heart of Clay have left her raw. If deranged necromancers were bad, you'd think Debbie and her slugs would be small potatoes, but Sam's life has gone straight back to hell in her senior year. Even with her high level hapkido skills, and a budding relationship with hockey hunk Rick Hansen, nothing seems to fill the gaping hole that Joshua and Duckie's disappearances have left . . .

But just as suddenly as he vanished, Joshua reappears with grave tidings, and Sam must decide what lengths she'll go to prevent her life—and her boyfriend's body—from falling apart.

Drug Wars Part 1: Lethal Dosage

Yellow Sunshine. More addictive than opium, more potent than cocaine, more dangerous than heroin. It ruins lives, destroys communities, and threatens the very country itself. It will take the River City police force everything they have to fight the scourge from street to bloody street.

Someone's dealing the worst drug the city has ever seen. THE REVENGIST is on the case with a brand new partner and a list of broken lives he's going to avenge. But to find the source of the poison, they'll have to go so far undercover that they might never make it out alive.

Drug Wars Part 2: Blood Money

MechaMountie. The secret CSIS project in cybernetics set to revolutionize the world of law enforcement. Stronger than ten gorillas with a brain faster than twenty IBM computers, the robot is laying down the law in a city under siege!

After the death of Eddie Camponelli, River City is in chaos. Rival gangs are shooting up the streets, attempting to gain control of the drug trade. The police are powerless until the government sends in their top secret weapon.

Now THE REVENGIST is in for the fight of his life to prove that no robot can do his job better than he can. He's going to show that he's still got it, even if it kills him!

Drug Wars Part 3: Iron Curtain

Ninja. The silent assassins. Using ancient martial arts techniques passed down through the secret orders of hired killers, they stalk by night and murder without a trace. Now they've come to River City and it's not to sightsee!

He might have killed the world's biggest drug supplier in Carlos Mendoza, but that only made the real bad guys mad. Now they're after him with everything they've got. In an all out battle for the future of Canada that spans the globe, THE REVENGIST is in a fight for more than just his life!

The explosive finale to the Drug Wars trilogy!

Go-Team # 1: Bitter Rivals / African Assault

The old Go-Team is gone, long live the All-New Go-Team. Led by Jessica "Doll-face" Dawes; they're sent in to infiltrate a tiny African nation in the throes of a bloody civil war. Their mission: to try to preserve the peace in the face of a brutal warlord.

But are the supreme sniper Brutal-Suzy and the kung fu assassin Hunglo enough to take on the American's better equipped, highly public, no-so-secret commando team: Uncle Sam Squad?

It's a battle between Bitter Rivals for the right to save Baangolo in an African Assault full of action, suspense, and… spring break?